FRAUD CHRONICLES
Part I

From
White Powder to White Collar

Darren Keys

Managed by

THE POPULARITY GROUP

FRAUD CHRONICLES Part I

F.K.I. Publishing Presents, from WHITE POWDER TO WHITE COLLAR.

This novel is a work of fiction. Any resemblance to real people, deceased or alive, actual events, entities, establishments, and or locations are only intended to provide the story with a sense of reality and authenticity. Names, characters, places, and events are either a product of the author's imagination or are used fictitiously as are those fictionalized occurrences that may involve real people and did not happen or are simply set in the future.

From WHITE POWDER TO WHITE COLLAR CopyRight© 2012 by Darren Keys

Published by:
    F.K.I. Publishing
    P.O. Box 34711
    Philadelphia, PA 19101
    www.fkipublishing.com

Library of Congress Catalog Card No. In Publication data
ISBN# 9780982730607

This story is dedicated to my fallen cousins, "Cecil and Elwood," may your legacy live on through remembrances. If only you both were around to see the books fly off the bookstore shelves as this Urban Fire is released to the public. And to see your brother "Tony Blackstone" in Beverly Hills making 'em cry laughing at the comedy clubs and doing the morning show with Tom Joyner.

It's destiny being fulfilled. So just know that although you are not here with us, you will always be remembered.

Rest in Peace.
Love your cousin,

Darren Keys

Acknowledgments

First, I would like to thank GOD for allowing me to create, to soar, and to entertain you with a reality-woven tale to remember. Next, I'd like to take this time to thank my mother and father for the tools that you provided so that I was equipped for the tasks of life and its splendors.

I would like to especially thank my wonderful and beautiful wife, Tari, for supporting my dreams in spite of her own.

I'd like to thank G.B. Johnson, my main-man, the Author of "Against the Grain" and countless other titles—for his inspiration and motivation that I gained watching him produce book after book and have each one highly anticipated by his loyal readers. I look forward to that same success and more. I can't leave out Kwame, the author of "DUTCH." Thank you for your interest in helping get this story into print and on the shelves.

Next, I'd like to thank THE POPULARITY GROUP for making it happen; that is, managing my career and first movie. That's what's up! Also to my people in Beverly Hills and L.A.—whom have read the manuscript and all advise that the story has "movie Appeal;" so I'm definitely open to have that dialog.

I'd like to also thank, Jerry Vick for his expertise in helping get the book "press-ready." We couldn't have done it without you.

"Special thanks to Dr. Hasan Oji for his awesome advertising and publishing consultation and words of wisdom. Look forward to the collaboration on the next project. Thanks for believing in this project.

"Special thanks also and a shout out to "Shorty Rock" the bread winner for this ideas and I'll see you at the top. Spitfire Records is on fire now with you on the label.

Last, but not least, I'd like to thank my Agent, Editor, and Publisher for believing in me and making this publication possible and most importantly, I'd like to thank you, my readers, for your loyal support and stay tuned for the next thriller….from the "FRAUD CHRONICLES"…

From WHITE POWDER TO WHITE COLLAR
PART II

"FRAUD MASTERS"

Prologue

"All rise. This Honorable Court is now is session, before the Honorable District Judge Stevens presiding."

"You may be seated. We are here in the matter of United States verses Dejohn Patterson. Case number 02-78651."

The world wide empire of fraud and deceit was now under attack and only in inexperienced jury would determine guilt or innocence.

The press occupied the back row of the courtroom like vultures waiting for a kill. The defense attorney's assistant sat directly behind the partition that separated Dejohn and his lawyer from the nosey and concerned spectators who partially filled the first two rows of cherry oak wood pew-like seating. Among the crowd was his loyal team facing the bench where His Honor sat peering somewhat anxiously over his spectacles.

It was still as clear as yesterday, the picture in my mind, a twelve-year old child sucking up the game like a sponge. Watching everything from the girls my older sister had as overnight guests, who sometimes wore see through night gowns and my mother's girlfriend's daughter Neicy from Atlanta—who I think turned me out back then, by putting her juicy mouth on my lil (12 yr. old ding-a-ling) and making me lick what she called her "hairy peach," until she started breathing really hard, and juice started coming out - when I walked in my mother's bedroom and caught her playing with her P-U-S-S-Y and I threatened to tell my mother that she was sneaking and watching my mother's nasty movies. Not to mention, "the street numbers man" with whom my mother would play her .25 cent and .50 cent numbers combinated, straight, and boxed.

Those were the days. My mother would treat us to a new pair of tennis shoes when she'd hit the number, especially when one of her four children's birthday came out in the four digits. Now that I think about it, that's why I'm addicted to sex and numbers today. Hot sex and real numbers. Filthy rich numbers. The kind of numbers that make federal prosecutors indict you and cheat to convict you, in order to "rob you blind" in what the feds call a "criminal forfeiture," where they claim everything you own came from illegal activities. These Federal Boys are the real mafia, one of the only groups that come and take everything you had and there's nothing you can do about it, unless you have an attorney like Johnny Cochran.

Speaking of the Mafia, the only Mafia we knew growing up in Baltimore, were the Jews, who seemed to own everything damn thing. Then there were the Italians in Little Italy downtown, and the Baltimore City gangs we called "clicks." I grew up in a middle-class family with two parents from the projects – where as a child, you constantly looked up to kingpin drug dealers. Just the way they lived; the respect they had; the money, clothes, jewelry, and the cars you aspire to be, not just like them, but even better than them someday. In fact, I wanted the power they had, but I wanted to wear a suit and tie.

Now that I think about it. I had the best of both worlds. My Father, a steel-worker, ruled with an Iron-Fist and was quick to strike if he thought that you had disrespected him. He was a self-studied intellectual who commanded the English language and would slap my sister and I in the mouth when we failed to speak proper English. He always instilled in us that "no matter where you come from, the way you communicate can determine how far you go." So while in the projects, I learned street slang. English was definitely the 'first language at home.'

My Mother was the aggressor. She could get anyone to do anything. She had the gift-of-gab and the street-savvy of a pretty project girl. She would take us to the Pimlico Race Track to watch the horse races on the weekends while she bet the horses. So she stayed looking good and kept us looking good. And always told us "if you want something bad enough, "GO FOR IT!" If somebody gets in the way, then move them out!" But what really stuck with me was her saying "if anybody hits you, you hit'em back!"

Although I was a puny 130 lbs. growing up, I stayed in a fight and getting sent home from school. It was not long before the gang "The Untouchables" adopted me as one of their own. That's where it all began. I went from selling candy and joints of weed in school to becoming a young-unsuspected drug smuggler. The drug ring that I was down with had gotten a connect in California for 'Indo' or 'greenbud' and the 'Bolivian-Fishscale cocaine that made Cali the West Coast Mecca for cocaine.

Although I was starting at the bottom, it was still like a dream come true when Lil Mo, one of the P-Nut Kingsley's lieutenants, came through the spot in his Beemer and surprised me when he rolled down the window and told me to get in. I was scared at first, because he never really talked to me like he talked to the other workers.

I rode with him across town to North Ave. and Washington Streets to drop off some work. During the trip, he told me he'd been watching me and he liked the way I carried it. Some people that took a ride with Mo never came back. So it was music to my young 16 year old ears to hear him say, "So you think you ready to move up in this game?" The serious look on his face, made me hesitate a little bit, but the thought of becoming rich quickly overcame my fear.

"Awight, shawty, this is what we need you to do right. We gonna pay you $500 and pay for all expenses. You know, like your plane ticket, hotel, and shit. You gone dress in baggy clothes, fly out to California, meet this dude, have a little fun, and bring back a package. It's that simple! So you tryin to go or what?

He did not have to say it twice. I responded immediately. "I'm with it. Na Mean."

I was young, I didn't think about the consequences. All I thought about was the money and now that my mother had separated from my father, I had to step it up and be the man of the house. "We lived in the heart of one of Baltimore's most notorious neighborhoods, Park Heights where it was nothing to see a dead body on your way to school in the mornings.

And although our crew was selling "g-paks" of $10 caps of heroin, about 3 per week and making $300 off each one. We still had to split it between four of us. We spent that on weed, clubbing, clothes and girls.

So that $500 extra in my pocket at least 2 weekends out of a month and catching planes like I was a millionaire, made me feel important and although I came close to getting caught a couple of times, I never did, but other people did. So they switched the game up and started sending the drugs in the mail by Fed-Ex, and UPS.

I was in charge of getting the addresses to ship the drugs to and most of the time it was a single girl with kids who needed money, but to keep them out of it, we'd have people there waiting on the packages so if anything happened, like a sting operation or something. The girls could say they didn't know about the deliveries. We kept new addresses coming in all the time. Sometimes I'd even have to be there myself, if my best friend Splizzy wasn't around, to make sure nothing went wrong.

P-Nut and Lil-Mo got indicted for murder and R.I.C.O. drug charges, which caused a temporary drought on the good shit in Baltimore. Some of the customers started calling me, at Mo's request, and I would take their money and send it to the connect Jay in Cali and he'd send the coke in the mail. This lasted for years until they caught on and started x-raying the packages. I was the middle-man and never had to get out on the corners anymore, I decided to go to Towson State College part time with my main-man Splizzy. So if I ever got locked up, I could get my lawyer to say that I am a college student who just made a poor judgment and deserves a second chance.

I always believed in that saying. "Everything happens for a reason" but, I never thought that something which appeared, at the time, to be so wrong could turn out so right.

It was the spring of 2000, the trip to California to pick up what was left of a half of the best coke on the west coast, at least that's what my customers on the east coast said, before twelve ounces came up missing in the mail. I'll never forget it, it was a little after 10:30 a.m., and Fed-Ex had just delivered the package. I signed for the box, closed the door, and locked all four locks and the deadbolt. Only to open the Fed-ex box for the shock of my life, I pulled the oversized zip lock bag from the box, and although it had the powdery white cocaine residue all over the inside, there was no cocaine, only little black and white grayish rocks like that found in a parking lot. Someone had taken my client's coke and I was responsible. I never planned for any shit like this. When I made my money, I spent it almost as fast as I made it.

I snatched up the burnout and called California to ask my supplier, Jay "What the fuck happened?" He reminded me that I asked for "all hard" instead of a bunch of shake he usually gave me. It wasn't until I explained that the rocks that I received was gravel from a parking lot or fish tank, that he assured me that he personally took the package to Fed-ex this time and the problem had to be between L.A. and Baltimore.

There were only six more ounces left that were to be sent the next day, but due to this mishap we agreed I needed to take a flight to pick them up. Now I just had to call a meeting with my client to explain what happened. It was 9:30 am; we met at Burger King in the Mondawmin Mall. I had a feeling that this news, I was bringing may cause a problem so I brought my nine with me. I sat in the car with the Fed-ex box on the passenger seat, and waited until he pulled into the parking lot in a shinny metallic silver 430 SLK Benz with the top down showcasing the customized burgundy leather package. He always wore a baseball cap and sunglasses like a movie star, but everyone still recognized him. I didn't get it. Anyway, it wasn't until he pulled in next to me that he realized I was still in the car. As I lowered my window, the sound of Sade's 'Smooth Operator' emanated from the Bose speaker system.

"I thought you'd be inside already." He said to me like I may have wanted to be inside where the people could see me rather than outside in the parking lot alone, but I'm sure he was smart enough to know that neither of us would come alone. I had Nina and he had some guy I had seen at his barbershop with him in the passenger seat.

I inquired.   "Are you hungry?"   Just making conversation because I could have cared less whether he was hungry. 'I' responded rather curtly, "naw, I'm not hungry but we can go sit down though."

I got out of the car, looked around as I always do, then I remembered the box. I turned back to the car, reached inside and grabbed the box and caught up with him.

As I opened the door to the mall's Burger King Entrance, we were greeted by a girl who we both met two weeks ago in the strip club. I was aroused and got hard instantly looking at her mini skirt revealing her long sexy legs as she spoke to 'L', and the seductive fragrance she wore lingered on me after I hugged her, getting a quick feel of her soft ass without anybody noticing. She whispered in my ear, "Call me." It wasn't until she walked out the door that I remembered her name and wondered was "Shareal" was her true name or a stage name.

Although I was a true flirt, this was not the time to be thinking about some pussy. I was about to find out whether one of the biggest and deadliest drug dealers in my city understood what I tried to tell him on the phone when I said, "We got a little problem. We need to talk." He knew there was a problem with the package because normally I'd call him and say, "It's a go. I'll be at such and such place, or at the spot from last week at a certain time." And he'd say, "Alright, I'm sending the girl", or "My man."

We sat down at the table in the back away from the rest of the customers; the smell of hash brown permeated the room. I pulled out the zip lock bag of cocaine residue covered rocks or gravel that interestingly weighed twelve ounces, just as the missing cocaine would have weighed. 'L' looked around when he turned to me with this cautious but disturbing look on his face. I suggested he look under the table at the bag. He looked under the table and noticed the bag had no coke in it. He stared at me with a very grimace smirk and said, "What's that? Why you showing me that?" As he smiled and peered over his shades at me with his beady eyes.

I responded, "This is what I got in the mail." He just looked at me and said, "So when are you going to deliver what I paid you for?"

I retorted, "Wait a minute, you sound like you don't want to share the risk and loss with me. I mean you do know that this comes through the mail and that this could happen at any time. We discussed that years ago when we first started doing business, and although we never had any problems like this before, we always knew something like this could happen."

'L' looked around again as if he was being watched or something, leaned forward, and said, "Check this out, I don't know what you trying to tell me, but ah, you need to call me when the plate is full. I'll holla at you later." He got up and walked out.

Although he told me to call him when the plate was full, implying that I had a little time, I didn't and I knew I didn't. All I could do was watch this 5'6" linebacker built, possible newly acquired enemy and his henchman who towered over him standing 6'4", every bit of three hundred ten pounds, walk away.

My cell phone vibrated. Looking at the caller I.D. It was my daughter's mother Irisa, reminding me that my daughter's Naisha's birthday party was this afternoon and I was to pick up the cake at 1:00 pm.

She put me on hold, another called vied my attention. I answered, "Hello." They asked for someone by the name of David. "You got the wrong number." and clicked over to my baby's mother who had hung up.

I couldn't help but wonder what that call was about. I turned my right blinker on to make the right out of the parking lot, and as I looked in my rear view mirror, I noticed a blue Crown Victoria also putting its right blinker on. Call it paranoid or whatever, in this business you must pay attention to everything. It could be the police, the stick up boys, or even someone paid to make me disappear.

When the traffic a short, four or five car lengths away, I made my dangerous right, almost getting rear ended as the driver was forced, by my maneuver, to slow down. He expressed his anger by blowing at me several times. Looking in my mirror, I blurted out, "Ah, shut up!" I quickly sped up and changed lanes so that I could take the next left to find out if I was being followed. I picked up the cake at Mulher's Bakery and realized the Crown Vic was no longer visible.

As I pulled up to my daughter's mother house, she was in the door looking at me like I was stupid. "What? Why are you standing in the doorway with your hands on your hips? Help me... get the balloons and stuff in the car."

Sucking her teeth and rolling her eyes like it would hurt her to help me, she came out and I went in with the birthday cake. I must admit, I was shocked that she didn't have company, as she called it. We passed each other again as we switched directions, this time I was going back to the trunk of the car to get the bags from Nordstrom's kids and she popped two balloons as one touched a plant hanging from the ceiling and another the stucco just above it. I couldn't help but look back at her ass, that I loved so much, jiggling as she walked by.

"Stop looking at my ass. I know you just looking at my ass to be nosey to see if it got bigger 'cause you don't want none."

"How you know what I want?" I said as I held the screen door open on my way to the car.

"Please... You come over here almost every weekend and pick up Naisha and all you say is 'What's up', or 'I'll see you Sunday, do you need anything Irisa?'"

"Hold that thought, I'll be right back. Let me get these bags out of the car and lock the doors." I walked down the stairs looking at every parked car in sight to see if I saw that blue car from earlier. I saw silver Volvo SUV across the street that was not there when I turned on to the block from that corner. I went inside and closed the door. I walked to the corner behind the couch to my favorite spot to look out the curtains without anyone seeing the curtains move or my face.

"What are you doing? Why are you all in my window?" Irisa said, apparently concerned.

"Whose silver Volvo is that across the street? Have you seen it there before?"

"That's umm, umm. Damn what's his name? Anyway, that's Debbie's boyfriend, the girl with the long hair that walks her dog all the time. It belongs to her friend. Why?"

"I just wanted to know, cause it wasn't there when I pulled up."

"I see you still paranoid as ever."

"What you got on? Come here." Reaching out and waving her over, sniffing her.

"Boy, what the hell you sniffing me for?"

"Damn you smell good. What's that?"

"Be Delicious. It's new, you like it?" Smiling and giggling.

"Hell yeah. It smells like something to eat."

"Yeah, whatever. You scared of this cause you know I'll pussy whip you like you was before I got pregnant." We both laughed.

"Ha ha ha, girl you a trip. The reason I won't fuck with you like that no more is you represent drama. You always gotta bring up old shit and throw it in my face. You just like to argue and I ain't with that shit." I was getting hard just looking at her standing in front of me, 5'4", her cocoa brown skin and red hair, I could see her nipples getting hard too. I wanted her just as bad as she wanted me, but I couldn't let her know.

"So what's up? It's just you and me." She said as she pushed me back on the couch and started to pull down my zipper. "Look at you. Scared to death. Scared I'm gone blow your mind."

"Damn, uhm, uhmmm…" She was right. This is why I stayed away because I am addicted. She's got the best head out of all three of my baby mothers, especially the way she licked down the side and played with my balls with her free hand. I grabbed her head with my left hand and pushed lightly as her head went up and down.

"You miss me don't you? Tell me the truth." Rissa said as my semen looked like clear rubber braces in her mouth.

"For real… You just keep getting better and better." And I meant every word of it.

"Yeah, hurry up and get it back up so I can get mine. You act like you ain't had none in years, all the cum that was backed up in you." Rissa said in her most sexy voice.

"Nah, you bring out the best in me, that's all."

"Bzzz, bzzz." My two-way pager started buzzing on the table.

"Damn, turn that thing off."

"Hold up." I checked my two-way, saw the message 'Call Splizz'. I immediately picked up my phone, Rissa still stroking me, trying to get me hard.

"Yo, Splizzy let me caalll you right baaaccck." Rissa had me in her mouth again. I felt my love muscle growing in her mouth; she lifted her pleated white tennis skirt and moved her thong over as she straddled me. Looking into my eyes, she started to ride me as I massaged her breast. It felt so good to be inside her again.

Chapter 3

"Yo kid, I'm leaving my daughter's house dropping off gifts for her birthday. Where are you, because I need to see you so we can talk? I got a problem... Six o'clock? Where? Oh, yeah, across from the dealership, the place where we went for seafood that day? Okay, see you then. My song is on.

'I won't tell your secrets. Your secrets are safe with meeee.' By Alicia Keys. "I know that's not the same fuckin' car from this morning... "I thought to myself as I hung up the phone and began watching the car behind me.

I tried to be discreet in examining my rear view mirror, but I couldn't help but move my head instead of just my eyes. In fact, I pulled over into a driveway and grabbed my gun from the glove box. As I rolled down the window, I noticed someone looking at me through an upstairs window, which meant they could see me holding the gun. The car went by and I pulled out and became the hunter, an obvious one at that. I followed this car for almost twenty minutes before I realized I was two blocks away from the restaurant Defacto's where I was to meet Splizzy in forty-five minutes. I thought I'd get there early and order appetizers, plus I'd have a chance to think.

My phone came alive with its distinctive ring catching me in a moment of deep thought. "Hello!"

"Dee your daughter is a spoiled brat. You got her rotten. She wants me to buy her these Durango boots for

$110 dollars. So I'm calling you to make sure I can get my money back from you. If I buy em?"

"That goes without saying Kim, it's her day. Whatever she wants I got chew awight."

"Awight then."

"Awight just get back at me." I ended the call just as Splizzy was approaching the table.

"Young Splizzy, what's up kid?"

"What's up Dee? Yo, this must be real important, 'cause yo ass ain't never on time yo, for nothing and you beat me here. So holla at you boy... What are these?" Reaching for a baba.

"Go wash your hands yo. You just come off the street and come sticking your hands in the food. What's up wit chew?"

"Nigga, I know you ain't got all proper on me. Shit, as many times as you came off the street and opened my frigerater. So what's up? What you wanna see me about yo? And give me that menu. I'm starving. These joints is good yo. What is it?"

"It's lamb, tenderloins of lamb, and the green stuff is mint jelly that you dip it in. Yo, you know who I keep thinking about?"

"Who?"

"That girl you introduced me to at the strip club."

"Who? I introduced you to a whole lot of girls at the strip club." Splizzy responded, looking at the menu.

"I think her name was Shereal, she keeps poppin' up on my mind."

"I know you didn't call me all the way down here to ask me about no damn stripper."

"Come on man, this is serious. I got problems man...

"What? What problems you got? You ain't got no problems. Hey waiter."

I went straight to the punch, "Splizzy, I need your help yo. I need ten thousand yo, and I'll get it back to you within a couple weeks."

"Ten thousand? For what? What you get yourself into yo? I told you about messing with them horses man. You ain't learned yet. So what's up?"

"I ain't mess up no money. I ain't been to the race track in over three weeks. Splizz, I been doin' good, until this shit happened."

"What shit?" Splizzy looking hard at the table across from ours. "Damn she fat to death." Looking at the blond woman with the form fitting black dress exposing back and her black girl shape.

"Yo, Splizz this is serious man, you playing. That girl is with somebody and please don't start nothing up in here. Seriously. Listen man."

"Alright, talk to me." He said, turning with a serious look on his face.

"Yo, I need ten g's like yesterday. Some wild shit happened to me yo. You know the boy 'L' I been fuckin' with for years, selling him coke?"

"Go ahead, I remember." He said with concern.

"Well, he gave me money up front, like he always do, for a half right. So I sends it to my connect in Cali and he mails me the coke Fed-Ex. Now keep in mind, we been doing this for years, and Fed-Ex is always there by 10:30, you feel me? Fed-Ex was on time this time too but this time the coke wasn't in the box; it was some fuckin' gravel that you find in a fish tank."

"Hold up, so what you tellin' me is that you got robbed before you even got the coke?" Laughing. "My guess is it was never sent to you."

"Yeah, that's an easy solution, and the same one I came up with. But one thing that overpowers all that shit, is the fact that we've been doing business for about nine years, and these people are filthy rich, driving Ferrari's and shit. It just don't add up, Oh yeah, the same night, 20/20 did a special on Fed-Ex thefts. They showed some dude get locked up and showed the items recovered from his house. They found diamond rings, guns, watches, seven ounces of coke and several thousand dollars in cash. Was this what happened to my shit? Maybe, maybe not."

"Damn yo, so what happened to the rest, you said it was supposed to be twelve, there's six more somewhere." Splizzy said doing the math.

"I know. The other six I gotta go pick up. I'ma have to fly out there and get them, but that's just one third of what I need. So now that you heard why I need the money, are you gonna loan it to me?"

Splizzy now looking out the window in deep thought, turned back and said, "Damn. Yo, I just opened up a recording studio on Park Ave... That's where all my money has been going and I ain't got no ten g's. Yo, the best I can do is thirty-five hundred. Will that help you? Give me a couple weeks and I'll try to put something together for you. Yo what the boy say about all this?"

"Man you know how niggas is. He didn't even wanna hear it, like it's all on me. He tells me call him when the plate is full."

"So call the nigga up and tell him you got thirty-five hundred and you'll get'em the rest later."

"Splizz, this boy ain't like that man. He want his shit or his money man. Remember, I been dealing with him a long time and I've seen him tell dudes that had over half the money to get with him when they got all of it. So it's not about money, it's about principle, and I respect him like he respect me. But this is a guy who everybody thinks he had his own cousin killed for not giving him all his money. So to avoid a "Death Hunt" by him or myself, I'm just gone get his shit or his money..."

Chapter 4

B.W.I. Airport

I handed my newly purchased ticket to the flight attendant and was led to my window seat, next to a woman who seemed to be writing what appeared to be a report of some kind. I tried not to be so obvious, but she was very attractive and it was a six hour flight to Los Angeles.

I was all too happy to see the seat belt signs go off and the flight attendants begin their in flight service of miniature relaxers. I preferred vodka. I had three of them on the rocks before finally falling asleep.

I was awakened by the sound of a crying infant, only to find the young beautiful writer admiring me as I slept, or at least that's what it looked like to me because she turned away so quick.

I opened a conversation by asking, "How long before we reach our destination?"

"About two and a half hours." She replied.

"Excuse me, but what do you do?" I asked her.

"I write movie manuscripts." Reaching into the pocket of her purse for a card. "Why do you ask?"

"Well I like to pride myself on being a great pooler of resources and I have found that success only by greeting, meeting and rolodexing individuals like yourself, only not as beautiful."

"Well, thank you, and what do you do, might I ask?"

"I'm a merchant broker. A need fulfillment specialist."

I could tell from the look on her face that she was intrigued by my answer. I had just sold mystery to a woman who probably made a handsome living writing and selling mystery. I guess the saying holds true that 'He who sells is easily sold'.

"Now you've got me curious." She said as she slightly turned her body towards me, crossing her left leg over her right to give me her undivided attention. Her woolen skirt retracted, revealing more of her beautiful legs. "What are you, a giggilo or something?"

"Why you ask me that? I mean, what about me made you even entertain that question?"

"Well, first of all, you dress very nice. I notice you're wearing Faragamo shoes, my favorite. You have the most beautiful golden brown complexion..." I cut her off.

"Wait a minute. What are you about to sell me?" I said, laughing.

"No, I'm serious. You're a very attractive man, and then you look like you're in shape. Do you work out?"

"Three times a week, for the last six years. And you, do you work out?"

"I have a gym in my home. I work out a least once a day when I'm not traveling."

I couldn't help but think about Splizzy and how he used to push me to work out every day in college. Just to make the football team so we could pull all the girls. Even though I was only 5' 9" and one hundred and eighty five pounds, I was cut up with washboard abs. Rissa used to say I had a body like Bruce Lee.

I could tell we had chemistry and that this chance meeting would not be our last, at least if I played my cards right.

"Forgive my manners, reaching out my right hand, "My name is Dee, or that's what my friends call me, but my name is Dejohn Patterson and you are? How do you pronounce your name?"

"It's French, Brishh-ette. The emphasis is on Brishh, like swish in a basketball game. So do you play basketball?" She asked as she was bumped by a drunken passenger headed back to his seat.

"I play occasionally, but my passion is football."

"So you like contact sports?" She asked.

"I love it; especially one-on-one." I responded, with a straight face. This was no ordinary woman. There was something special about her. Maybe I've finally met someone who could excite me to change, whatever that is. One thing for certain, there is definitely chemistry.

"Really? I'm not going to ask you what type of one-on-one contact sports you like, we'll save that for another time. So explain this need fulfillment specialist thing to me, I'm so curious." She did well dodging the subject.

"If I told you, I'd have to kill you." I laughed it off, but could tell she was really interested in knowing more about me. So I took advantage of the suspense factor and left her to wonder while I excused myself, going to the restroom. She had returned to what I learned later to be her movie manuscript, called 'Sound Proof. A story about a famous lawyer who has an automobile accident and was nearly killed but suffers from a neck injury that left him unable to speak. But continued to practice law through a machine invented in Sweden called the "Voice Actor".

I could only imagine what it would be like to have a woman who could write her fantasy on paper and have it acted out. What would a woman like this be like in bed?

Would she role play, act out scenes and different positions.

"So, where are you from?" I asked as I returned to my seat, leaning over to admire her cleavage from my angle.

"L.A. Well, I was born in France and moved here to the United States when I was nine years old. My mother is French and my father is from New York. Why am I so comfortable talking to you? I can't believe I'm talking to a complete stranger."

"That's because I'm no longer a complete stranger. Remember, you just gave me three phone numbers, your office, fax and cell phone on your business cards, and I take that as an invitation to call one of them. I think I'll do that, and then maybe you can show me around."

"Just give me a call. If I'm free I'll be glad to show you around."

It wasn't until I heard the 'Return your tray tables to its upright position' that I remembered my fear of flying or taking off and landings were real from the instant butterflies in my stomach.

I got a voice mail from Kim, while in flight, telling me that I'ma have to cut her a serious check. I guess her and Isha bought the mall. She also said she ran into 'L' and he wants me to call him.

Chapter 5

As I made my way to baggage claim, checking out Brishette's shape alongside her sister, whom she introduced me to as we exited the plane at gate E-17. Just the way she walked turned me on. Suddenly, as we approached baggage claim, I heard my name called. I turned and immediately recognized Jay's younger brother Kevin waving me over. I grabbed by baggage and said goodbye to Brishette and her sister.

"What's up, man? How was your flight?" Kevin asked reaching for my bags.

"It was alright. I just don't like the takeoff and landing part." "My brother had me come pick you up because he's busy taking care of some business. He's gonna meet us at Dimagio's. Remember the restaurant we went to the last time you were here?"

"I could use a drink after all that flying?"

"We'll be there in ten minutes, it's not far."

"It's a three hour difference right?"

"Yeah, that's right?"

"I need to call my daughter and wish her happy B-Day." Immediately thought about Rissa and how she had a way of taking up space in my head.

"Hello. Hey... What's going on? Where's my little princess?"

"Hold on." She screamed downstairs, "Isha, your father is on the phone. I thought you were going to stay when you came by."

"I had something to take care of. I'm in California."

"California? Boy stop playing?"

"No, I'm serious. When I left you..."

"Hello." My daughter, Naisha picked up the phone.

"Hey Isha. Happy birthday baby."

"Daddy where you at? Why didn't you come to my party?"

"Isha, daddy had an emergency, but I should be back in a few days. Okay?"

"Okay, I love you daddy."

"I love you too baby. Put your mommy back on the phone."

"Hello, wait a minute. Go get your bath water ready so you can get your butt in the bed. Okay, I'm back. So what's up, what are you doing in California?"

"I had to take care of something."

"Oh that's right, I almost forgot. Lil Kim and Isha saw some guy named L'..."

"Saw him where..." I said in my most concerned voice. "What he say?"

"He said you knew who he was and to call him." Rissa replied nonchalantly.

"She left me a voice mail but she didn't mention details. So how did he know Kim?"

"He said he thought Kim was me. I guess he recognized Isha, and Kim do look like me a little bit."

We arrived at the restaurant. "Waitress, what's your name?"

"Sophie." She replied with an accent of Italian.

"Sophie, I'm gonna have the Chicken - Lobster Alfredo, and let me have an Absolute Vodka from the bar." I ordered first. Kevin was still perusing the menu.

"Sorry I'm late..." Jay said as he pulled up a seat and shook my hand. "So where are you staying?"

"At the Hyatt on Wilshire. The Sheraton was full; they said some convention was in town." I said, taking a sip of my drink.

"Sir, I'll give you two some more time to make your selection." said the waitress.

Jay responded, "I don't need any more time. I'll have an order of Baba's for the appetizer and I'll have the two pound lobster with prime rib, medium well, and let me have a bottle of Chateau Lafit Rothschild nineteen sixty-three. And here's a little something for you." He said, handing the beautiful Italian waitress a fifty-dollar bill before she disappeared into the chatter-filled restaurant.

Kevin's phone rings, "Hello. Yes this is he. Yes. Is she okay? I'll be right there, thank you for your call."

"What's that all about?" Jay asked his brother.

"It's my daughter at the hospital. She's got a fever of a hundred and four degrees. I gotta go. I'll see you guys later. Enjoy your meal." Kevin got up, pushed his chair in and turned to leave.

"I hope she feels better." I said with sincere concern.

"Call me and let me know how she's doing, okay?" Jay stated to his brother.

"Alright. I'll call you." Kevin returned as he walked towards the door.

"So what's going on? What do you think happened?" Jay began to question me.

"That's what I wanna know. Well, one thing we can almost rule out is the feds, because that would have affected interstate commerce and gave the feds a case." I said as he looked at me with a strange look and then responded.

"Yeah, that went through my head as well, and you're right, almost was a good word because they will make you think you got away and just be settin' you up."

The waitress interrupted our conversation with the meal now accompanied by another waitress even more beautiful than she - and I had now had two drinks and was just warming up. We began eating our meal and Jay insisted I join him in consuming the wine.

"Come on Dee. This wine is two hundred seventy-five dollars per bottle. It's hard to find this wine and they ordered it for me, and I'd be insulted if you didn't have some."

He started to sound like some mafia boss trying to make me drink some poison, but he was only trying to show hospitality. We finished eating and the waitress asked if we'd be having desert.

"No thank you." He and I both almost said it at the same time. We paid the tab and went out to his Maserati.

"We got to get you to the hotel. So which Hyatt is it? The Wilshire or Beverly Hills?"

"It's the Wilshire." I answered as my phone rang. This number was not familiar.

"Hello?"

"Hey DeJohn, what's up baby. It's Karen."

"Who? Oh yeah, what's going on stranger? You're not gonna believe this, but I was thinking about you earlier."

"Yeah right, tell me anything. I got a little treat for you when you come over here. I went shopping with that money you gave me and I got some goodies from Victoria's Secret."

"Is that right."

"I hear music, where you at, in the car? So are you on your way over here or what?"

"Unfortunately, I'm not gonna be able to make it because I'm in California and I won't be back for a couple of days."

"I bought some body butter and I got a surprise for you."

"Oh you do huh, what kind of surprise you got for me?"

"You'll see."

"Okay, we can talk about that when I get back to my hotel. What number do you want me to call you back on? Is this one okay?"

"You're not dirty are you?" Jay said with this scared look on his face.

"No. Why?" I said as my heart started racing because I hate police.

"Don't look back, but this police is behind us and has been following us since we left the restaurant. You got some change on you? I'm gonna pull over, you get out and get a paper out of the machine. That's why I hate coming down here driving one of my vehicles. These police be so jealous of young looking black people with money. I wish you would've got the hotel by the airport like last time."

"I tried. They were booked." I said as the car came to a sudden stop. "Okay. Here we go... Okay, he's pulling over too. Okay go ahead."

The officer got out of the car and walked over to the Starbucks Coffee store right in front of the news stand. I got back in the car, and we pulled away.

I broke the momentary silence, "Yo Jay, we been doing business a long time and made a lot of money..."

Jay cut me off saying, "I already know where you going. I got you. I put something together for you. I gave you the six that was left and another twelve. Just take care of me when you can."

"My man. I appreciate that Jay?"

Though this was enough to take care of 'L', I decided he was gone have to wait until I flipped it, then I'd pay him.

Chapter 6

I was awakened by my cell phone, which blared forth from the nightstand. "Hello?"

"Hi, are you up?" I knew immediately it was Brishette from the plane."

"Yeah, I'm up. This is a wonderful surprise. What time is it?"

"It's ten minutes till eleven." She returned wither sexy French accent.

"What? Eleven o'clock? I didn't mean to sleep this late. Let me get myself together and call you back..." Brishette caught me totally by surprise as she cut me off.

"You've been on my mind since yesterday, and so I thought since I have a little time today, I would show you around and we can start by doing a late breakfast or brunch. So I'm gonna pick you a few things and swing by your hotel, have a bite then we can head out."

"Wow. Okay, I guess I'll wait for you." I must have made quite an impression I thought to myself.

"So what hotel are you staying at? And what 's the room number?"

"The Hyatt on Wilshire and my room numberis 1206."

"Okay, I'm on my way."

"Then I'll see you when you get here."

"Buyyy." She sounded so good.

I couldn't help but wonder whether anything had changed with Jay. Would he still contact me or do I contact him. So I dialed his cell.

"Hello. What's up Jay, what time you want to get together?"

Jay responded, "It'll be later. Get some rest. I'll call you later around dinner time."

Perfect, I thought. This would give me a chance to see Brishette. I took a shower and left the bathroom door open so I could hear her knock. I wasn't in the shower twenty minutes before I heard the door. I immediately sprayed some cologne on and went to the door-dripping wet with a towel wrapped around my waist. I opened the door, she entered, smiling, eyes wandering up and down my body somewhat surprised that I was practically naked. She had two bags in her arms. I reached to help her with the bags and my towel fell, exposing all of me.

"Oops. Here, let me get... Ah," as she bent down in front of me to get my towel, I started to get aroused by just seeing her bend down in front of me and she noticed, "your towel. Boy, are you glad to see me." She said laughing. "Maybe you should go and put something on before I jump on you."

"I'd be honored to entertain your jump." I said as she pulled the late breakfast out of the bag.

"So, I see you haven't broken the seal on your wet bar." She responded.

"I was waiting on you."

"Oh yeah. You didn't even know I would come here."

"Yes I did. I knew that wouldn't be the last time I'd see you."

"Umm. That smells good. What is that?" She asked, closing her eyes, enjoying the fragrance, smelling me as I got closer to her.

"It's called 'Eat Me' by Escada."

"It smells edible too." She said as I reached for her hands and pulled her close to me, pressing our bodies against one another.

"You look and smell so good." I said, heart racing. As I lifted my hands, she grabbed me. We started kissing passionately. I lowered my hands to her lower back, and then I grabbed her soft ass. She then grabbed my hands and put them on her breast. I couldn't take it any longer; I picked her up and took her into the bedroom. As I laid her on the bed, my towel fell. I took her shoes off, and then I reached for her blouse to release her now hardened nipples from her bra. I knew this was a zone I needed to work.

"I don't normally do this on the first date, but I feel more than comfortable though, sharing my body with you." Brishette said, slightly panting.

"Shhh. Just enjoy this moment." I said as I took off both her stockings and panties at the same time.

I was so hard she bent down and took me into her mouth. It felt like I had died and gone to heaven.

"Uhh. Da-ham girl." I moaned as she started stroking my balls with her left hand.

Then she pulled me on top of her. As I crawled between her legs, my cell phone began to vibrate on the night stand. I ignored it and went to work on her pussy-so-soft as she took me into her and guided me in.

"I knew it was something about you. When you first boarded the plane I was hoping you sat next to me." Brishette, out of breath managed to get these words out before she screamed.

"Oh, yesss. Oh baby, it's your pussy. Oh yeahhh, it's yours!"

She made so much noise I wanted to cover her mouth but her voice just turned me on and made the animal come out of me.

"Tell me you love this dick baby. Come on... Yeah that's right, pump back. That's right baby, work that pussy." I joined her verbal visage while meeting her body's every rhythm.

I turned her over on her stomach, pulled her legs beyond the edge of the bed until her hips were at the edge, then I entered her from behind and began banging with all my might.

"She began screaming, "Ooh, ooh, ooh. Fuck me Dejohn. Fuck me baby"

I couldn't hold it any longer, and just as I was about to cum, she screamed. "Oh baby, I'm cumming. I'm cumin!"

Her body started jerking with convulsion-like movement and I just grabbed her hips tighter and blasted off. My back arched and I came to a slow stop.

She turned on the bed, I followed and lay next to her, watching her shake.

"Are you okay?" I asked, putting my arms around her.

She put her arms around my arms and responded, "Am I alright? That was the best. Oh my God you are something else."

"No. You are something else." I whispered in her ear.

Her eyes closed and I rested my head back on the pillow and looked at the ceiling trying to catch my breath. As she fell asleep, I turned around and reached for my cell to find out who called. I checked my messages only to find that jay had called and asked me to meet them at Angus Nights restaurant at six thirty. I had almost four hours. I stared at the clock on the nightstand reading two forty-five; we had been at it almost from the moment she arrived at eleven twenty-three. So we had a two-hour sex-a-thon. I turned facing Brishette, kissed her on the shoulder and took a nap holding her as if I had no worry in the world.

Chapter 7

6:28 Angus Nights Restaurant

I arrived at the valet parking entrance. The uniformed attendant escorted me out of the car and pulled away.

"Hey... You're just in time. We just ordered appetizers. Let me introduce you to my friend Shine. This is Dee form the East Coast."

This girl was so fine. She reminded me of Nia Long and Janet Jackson mixed.

"Hello. It's good to meet you. So how do you like the West Coast? Or have you been turned out yet"? She asked with a dimple-induced half smile.

"That depends on what you mean by being turned out." I gainly returned.

The waitress interrupted us, she asked could she take our order for entrees. I ordered Surf and Turf. Shine and Jay both ordered, lamb and lobster fettuccini. After the waitress took our order, Jay excused himself to go to the restroom, probably to answer one of the many calls he received since I had arrived.

"So how long have you been knowing Jay?" Shine asked with a very sinister grin on her face.

"A long time. Almost twelve years. Why do you ask?"

"Oh, I just wanted to know." She replied.

"And what about you? How long have you been knowing him?"

"Jay and I are just good friends. He used to be with my sister and she was killed in a drive by shooting and we've been tight every since. Everybody thinks we are closer than we are but it's not like that. He's like a brother to me. We just watch each other's back. You know what I mean?"

There was something in her voice. The way she said it, it was insincere. I had an eye or innate sense or something. Whatever it was, I had it and she was not right.

Jay returned, as if this was a script, and he'd come in on his part. He interrupted saying, "I'm hungry. Where is that waitress?"

Two minutes later, here comes the food. The timing was like a movie. Then I got the call...

"Hello."

"Dee, Kim is in the hospital, Somebody kidnapped and raped her and sh...eee; Whh...." Either because she was fast-talking like a auctioneer or because every other word was followed by crying. I could hardly make out what she was saying.

"Wait Rissa, slow down, she said what? Wait a minute, calm down so I can understand you. Stop cryin, and tell me what the fuck is going on!" I raised my voice in anger..

I felt my world crushing around me as I listened to her tell me her sister was raped and she thinks 'L' had something to do with it because he called and left a message on her machine for me to call him or there will be problems.

"Okay. I'm gonna send Splizzy over there to find out what happened. If he did this we gone deal with it, as long as you're okay? Let me go so I can make some calls. I'll get back to you. I love you. Tell my daughter I love her and I'll call you back."

Jay, now concerned asked, "What's going on Dee? Sounds like drama. Everything okay."

I didn't want to get into details, so I simply said, "Yeah, a little problem but its cool. I need you to excuse me. I need to make a couple of calls real quick."

I got up from the table and walked off, passing a table of Chinese girls who seemed to be gossiping in Chinese. I found my way past the noisy corridor leading to the kitchen, turned right following the overhead restroom sign with the arrow pointing to the restrooms. Once inside the restroom I dialed Splizzy's number. He never answered; he was probably asleep. Then I remembered it was a three-hour difference in California. He must have been with a girl or something because he never went to bed this early. So I left him a message to get back to me.

Chapter 8

Marriott Hotel, L.A.

It felt as if I was being followed. As the sliding glass doors opened, I quickly walked across the well-marbled floors towards the elevator. As I passed the giant waterfall display that attributed to the hotel's five stars, I noticed a man appearing to be in his mid thirties turn away as I looked his way. This felt like a set up. Maybe the mysterious missing package delivered by Fed-Ex was not missing after all. Maybe they had gotten to Jay. Maybe the FEDS had arrested Jay at Fed-Ex as he dropped off the package and promised him a deal if he delivered me. This would explain why he didn't pick me up from the airport, or why the police was following us to my hotel, and it would also explain why this girl Shine, who says she and Jay were just good friends and never been intimate, began asking so many questions when Jay went to the restroom.

"Sir, what floor?" The bellman asked.

"Seventh please." I responded from my dazed state.

I picked the seventh floor and exited on the fifth floor as a woman stepped off the elevator. I knew I could not go straight to my room on the sixth floor. I quickly located the laundry room. It was empty, thank God. I removed the shoebox containing the coke from the Neiman Marcus shopping bag. I then climbed up on one of the washers and pushed a ceiling tile to the side and hid the cocaine. I walked down the hall passing a couple who obviously couldn't wait until they were inside, fondling each other. I slid into the stairwell unnoticed by the two extionbitionists. I quietly walked up the stairs one flight to the sixth floor. As I opened the door, I was met by a woman who appeared to be drunk, but startled as she looked me in the eyes. My heart was beating faster than normal. I didn't like this feeing. I stuck my card into the door, it beeped and the red light turned green. I entered and immediately began looking around to see if anything was moved.

All sorts of things were running through my mind. As I closed the curtains I was startled by the unexpected vibrating of my phone in my pocket. It was Splizzy.

"Yo Dee. What's going on man? I couldn't get your call because I just left the hospital talking to your sister-in¬-law Kim. She said she don't know whether 'L' got anything to do with it or not. She says it could have something to do with the Jamaicans that she used to sell weed for. She said she still owe them about nine hundred dollars and the last time she saw the dred dude, he tried to put his hands up her mini skirt.

"But she was fucked up man. At first she didn't want to talk about it, but I explained to her that if she told me how it happened and where, then we would have a better chance at finding out who did it."

"So what happened, did she tell you?" I asked peeping out the peephole of the hotel room door to see if anyone was passing.

"Yo, she said it was three dudes. One of them approached her in the mall's underground parking lot and asked her for some jumper cables, and if she could give him a hot shot. She said no she didn't have any, then as she stuck her key in her car door she noticed he had pulled out a gun. She looked around to see if anyone was in the parking lot and nobody was around. She thought he was gonna rob her, then a man pulled up in a SUV. She screamed help and the vehicle stopped. The man asked was everything all right. She said 'Sir, this man is trying to rob me, please help me.' She said the man got out of his car, told the guy 'Put the gun down. I'm a police officer.' He pushed his jacket aside with one hand revealing his badge; with the other hand he pointed his gun. The first guy then lowered his gun, placing it on the ground. The man presenting himself as the police then walked over pressed the barrel of the gun against her forehead and told her if she tried anything he would kill her.

The other guy grabbed her from behind and before she could scream he had covered her mouth with a cloth smelling like some kind of chemicals. Next thing she knew, she was tied hands and feet to a bed with four posts. When they removed the blindfold, all she saw was three blurred men with stocking caps on their faces. She said wherever she was; it was real cold because she was shivering. And she remembered one of the guys said something about her nipples being hard as he started feeling on her. Then the second walked over to her and held a gun to her head and made her suck him off while the third one forced his way inside of her, then they switched positions. That's when one of the guys got real ruff and started pulling her hair as he humped her face calling her names.

"Yo, she told you all that? Man, I knew that bitch was a psycho yo. Yo, just tell me how the fuck she got away."

"She said when they finished with her, one of the guys said he was gone kill her because she saw their faces, But one of them said the lights were real dim in the parking lot and we had on masks when she woke up, plus that pussy was good. I want some more so it would be a shame to waist a perfectly good piece of pussy. They put the blindfold back over her face. She said she didn't see where she was, but she heard the sound of a garage door open."

"So how did she get to a hospital?"

"She said they dropped her off in an alley with her hands, mouth and feet taped up. A delivery man found her..."

Chapter 9

"Hello baby. I was hoping you called me because I've been thinking about you since you left the hotel." I said as I answered Brishette's call.

"I've been thinking about you too and I want some more of you. Do you have a problem with that?" Brishette purred in her sexy-assed French accent. That shit was a real turn on.

"A problem? My only problem is not knowing when I'm gonna see you again. I replied now thinking about the coke and whether it was safe and was my phone tapped.

"What do you mean you don't know when?" She said in what seemed to be her sexiest voice.

"I mean I'm ready to see you now, and anything later would be uncivilized." I answered with a semi cool smile on my face. "But this time I'd like to go somewhere different."

"Like where? Where do you want to go?"

"I don't know. Just somewhere other than here."

I knew that if I was being setup, this was as perfect a time as any to change up the game a little bit. I was always told that there's no target harder to hit than a moving target. So we agreed we'd talk about it when she arrived. As soon as we hung up I began packing.

As I sat on the bed I started to reflect on the days when I was a member of the "Untouchables". A gang that everyone seemed to be afraid of, or at least that's what they made us think. We were notorious and deadly. We all were students of Lee's Karate since we could remember. Only two of the members were without a

Black Belt and that's only because they were new additions. One of the member's cousins sold guns so we always kept heat.

I knew my reputation depended largely on how I handled these next moves on the chess board of life. I had to remind both of my associates that I am still an "Untouchable".

I picked up the phone and dialed L's number. His caller I.D. revealed I was calling from a California number. He answered in a cold coniving tone, "Yo, speak."

"What's good? Can you talk or you want to call me back from a pay phone?"

"Nah, go 'head."

"I think the fashion show is gone jump off close to schedule. I got nine girls for you so far. I'm working on the other nine and I should have them rounded up in a bout a week. So..." He cut me off again.

"A week?" L impatiently retorted. "Yeah okay." As if to say I was pushing my luck.

"So what's up? You tryin' to entertain the first nine girls or you trying to wait until all eighteen models come together? I said in a short tone, aggravated by his earlier statement.

"Why don't you just bring them all at once?"

"Aw 'ight. I'll get back to you when I round up the other girls. You just get the money ready for the fashion show. And oh yeah. You got my cell number right?"

"Yeah. why you ask me that?"

"Because you called my baby's mother when you could've called me direct."

He seemed disturbed and answered, "Yo check this out. I called your phone and got no answer so I tried the other number you always called me from."

"Yeah awight. In the future, call me and not my girl."

"Peace." We hung up. On that note and although he never responded, he got the message.

Even though I'd been doing business with him for a few years, he was never to be trusted. But neither was I if you'd become an enemy. I had great respect for Splizzy's street credibility because he had an uncanny way of finding out shit on the street that not even a detective could find out, and if L had something to do with Kim's rape, Splizzy would find out, and his enemyship and fate would be confirmed.

Brishette phoned me from downstairs, asking me if I wanted her to come up or was I coming down. I told her to wait for me; I'd be coming down. I located a luggage cart in the hallway, loaded it with my luggage, and entered the elevator where I squeezed an overweight Caucasian man who wore a poorly attached tupe barely covering his baldness, into the corner. The smell of garlic and cigar smoke emanated from the olive skinned man in the elevator. I experienced sudden relief as the elevator doors opened to the hotel's lobby. I observed the patrons parading throughout the adorned lobby. I was surprised by the hotel manager's efficiency as he had my statement all ready, inducing a smooth check out. I paid and made my way to the glass sliding doors where I saw Brishette waiting.

She seemed somewhat surprised, "I thought you just wanted to go to another place to hang out. I had no idea you wanted to change hotels." She said as she popped the trunk of her white 745 BMW that seemed so complimentary to her style.

"I'm just not comfortable with the service. Maybe I'm just used to staying near the airport."

"So, I have an idea..."

"What's that?" I replied.

"Well we can take you to the Sheraton near the airport. I've stayed there. It's really nice."

"That'll be fine." I said as I pressed the lever on the side of the chair, reclining my seat back.

I couldn't help but remember the look on Jay's so-called friend Shine's face, coupled with the probing questions that flowed so naturally from her mouth. She questioned me as if she was a professional. But more disturbing, was the statement she made about her sister being gunned down. I had seen my share of movies, both on the silver screen and on the screen of the streets. Her connection with jay seemed, like she said, precipitated by her sisters death.

"So do you want to stop and eat first, or check in first? I..."

I cut Brishette off saying, "Let's eat. Your choice, I'm hanging out with you."

"Okay, fine." She said, giving me a quick smiling glance, and then returning her attention to the road. Whatever she had in mind I was sure to enjoy it. There was just something about this woman that soothed me. She was the calm in the midst of a storm.

Suddenly the ring of my cell phone broke the temporary silence. It was Splizzy's number on my caller I.D. I excused myself.

"Yes Sir. What's going on?" I asked looking away from Brishette out the window, into the nightlife we passed by in route to the restaurant.

"You're not going to believe this." Cutting him off, I asked,

"Believe what? What are you talking about?"

"Kim yo. Somebody just broke into her house and took everything that was valuable."

"She must owe somebody."

"Yeah, and I spoke to the boy Fat Cat. He tells me that Kim not only owes the Jamaicans money, but the weed connect guy she turned them on to, was bad. So they are hot with her."

"So you don't think 'L' had nothing to do with this then?"

"Nah man. This is the Jamaicans' work." Splizzy said rather confidently.

"Okay. Well get back with me. Let me think about that..."

"Okay. Peace."

I noticed Brishette looking at me while I was talking to Splizz almost as if she was trying to figure out the direction or context of my conversation, but she never opened her mouth to ask me any questions. That was a good sign, she minds her business. Already I was feeling her style.

"You know, I never asked you what kind of food you liked."

"I like seafood, ah... turkey, lamb, no beef, and no pork. Oh yeah, chicken of course, but you want to know what I really like to eat?"

"No... What?"

"You. You are the best thing on the menu girl."

"Is that right?"

We had arrived at Nikko's Restaurant on the hill overlooking the entire Los Angeles. The puny Japanese man dressed in a red sports jacket, white wrinkled shirt, and black slacks welcomed us and took our vehicle. She entangled my arm with hers as if to let the world know we were together. I was actually impressed. It felt good to know that I wasn't just attractive to the girls in the hood, but also to the women of the professional world. As we entered, we were greeted by a very beautiful Japanese girl.

"Party for two?"

"Yesss." I answered somewhat sarcastically. Wanting to say Daaahhh!!!

Brishette yanked my arm, whispering, "Stop it." The waitress escorted us to a quaint table in the back with a scenic view. It was beautiful. I felt so relaxed in her company. She was different, she was genuine and she gave me an opportunity to be as versatile as I had always wanted to and bragged about being. I had always said I could communicate with the best of them from the projects to the White House. It was crazy, butI could. When I was around Brishette, I had to step my game up and speak correct English because if I didn't, she'd find me less intelligent. It was just the opposite in the hood, if I didn't speak broken English I was acting proper and even white to some. All the self-help books I've read, all said if you wanted to be a winner, you had to act like a winner, speak like a winner, and surround yourself with winners. And Brishette was definitely a winner.

Brishette, looking at the menu as the waitress inquired about our selection, ordered warm sake and sushi appetizers to start the evening. "That'll be all for now.

We'll need a little more time to choose the entree." She informed the waitress.

Brishette had eaten here before but this place was foreign to me. So I didn't know what to order. I perused the menu looking for something familiar to no avail. I was a diehard Chinese food man because on the east coast there was a Chinese restaurant on every corner. The waitress returned with little white hand painted floral porcelain; half sized tea cups and poured peach scented heated sake into our cups.

"I'm ready to order. What are you having Dejohn?"

I said, starting to laugh "I'm gonna go with your choice, just make certain that it has some chicken in it. Now if we were at a Chinese restaurant I could tell you everything on the menu. General King Pao, Dun chow pow, SunChow Fun, King Kai..." We both burst out in laughter. The waitress gave a phony smile and pulled out her order tablet from her apron.

"Let us have ahh... An order of your Sukiyaki Chicken and an order of the Tempura Shrimp and some teriyaki sauce."

"This sake isn't bad." I said as the taste started to grow on me.

"Oh, you like that huh. I thought you'd find it soothing." She said with a sinister but seductive look on her face. She refilled our cups for the fourth time. I could tell this sake was starting to take affect.

Brishette had gotten comfortable and took off her shoes. It wasn't until her foot traveled up my leg to slowly seduce every inch of my groin, that I noticed that she was drunk. She had six cups of plumb flavored rice wine. We ate our meal and both decided it was time to go to the hotel. I drove and on the way she kept me excited, as well as anticipating her, by rubbing and stroking me through my pants. I checked in and got the hotel key card. As soon as we were alone on the elevator, she began kissing me passionately. Her tongue tasted like candy from the plumb wine. We were interrupted by an Indian man with a beautiful girl half his age. Either this was his daughter or he was paying to play. At any rate, we had to endure the temporary separation until we made it to the room. We had only two more floors to go. Suddenly Brishette's cell phone began to vibrate. The man reached into his jacket for his phone and found it was not his. Before Brishette could get into her purse, the vibrating stopped. Brishette turned on her ringer.

Once inside, we started undressing each other. Before I knew it, we were on the floor in a sixty-nine position, both sucking and licking each other as if we were auditioning for a porno movie. I could feel her warm, moist tongue travel from my balls to my ass and back to my shaft again. Damn, she must of went to school for this shit.

"Ohh... Shiitt." I was shivering partly from the cool room because we had no time to turn on the heat.

Brishette began moaning as I inserted to fingers inside of her sugar walls while gently planting my pinky finger at the opening of her ass hole. I held her vaginal lips apart with my thumbs as I blew softly on her clit, and then followed up with my warm tongue. She started to shake and suck faster and faster. Brishette started to return the magic. She started blowing up and down my throbbing manhood followed by her warm silky mouth sucking me with such precision, and just as I was about to cum, Brishette slid her mouth off very slowly and began blowing cool air around by shaft. Then as I shot my load,

Brishette quickly put my pulsating monster back into her mouth, swallowing every drop. I shoved my two fingers as far inside her as I could, at the same time back and forth with my tongue across her little boat, causing her to begin moaning loudly.

"Oh... Sssh.. . Oshiiit.... . . Whooo. Oh yeah. Oh ye.. .aeh. Huh huh. Whooo. Yeah baby. Ooooh." Her body convulsed as if she were having a seizure and she let loose. Her juices began flowing, soaking my face. We both got up and went to the restroom.

"Damn. You made me cum multiple times." Brishette said with a smile on her face. "You taste wonderful."

"So do you." I said as I stood there I began getting hard again looking at her sculpted body. Her workouts were really paying off

The later episode in the shower had gone on thirty-five minutes until suddenly we were interrupted by her cell phone ringing again with its distinctive ring of Beethoven's 'Moonlight Sonata'.

Brishette conversely stated, "I wonder who that could be calling me this hour." Just as she annunciated her last syllable, the phone rang again.

"Hello. What? Oh my God. Where is she now? What hospital? Where's Jasmine? Okay. I am on my way."

"Is everything okay?" I asked, genuinely concerned for her.

"No. My mother was just rushed to the hospital. She fell down a flight of stairs. She just recently had a hip replacement. I gotta drive to San Francisco because there are no flights until tomorrow and they don't know if she'll make it." Tears started rolling down her face.

I quickly embraced her and stated, "I'll go with you because you're in no shape to drive alone all the way to San Francisco."

I had experience driving at night with little rest because of my drug trade experiences where I'd have to drive at night when no one else was on the road. So me being there for her would mean a lot to her and I felt I'd have an opportunity to really get closer to her. We went to her house so she could pack an overnight bag.

"You know you don't have to do this." Brishette said as she and I headed for the door.

"When you need me, I'm there for you and if I ever need you I hope you'll be there for me."

"You're so sweet. I'll drive 'till I get tired and then you can take over."

Chapter 10

We arrived at 7:41 am. The hospital looked deserted, as if all the action had come and gone. We went straight for the emergency room. The security desk officer asked if we needed to see the triage nurse. We told him we were looking for Madrid Lionne. The Officer phoned patient services, located her and directed us to her room. I thought it best to wait in the waiting area on her floor while she visited with her mother.

I had fallen asleep for what seemed like several hours. When I awoke I notice everyone in the waiting area seemed to be drawn to the news flash, and it wasn't until I saw my cocaine conect Jay's picture projected upon the screen that I too tuned in. The newscaster announced that the "Authorities are searching for this black male, and anyone having information leading to whereabouts of this man should call 1 -800-CATCHEM. He is wanted for the shooting of an FBI agent who infiltrated his organization.

I thought immediately upon seeing the photo of the agent, I was right about the girl 'Shine' who I suspected to be bad when Jay introduced us at dinner. It was something about her. She was too nosey and accommodating at the same time. I wondered how much Jay told her about me.

"Hey." I noticed Brishette as she broke my trance from the overhead television. "How's your mother?"

"She's gonna make it. She's a strong woman. I'm hungry. You wanna get something to eat? Plus I still got a hang over from last night."

"I know what you need." Standing to my feet and yawning. I reached out and she instinctively moved into my arms like she belonged. My yawn caught her and she too began to yawn.

"Ahhh. Somebody is sleepy."

"Maybe I'll get some energy after I eat and get some caffeine in me. Oh yeah, my sisters want to meet you. I told them I'd bring you in when we get back."

My cell vibrated again and displayed Splizzy's number. I excused myself "Hello. What's up yo? What's going on? Yo Splizzy let me ask you something. Are you still going to be able to do that what we talked about?"

Splizzy responded, "I thought you was straight. You still in California right?"

"I started to whisper, "Yo, I'm fucked up. I need that money Western Union. I still got the stuff put up so I ain't even got enough to hold me."

"Aw-ight. I'm gone send you two g's yo. That's all I got right now. I know I said thirty-five but all I got is two thousand right now. I'll call you back once it's in and give you a confirmation number. It's a Western Union on my way uptown."

"Okay. I appreciate that and I need to talk to you when you call back. Aw-ight. Peace." I hung up the phone and noticed a look on Brishette's beautiful face as she stared at me as we entered the elevator.

"What?" I asked, grabbing her hand.

"Nothing. I just had a thought go through my mind, that's all."

"Like what?" the elevator opened and we entered a hall full of medical providers and patrons.

"I'll tell you later. I promise." She said displaying her million-dollar smile.

We found our way to the cafeteria. I was not trying to be around a lot of people. I felt like I might be wrinkled or something after driving all-night and sleeping in a chair. But it was just my imagination because when I went to the bathroom to wash my hands, I checked myself out and I still looked like the fly guy I was. There were very few guys I knew, who knew about, let alone wore Salvatore Ferragamo shoes. Even though it was my first pair, it wouldn't be my last.

I returned expecting to stand in a long line to order my food only to find that Brishette had read my mind. She kept it simple.

"I got you a cheese egg croissant and an orange juice. And just in case you drink coffee, I got you a cup with cream and sugar. if you don't there's more for me."

Damn, that beautiful smile just melts my world, even with all the drama going on in my life.

"How did you know I liked cheese egg croissants?"

"I just thought you would prefer that instead of scrambled eggs and grits, or pancakes with bacon because you did tell me you don't eat pork, right?"

"Yeah that's right. Wow, you don't forget anything do you?" I said smiling and thinking that she could be wifee material because the girls in the hood would have bought me something crazy like bacon and egg sandwich.

It was easy to tell that Brishette hadn't had any sleep. Her eyes were bloodshot red and looked as if they would soon need toothpicks to hold them up. So the money that was being sent Western Union would come in handy soon enough.

We walked into the room; I immediately got this queasy feeling in my stomach. Her mother was in traction and her face was covered as if she was burned in a fire or something. I felt so bad for her. All I could do was imagine what may have happened. Had she sustained broken bones falling down the stairs, or was she pushed, or what? You never know these days.

"This is my sister Mardella. We call her 'Mardy'." Brishette introduced us. The other sister had left ten minutes before we arrived.

"It's good to meet you. I'm sorry about your mother's accident and if there's anything I can do, please let me know."

She called me baby and told me that I have done more than enough by coming and supporting this family and that "My sister speaks highly of you."

"Oh yeah?" I said smiling and looking at Brishette.

"That's right." Brishette said, grabbing my hand.

I knew when we finally get to sleep, our loving will be explosive, and I couldn't wait. Suddenly the vibration of my phone startled me. It caught me off guard and you'd think I'd be immune by now but it continues to catch me off guard.

It was Splizzy. I excused myself, and stepped out the room to get the confirmation number for the money transfer. He seemed to be in a hurry. He must have had a girl with him and about to do something. It must've been around 1:00 pm on the East Coast because it was close to ten o'clock in San Francisco. He gave me the confirmation number and we quickly hung up.

I then dialed 411 and asked to be connected to Western Union to find the closest location. I was given a Market Street location. The location was three blocks away from the San Francisco Marriott. I knew that we'd be hanging out, but we needed some rest first and the Marriott suited me and the occasion just fine because

Brishette was a class act, nothing like Missy or Lynetta from the hood.

I returned to the room moments later, and not long after, the nurse entered and asked that we step out while she check her patient. Probably to check her to see if she had used the diaper they furnished her. It was time for me to get some rest anyway. I told Brishette that we needed some rest.

Meanwhile I couldn't help but wonder why Jay had, or if he had, shot that girl. Was it because she betrayed him? He was always talking about loyalty was big on his list.

Brishette waited until the nurse was done and entered the room to see her mother again before we left. I let her have her time with her mother while I walked down the hall, used my cell and called to check on my daughter and find out what was going on back on the East Coast.

Irissa answered the phone, "Hello."

"What's up? 'Where's my daughter?"

"Where you at? Why it take you two days to call back? We been waiting for your call."

"You a trip. You act like you all concerned and shit. If yo ass would have showed this much concern when we was together, we'd still be together."

"Whatever... Hold on, let me get Isha." I knew she still loved me because it was me that walked away, not her, and that makes a woman want you more because you make them feel insecure, like it was their fault, or at least that's what my uncle used to tell me and my cousins.

"Hello... Daddy?"

"Yeah."

"Hey Daaady. What you doin'? When you coming home?"

"I don't know what day because Daddy is taking care of some business. Okay?"

"What kind of business Daddy?"

That's my little girl, always asking questions. Never taking anything without questions and proof. I always told her to believe none of what you hear and only half of what you see.

"I'll explain it to you some other time Isha. So how is everything in school? Are you getting good grades?"

"Yesss. My teacher said I'm her best student." Isha said this with such enthusiasm, as if praise was the key to her success. So I told her how proud I was of her doing well in school, and promised to take her shopping when I got back. Whenever that was.

Brishette returned to the waiting room, eyes puffy from the tears she shared with her mother. I could tell she was a product of a loving family just the way she cared for and mourned this untimely accident which has her mother in traction.

"Are you ready?" I asked, beginning to yawn, indicating my sleep deprivation. But it was quite worth it because I had prevented a possible arrest or delayed it because I don't know what this FBI agent was told about me.

She and Jay seemed pretty close, but I know Jay, and he would kill, and has killed for betrayal and this girl posing as his friend when her sister was killed, turning out to be an FBI agent I'm sure pushed him to kill, or in her case attempt to kill.

I felt that drama was following me everywhere I went. First, the situation at home with 'L', making him the enemy because the coke came up missing. Then this situation with the FBI. If I stay here in California, the FBI may be looking for me to arrest me. If I got back to Baltimore I could be killed. But this was my chance to have a girl that men dream about; independent, beautiful, and smart and she really cares about me. She confirmed that she was ready to go.

We checked into the hotel and took a shower. Seeing her vanilla body, looking like Mariah Carey, sexy as a porn goddess, I got a second wind, probably from the shower. The kissing and caressing led me to bending her over in the shower and hitting it from behind. We made it to the bed because we couldn't sleep in the shower when we ran out of gas.

She was more passionate than ever. She took control by getting on top and riding me all crazy. I could tell she was acting out the aggression of dealing with the possibility of losing her mother. She has this look of seriousness on her face as if she had something to prove. Like she was in a fucking competition that she was determined to win. She rose up and came down harder and faster like a cowgirl at the rodeo. Damn, that shit felt like wet silk. I grabbed her waist and met her returns with an enthusiastic thrust then she exclaimed violently, "Oh. My ggod. I'mmmm cummmin'. Hh Ooooh yessss oh be baby."

She climbed off and realizing I had not cum yet, she lowered her head and began to introduce me to heaven. She did some tricks with her tongue that I had never experienced before. I gently grabbed her head trying not to offend or choke her, but it just wouldn't have been right if I didn't run my fingers through her long, soft hair while holding her head. She started licking the sides of my shaft up and down then taking the head into her mouth. I felt the clouds move outside, and my loins move inside, it was definitely time. She slowed down with perfect rhythm without me saying anything, then she paused briefly then slowly sucked me to a slow jerk and she savored every drop. I didn't even feel the urge to push her head away; when I usually do because it was too sensitive after I came. Most women don't know when to stop. Brishette just made dick-sucking history.

We slept until almost two o'clock, and ordered room service. I had a turkey burger and a Kaiser roll and fries. She had a melon smoothie, whatever the fuck that green health shit was along with a Ruben sandwich with chips and a slice of pickle. When she put the pickle in her mouth, I got instantly hard again, just thinking about how good her head was. She saw my throbbing member calling her, she said "Awe, poor baby. You miss me huh?" If my dick could talk, it would have said 'hell yeah. Please give me some more'.

We took another shower and fucked again. I couldn't keep my dick out of her. Let the truth be told, we both were addicted, especially since I gave her clitoris the hot and cold treatment. She'll never forget that shit., I put hot water in my mouth to warm my tongue while I sucked on her clit, at the same time I had two fingers planted inside of her, touching her "G Spot". I switched to the ice cold water. These two sensations caused a storm of pleasure. I liked it because if you think about it, that's what happens in nature when the cold front and the warm front meets, it starts to rain, sometimes it thunders and lightening fills the sky. Well the same happens when I perform my specialty, the hot and cold treatment. Anyway, both our oral skills were on one thousand.

Chapter 11

San Francisco, 4:45 pm

We arrived back at the hospital around 4:45 p.m. This time I was well rested and ready because I knew I would meet more of her sisters, who would be interviewing me. One of her sisters Rhya looked like J-Lo with a fat ass and small waist. Brishette introduced me to her and a friend of the family, Carla. They were the only two there when we arrived. Their mother was still unconscious or sleeping because they were talking in a whispering tone. Her sister kept looking over at me as if she were talking about me. Either she was feeling me or she was trying to figure me out. Whichever it was, I was the object of her attention. I was suddenly saved by the bell, my cell vibrated and I politely walked about into the hall. It was Splizzy's number on my caller I.D.

"Hello."

"Yo. Who's around you? Go somewhere where you can talk." I started walking down the hall, listening to Splizz, almost knocking down a nurse who was carrying some kind of containers in her hand; my heart beating at an irregular pace.

He said the words, "I seen the boy.'

"What boy?" I knew exactly who he was talking about.

"The boy you owe the money to."

"What he say?"

"He ain't say nothing. I didn't say nothing to 'em. He didn't even see me I saw him and his little entourage on the first level walking through the mall as I was coming down the escalator."

The shit hit me like a ton of bricks. I realized just how fucked up my life was. I had two g' s to my name and a few ounces of coke. I was afraid to even go back to the hotel because the girl Shine, the FBI agent, may have known what hotel I was staying at and Jay was on the run for shooting her. They definitely wanted to talk to me, probably hoping I knew where he might be, and of course, drug conspiracy charges.

I didn't have L's money so I couldn't go back yet. I couldn't send him the only money I had to live on, but I needed to send something because I don't know what's up with this boy. Whether he would hurt my baby's mother and daughter because he knew where she lived. I didn't know whether the airport was safe or not, now that the same FBI agent who had just nights ago sat in front of me asking too many damn question, got shot. But I knew I had to face the music soon. For now I would get back to the coke, find me a place to stay, and sell some coke and flip it until I was able to pay back the ten thousand dollars.

I had a lot to suddenly think about in spite of the beautiful feelings Brishette gave me. Which was another problem I needed to think about, that is, keeping Brishette, because she might run away if she found out I was a struggling drug dealer? It was time to step my game up and whatever I was made of, it was time to try it out.

Splizzy broke my daydreaming trance.

"Did you get the money?" And I needed ten times that much to get me out of this hole.

"Yeah, I got that thanks. I thought you would have mailed it, but that was cool, I had my license on me. Man this money is half gone already. As soon as I got it six hundred was gone, then eating and flowers for the girls mother, which reminds me has not arrived yet."

"Yo. You alright out there?"

"Hell no, but you know me, I'm gone come up. I ain't got no choice, I'm a survivor.

We hung up and I returned back to the room. Her mother was trying to talk, and wouldn't you know the nurse came in there getting in the way. I asked the girls would they like something to eat. They joined me for dinner. I should have gone to the hospital cafeteria and got sandwiches, but I didn't want to appear cheap. So we went to the Italian restaurant Carraba's that we passed on the way to the hospital. It cost $112 and under normal circumstances that was nothing, but I was way in California with no family, and no support out here and I needed to get an apartment or a room or something. Not just anything because I would need to entertain Brishette somewhere.

Anyway, we stayed another day and returned to L.A. I got a call from Jay's brother Kevin. I met him at a club on Crenshaw. He told me Jay said to stay away from the hotel because the girl heard him talking to me on the phone and he might have mentioned the hotel, and definitely get rid of the cell phone because I could be tracked by the phone. Damn, this shit was getting crazier and crazier because now the hotel might be hot, and I was thinking heavy on that word "might." What if he did say something anywhere I was staying and she heard it, and then they'll be waiting for me, when I go to pick up the Coke? But that's the chance I'll have to take tonight.

Kevin was well known at the club because they treated him like a V.I.P., probably because of Jay. Jay was rich since he was a young boy. He said he was 11 yrs. Old when he started selling coke and that his mother's boyfriend or his step-father was Columbian. Jay used to steal from his father until he noticed that his product had been tampered with and told jay if he is man enough to steal he is man enough to die. Jay told him he was doing it because he needed money. So his step-father gave him his first package at 16 yrs. Old and he never looked back and Lil Kevin, being his younger brother, he followed suit.

So everybody knows him and how powerful he was. The waitress kept coming back like her only job was to wait on us. Kevin kept ordering Cristale like that shit was water and free. I noticed-at the table across from us-there were two beautiful girls; one of them was dark skinned, fine as hell, and an ass that was calling me from inside her jeans.

"Yo Dee, them girls over there are checking you out. They like new dudes down here, especially from the East Coast. Shiiit. Go holla at 'em, if they want to hang out we can take 'em to the telly." He said slurring and getting loud on me. I was hoping they couldn't hear him.

"I got this." I started walking towards their table as I watched the one I liked turn some guy down when he asked her to dance.

"Hi yaw doin' ladies? I'm Dee." I said, reaching out my hand.

The light skinned one reached out first. I just shook her hand, but when this pretty chocolate thing extended hers, I took it and kissed it and made eye contact with her. She knew I was wanted her.

"Hi, my name is Candice, and that's my sister Sharice. So I see you hangin' out with Kevin."

"Oh, yaw know each other?"

"No, not personally, but lets just say I know of him because he's here all the time and you always see all these girls up in his face."

"Oh yeah, well I was coming over here to ask you did you want to dance and could I share this bottle of Cristale with you two beautiful ladies, but I saw you turn that guy down..." She cut me off.

"That ain't for us. First of all that song, I didn't like and the guy wasn't my type, and yes you and the Cristale can join us."

I liked her answer. She knew how to play the game. If we became nothing but friends I could deal with her. I liked her style.

"So what is your type?" I asked, giving her the look and running my tongue across my bottom lip.

"Let's dance, and we can talk later." We went out on the dance floor, En Vogue's 'Hold on to your love', the remix, was playing. She said it was her favorite song. I could tell because she was dancing all sexy, and then out of nowhere, her sister appeared and they sandwiched me. This helped me to make my choice, of which one has the softest body. I was hard as a brick when Candice turned around and put her butt on me and her sister's pussy was pushing against my ass. I know she felt how hard I was. It was like they were fighting over me on the dance floor.

After we danced two records, everybody started doing the electric slid. We went back to the table and began talking. I told them I was from Baltimore, like the D.C. area. They acted like they knew what I was talking about but they really didn't. But they knew I was from the East Coast and when I told her we could go kick it at the hotel, she responded, "Why would I wanna kick it at a hotel when I got a house and we could kick it at my house?"

"Yeah, but I still got to pay for the room because that's where I'm staying. I don't have any family out here and I don't know how long I'm gonna stay, but I know it will be at least a few weeks."

When I finished speaking, I noticed a sincere look of concern and opportunity. I always told myself that I would never move in with a woman because she would never get a chance to put me out. Candice began asking me questions like do I have a problem putting the seat down after using the bathroom, did I ever live with a bunch of girls before, and can I cook.

"Where are you going with all these question?" I had to ask because she was starting to get on my nerves and fuck up my Cristale buzz.

"The reason I asked you those questions is because we have an extra room and we could use a man around the house to help with the bills, and especially a Mr. Fix-it." Both sisters started ginning as if to say 'you could fix it anytime you like.'

I thought to myself, either my problems just ended, or just began or both. I guessed it was both because two sisters feeling me at once was not good at all, unless they were into 'manage-a-trois' because the one who doesn't get none would be the one that cause me problems or visa versa. Then if I do both of them, they both will have a problem with me being with other women. I didn't know what to do, but I knew I needed a place to stay. I just had to figure out how I was going to keep my thing going with Brishette, and either dodge or satisfy both sisters, who were both fine as hell, especially Candice.

She looked like Halle Berry, but darker and a little taller, and I could tell she wore about a 34B bra because her titties were perfect and stood at attention like a Chinese virgin. Then her sister, lighter like Alicia Keys with a look like Gabriell Union. They had to have different fathers or something because they both were gorgeous, but looked nothing alike.

This shit was crazy. You meet two bad assed women and they invite you to come and live with them, and don't even know you. But I guess people can spot "Good people" a mile away, or Kevin's status might have had something to do with their instant comfortbility.

"So how much would you charge me for a room for about a month?" I was hoping she said something reasonable.

When she said five hundred dollars, I was like okay, if I pay her for the month in advance, they might get crazy on me. So I told her I'd giver her two weeks in advance, that's if I like it.

"Oh, you're gonna like it because I am an interior designer slash decorator, and I put love in our house. So consider yourself fortunate because I don't let no any body in my house."

I said curiously, "So why are you letting me in your house." This response would tell me some things about her. I always asked these kinds of questions if you say yes, I'd say why, the same with no and my daughter was growing up to be just like me in that respect.

"Because I like you and it don't take a 1ong time for me to know a person's character and heart. Call me psychic or whatever, but that's how it is and that's how it's been, and nine times out of ten, I call it right."

Her sister said something so profound that I'll never forget.

"The person doesn't reveal the heart, the heart reveals the person. So like my sister said, it don't take forever to know a person because the heart is consistent unless or until it is broken, then it's a different story."

Man, that shit was deep. I was feeling that. She was right, and I could tell she was used to taking her sister's men on 'wit' alone. She was quiet and calculating. I also sensed a warning in her profound statement, as to say, "If you hurt me, I'm not responsible for what I may do." I didn't get this far being stupid. I knew I needed to stay away from her because she was the one to watch, and that's from a distance.

"So when can I see the house?"

"You would have to see it tonight in order to stay right? No, I was just joking. Whenever you're ready because we hadn't planned to stay the whole time anyway." I excused myself and went back over to the table with Kevin.

"Damn Dee, I thought you was going to holla at the girls you went and joined the party." He didn't know it, but what he said was right on point.

"I did better than that. I got us going over their house and kickin' it, and I might be staying with them. They got a house in Inglewood."

"Damn." He said chuckling, "You the mutha-fuckin' man. You made all that happen with one bottle of Cris, in about thirty minutes. It takes some guys all night to accomplish what you accomplished. So which one I get?"

I really wanted to say neither one, I'll get one or two for you and I'll keep these two, but I really wanted Kevin to break up the tension that I was feeling for having to choose one over the other and possibly living with both. At least if Sharice was interested in him, I'd have Candice and wouldn't be trying to share myself with both sisters because I hate picking the wrong one and regretting it later.

"The light skinned one. But watch her'cause she seems like she's sharp, and that's a dangerous combination, to be pretty and sharp. You..." Kevin anxiously cut me off.

"So you got the chocolate one? She bad too."

"C'mon, let me introduce you."

We walked over and I introduced Kevin and got the strangest look form Sharice. She looked at me like she was mad that I brought somebody else to the party, or she wasn't feeling Kevin. I may have been misreading her, but I've been around and this was another sign that she liked me.

So we all left and went to our cars. I was riding with Kevin in the Mercedes 430, black with burgundy interior. The girls were driving a Lexus coupe, and they looked good in it too. I took down the address; Kevin knew exactly where it was. I told the girls we had to make a stop but we'd be over there shortly.

Chapter 12

Kevin took me to the hotel. I slipped in the side door with my key card, went up the back steps being careful not to be seen, but as soon as I opened the door to the fifth floor after walking up all those steps - I ran into a huge guy standing in front of an open door, two doors away from the laundry room. This guy was so big, he could have won a look-a-like contest for the wrestler 'Hulk Hogan'. My heart started beating faster, I was like "Shit!", so I kept it moving pass the laundry room. As I got further down the hall I heard a door close and a woman started asking him how long he's been playing football. I quickly turned around and started looking at numbers on the other side of the hall as if I was lost. I figured he had probably picked up a hooker and was calling it a night. As they entered the elevator, I entered the laundry room to make sure no one was in there, then quickly climbed up on the washing machine, pushed the ceiling tile over I collected my coke in the shoe box. I replaced the tile and rolled out. I took the same stairs and out the side door. It was easier than I thought it would be.

When we arrived at the girl's house, they had gotten comfortable. They weren't in pajamas or anything but they had on slippers and, Candice had changed her blouse and was now wearing jeans and a Tee-shirt that said "I bet you can't" on the front, and "Handle this" on the back. They took our coats and offered us some chicken wings. I smelled them ass soon as I walked in. It smelled like Kentucky Fried Chicken up in there.

Kevin went out to the car and got his stash bottle of Chris. We drank, snorted a little coke and ate chicken wings-hot out the grease-and they were pretty good too. It looked like the more Sharice drank, the closer her and Kevin became, but I couldn't get her look out of my head. I asked to use the bathroom so I could wash my hands and Candice made her move.

"I'll show you." She said grabbing my hand like a little girl would do her first boyfriend.

The stairs were carpeted with a thick, soft, beige carpet. The railing was a wood grain oak, the wall going up the steps were covered in a beige and white print wall paper. I was surprised, it was kind of classy, especially the little brass seagulls on the wall gave that special touch.

When we reached the top of the steps she started pointing to rooms. I interrupted her, "Let me wash my hands first, then you can give me a tour."

She laughed, "Oh, my bad. Here, let me show you the bathroom boo." Damn. She was calling me boo already. It just goes to show, if a woman meets a man and she's feeling him, she's going to let him know. Just like my uncle used to say, "It's ladies choice, men's game." He tried to explain it to me, but I was probably too young to understand. All I remember is him saying "A lady knows when she meets you just what she wants. In other words, it's not about how smooth of a talker you are, or how much game you have, because she already chose you when she laid eyes on you, and these guys go around thinking they got game, when the truth is, it's woman's choice... They choose us.' Now I'm starting to understand all those old sayings...

I was admiring her bathroom, she was right, I did like her house so far. Everything seemed to have a place.

There was potpourri in a wicker basket on top of the burgundy-covered toilet. The shower curtains were see-through but lined with a burgundy shower curtain behind it. The rugs were burgundy, oval shape on top of the beige carpet that ran throughout the house. But I was especially impressed with the wooden mini-blinds that were the same color as the banister coming up the stairs. I had to admit, the house was hooked. The towels hanging up were burgundy and the hand towels over them were beige.

When I finished washing my hands, Candice came in with a hand towel. She had just gotten it for me out of the hall closet. "Here's a towel to dry your hands. Don't use these towels hanging up, they are for show."

I reminded her that I know. The bright lights from the three bulbs going across the vanity mirror like that in a stars' dressing room, illuminated her eyes which looked hazel brown, sexy as a mutha fucka, as she got close to hand me the towel.

"Damn you got some pretty eyes." This is the first time I saw her in a well-lit situation because the club had dim lighting.

"Thank you. You got some pretty eyes yourself"

"I appreciate the compliment, but I prefer the word handsome instead of pretty. Pretty seems too feminine, so I don't get down with the pretty thing."

"Okay, Mr. Handsome. C'mon, let me show you around."

"Hold up. I gotta a question for you." It was the perfect time. I had to get it in, and her answer would tell me whether she was trying to go or not.

"And I got an answer." She had this seductive and intoxicated look on her face.

"I just want to know one thing..."

"What?"

"Of all the T-shirts..."

She started laughing. "Oh my God. You a trip."

"What 'chew mean, I'm a trip? You the one wearing a t-shirt that says 'I bet you can't handle this. I just wanna know did you put that on for me?"

"It's just a t-shirt."

"Yeah, but it's a challenging t-shirt and I love a challenge."

I stopped her and raised my arms above her shoulders, against, pinning her against the wall.

"Boy stop playin." She said, giggling, but never pushing me away.

I had gotten instantly hard just thinking about making love to her, plus I was buzzing off the Cris. I started to kiss her, and she closed her eyes like she'd been waiting to exhale. She put her arms around me, it was a slow motion video scene. Only I shocked her, I reached behind me and grabbed her hands and removed them. Her eyes opened with a look like somebody was coming then turned into puzzlement. She was fucked up by that move.

I said, "Show me around please. I can see right now I'ma have to stay away from you, 'cause you like a drug. One time is too many and a thousand is not going to be enough."

She laughed, "Whatever. This room right here," she said opening the door, "Is my sister's room. It's a little junky because we were rushing to get dressed. I was getting ready to leave her ass 'cause she so slow."

"You call that junky just because all kinds of perfumes are all over the dresser?" Her room was nice.

She had a black lacquer canopy bed and matching dresser, and beige and black curtains.

"Everything has its place. You'll see." What did she mean by that? I wondered.

"This room right here would be your room."

She opened the door. It wasn't much in there, a queen sized bed, probably a nineteen inch color TV on a stand, and a computer desk with a bunch of pictures on the wall. It was neat and comfortable. At least it wasn't a futon and a thirteen inch black and white TV. If I stayed any significant amount of time, I would make it comfortable for me, but it would certainly do.

"Well... Do you like it?"

"Yeah, it's cool. I like it."

"So... What does that mean? Does that mean you want it, or do you have to think about it? You can stay in there tonight and let me know in the morning if you want it or not."

"I already made my decision a long time ago. I just had to see it to confirm that I made the right decision, that's all. I..."

She cut me off, "Let me show you the master bedroom. My bedroom." She said it like she was anxious to show me her room, and I could see why when we entered the room. She had a Bang and Olsen CD player on the wall like the one on Nip/Tuck, where you wave your hand over it and the glass windows slide open. She walked over and waved, the window opened; she hit a button and Sade' came on. That fucked me up. Then I noticed her sleigh bed. It was red oak with a matching dresser. The comforter was beige to match the plush carpeting; it looked like a goose down comforter. There were like these little Chinese burgundy pillows with gold dragons on them. Her drapes looked like they were professionally done. She had a creme love seat against the wall, and a big picture of black cats' eyes. I guess symbolizing her own.

"Come here Dee. Let me show you my walk-in closet."

She was standing in front of a long mirror, which looked like three people could get dressed side by side. She slid the sliding mirror door aside and pulled a switch. The light came on and all I saw were shoes. I thought I was on MTV Cribs. I forgot I was in the hood. This chick was living ghetto fabulous.

I had to ask her, "What do you do?"

"I told you. I'm an interior designer. I show people how to live."

Yeah, she probably show people how to shop too because I got a shoe fetish myself and I don't even have all the shoes she does. I walked in deeper and brushed up against her soft ass as I passed her.

"Did that feel good?"

"Did what feel good?" I knew exactly what she was talking about. I tried to play dumb.

"My ass. You know what I'm talking about. You did that on purpose."

"You're right. I wanted to see how soft if was."

"Well... Was it soft?"

Those hazel eyes were fucking me up. Damn she was sexy. I just grabbed her and started kissing her. When she rose up for air, she grabbed the crotch of my pants and started rubbing on my dick. Then she got me back, She whispered, "Sssss... I ... Wanna fuck you soooo bad, but I'm on my period, and if I wasn't, I'd still make you wait because I'm worth it."

Damn. This bitch had game. She walked away leaving me standing there. That shit was cold.

I called out, "You want me turn this light out?"

"Yes, please." she answered.

I came out of the closet and closed the door feeling like all my control had just been shifted to Candice. Now I wasn't sure who was the sneakier of the two sisters. I liked their style though.

"Come on. Let's go back down stairs before they think we're doing something."

I commented on how nice her house was and we joined Sharice and Kevin downstairs. But I could not get it out of my mind, the way she did the hot and cold thing. It reminded me of a book I read called 'The Art of Seduction'. She must have read this book because I felt like a victim of what the book called "Coquette". I remembered these words,

"...We are only excited by what is denied us, by what we cannot possess in full. Your greatest power in seduction is your ability to turn away, to make others come after you. Delaying their satisfaction..."

That was my intentions, to stay away from her. Now I feel like I gotta show her I can get her.

She kept telling her sister I reminded her of some dude from the East Coast who lived around the corner named Mel.

"Are you always this cool?" Sharice questioned, again revealing her curious interest.

"Why you say that?"

"Cause you be chillin'. It's like.., you just... you know... smooth with your shit."

Kevin joined in, "Yeah, that's my man. He's cool as a mutha fucka though."

"Y'all just high as a mutha fucka. That's all that is..."

"We gotta introduce him to Mel. They gone hit it off, off the rip."

I had to ask, "Who is Mel?"

"It's this dude we know. He be gettin' just about anything you want. A lot of the stuff in here he gave us and what he sold us; we got it for half price. You'll meet him cause I'ma see him tomorrow anyway. I help him out in the mornings."

Chapter 13

It was around 11:15 a.m., and I just got off the phone with Brishette, telling her that I am staying with some friends in Inglewood. I could tell she wasn't feeling the location, so she wouldn't be coming over a lot or at all for that matter. That was fine by me because that would help me to keep the drama down and peace with the sisters until I could get on my feet and get an apartment. Brishette invited me to a movie premier tonight at the Manns Chinese Theater on Sunset. I was just about to get in the shower when I heard Sharice call me from down stairs.

"Deeee. Are you up there?"

Her voice began to get closer. As she came up the steps, the door was open and she walked right in all excited, "He wanna... Oh, I'm sorry."

I was sitting on the edge of the bed with my Joe Boxers on, with the smiling faces on them. "Nah, nah... You good. I ain't trippin' and I know you've seen boxers and a wife beater before."

She just stood there admiring me, then she said, "He wants to meet you."

"Who? What are you talking about?"

"Mel. the guy we were telling you about yesterday. He said he want to meet you."

"So how did y'all get on the conversation about me?"

"I told 'em you lived with us and I told 'em how cool you was and that he'll like you."

"What you mean, like me? What, is he gay or something?"

"Nooo, silly."

I cut her off, "Silly?"

"I'm sorry. I didn't mean to call you silly. What I meant to say is he's not gay, he's just always saying how country California dudes are, and he jokes about the way they, you know, like all the guys say 'partner or pawtna'. He says Californians are country. So I was just tellin' him how cool you was and he want to meet you, that's all. You'll probably like him too because you two can relate better than the dudes from out here..."

"Oh. I feel you. alright, let me take a shower and get some clothes on. So what, he coming over here or..."

She cut me off, "He wants me to bring you over there, but its right around the corner. It's walking distance."

When I stood up, my dick accidentally came out of my boxers. Before I even realized it, she had commented.

"Please put that thing away."

"That thing has a name, it's Lil' Dee."

"Whatever its name is please put it away." She obviously liked it because she was still standing there. "I'm going to fix me something to eat. Do you want some?"

"I'm not even going to answer that. Damn, you opened yourself up asking me do I want some. The answer is yes. Whenever you ready."

"What are you talking about? I'm talking about food. Get your mind out of the gutter. Plus you're on my sister's team."

"I'm not on anybody's team yet, and your sister is a tease, and you're probably just like her."

"I'm nothing like my sister. And you wouldn't be saying that about me." She seemed to get a little angry.

"Oh yeah? Why is that?"

"Because I don't tease, I please..."

I cut her off, "How would I know that?"

"You don't."

"I said, how would I...?"

"I said, you don't."

"Don't you mean, you won't." I said as she walked towards the steps.

"I said what I meant." And she walked down the stairs, but I caught that shit loud and clear.

Man, my uncle was right about women. They choose us because Sharice had just told me in so many words, that she had not ruled out giving me some pussy. I'd just have to lay back and wait and let this thing play out. No hurry for anything.

I took my shower, got dressed and followed my nose. Sharice had cooked some turkey burgers. I thought they were frozen until I saw the packaging in the trash. It was fresh ground turkey. Very impressive because I don't eat no pork. So we had a conversation about beef and pork while we ate.

I asked her did she eat pork and she said she didn't but her sister did. That was a plus in her column and I couldn't help but think about last night and my kissing her pork eating ass sister. I thought, at least if I kissed Sharice, I wouldn't be tasting a pig in my mouth.

"So how long has it been since you stopped eating pork?"

"I guess about eight years. Well, lets see, I was with Rahim for six years. We been apart for about two years, yeah that's right, about eight years."

"Were you or are you Muslim?"

"Well, it's funny you asked that. I was gonna take my Shahada, I think that's what you call it."

"Yeah, that's right."

"What happened was this when me and Rahim broke up, I didn't want to see his face again. So I stayed away from the Mosque. You know how that goes."

"Nah, I don't. So you're tellin' me you let a man keep you away from Allah?"

"No, not like that, but..."

"Listen. Nothing or no one should ever keep you from God. I don't care who or what they are."

"You're right. I just been reading my Qur'an and the Bible and staying away from men who represent drama."

"So what are you trying to tell me, you're a nun?"

"She laughed and said, "If me not givin' up none in about seven months means I'm a nun, then I guess I'm a nun 'cause I will stay a nun until the right one come along because giving up my goodies to just anybody is out with the bump. and you know how far out the bump is." We both laughed.

"So am I just anybody?"

"Where did that come from? Let's go so you can meet this guy."

"Hold up, let me get my coat." I went up stairs, grabbed my money and my black leather jacket and a black fitted NY baseball cap.

As we walked to Mel's house, I asked Sharice if anyone called her Reecee. She said no. Then I asked, "Could I call you Reecee?"

"I guess so. Look when we get in here try not to act like you like me because I think he likes me and I don't want to hurt his feeling by lettin' him know I'm attracted to somebody else."

I don't think she realized what she just said. She's telling me don't act like I like her, but at the same time, she doesn't want to hurt his feelings by 'letting him know she's attracted to somebody else. Man she keeps on letting it slip out. She was right about the heart revealing the person.

We walked into the guy's house, and it was like being in a store slash office. This dude had all kinds of shit everywhere. He had new clothes thrown over the back and across of the couch. There was a wooden kitchen table filled with catalogs in the living room by the window. He had statues on the coffee table, and he was on the phone talking like he was a country oil executive from Texas. Shit didn't add up to what Reecee just told me about this guy, nor did she tell me she had a key to his house and she just said that she hadn't given anybody none in seven months.

He got off the phone after handling his business.

"What up youngster."

I take it that means that he was older than me, and I did look good for my age. "What's up my man"?

I responded

"So, where you from youngster?"

"My name is Dee, and I'm from Baltimore."

"Oh, you don't like me callin' you youngster? How old are you?"

"I'm twenty-nine."

"Yeah, just what I thought. You know how old I am?"

"Nah. How old are you?"

"I'm fifty-one. I'll be fifty-two in two months. You want a drink or something to eat?"

"Nah, I   'm cool. I just ate."

As I looked around I saw boxes, both opened and still sealed. He asked me how long had I been knowing Sharice and Candice. I didn't know how to answer that because I didn't know what she told him so I said, "Ask her." I hope he didn't think I was getting smart because I wasn't. He asked her too.

I thought she was going to lie but she told almost the whole truth. She said they just met me last night but they used to hear about me a lot because I hang out with one of their cousins, who told them to look out for me. I must say, that was a good half-truth and it mad him feel better.

"Okay youngster. So what are you doing for money?"

"Nothing right now, I'm working on that but I'm a hustler so I'm gonna be awright."

He chuckled and said, "I see what they mean about you. You're not like these California dudes. I like you youngster."

He gave Reecee some index cards with some information that I later found out was credit card information. She got on the phone and started talking like a white person and was placing orders with the catalog companies.

He handed me an index card with some funny name like Bazzigani, and asked me how would I pronounce it. I pronounced it in a way that made me become the character. I don't know, but it was natural to me. Like when I would go into a Chinese store and I'm ordering my food, I talk to them like I'm Chinese or something. People always say that I should stop because I am mimicking the people. But it just came natural because I used to sit in front of the t.v. with my cousin as I was growing up doing imitations of everybody, form Stevie

Wonder to Robin Leech of the Lifestyles of the Rich and Famous. So I had a knack for changing my voice and speaking like anyone African, Ethiopian, Australian, Chinese or White. I guess I always wanted to be an actor, and today would be the beginning of what would become my career in the wonderful world of fraud.

Chapter 14

I was being casted in a movie that would forever change my life. Needless to say, Mel and I became good friends. Actually, better than that, we became like uncle and nephew and partners in crime. He needed me for what I knew and I needed him for what he knew. So it became a value to value relationship, no one lost, we both won.

He started pulling out all of his hard to pronounce names, and I would not only interpret them, but I also would become them in character like I was casting for a part in a movie as a foreigner. He was amazed and my new acting career was born, maybe not on the silver screen yet, but I was certainly getting practice on the phone acting out parts that no one else could. I was able to bring alive a whole pile of information that would have otherwise been trash. So it was true that 'one mans trash was another mans treasure'.

There was another good thing about these foreign credit cards. A lot of them were rich and that meant so were we. He even gave me an index card with a name and address of somebody who agreed to accept his packages through UPS and Fed-Ex for twenty to forty dollars a box, depending what was inside. He wrote down what to order and asked me to try it. I did, and I liked it. It was fun and I had a good ratio of success. What I mean is, if I made five phone orders, I would get three or four of them shipped out. That was good because each box had either something for me in it or something to sell. Either way, I would win when these boxes came in.

I'll never forget the words he said to me that day. "Youngster, we gone get rich. You don't know how long I been looking for somebody like you. Yeah, youngster I'm gonna take you under my wing and we gone get rich."

When I left his house that day with Reecee, I felt like a new man. Like I just got a job making a hundred thousand dollars a year at IBM, and all I had was twelve ounces of coke and five hundred dollars to my name. Well, that's after I give Candice her other two hundred fifty dollars because I gave her the first half last night. But I felt like a million dollars. I had already started counting money in my head. I figured if each box averaged three hundred dollars, and I set a goal of one hundred boxes a month that would be thirty thousand dollars a month, three hundred and sixty thousand a year and hundred boxes didn't seem hard. Shit, I saw ten boxes in his house from one days work, and he wasn't doing it like I would.

I was so happy I kissed Reecee on her forehead and on the tip of her nose as we got in the house.

"What was that for?" She said, smiling. She just didn't understand that her introducing me to him was big; it was the answer to my problems. I mean, it didn't stop all the drama instantly, but I certainly felt better about my future.

"That was a thank you kiss."

"A thank you kiss? For what?"

"Because you just don't know what you did."

"I told you, I knew you two would hit it off immediately."

"Oh yeah. Plus you told me, before we went, in not to make him hurt or something by making him think you were attracted to somebody else. What made you say that? Are you attracted to me?"

"Oh my God. You don't miss nothing do you?"

"I'm just going by what you said."

"Can we leave that alone?" She sucked her lips and sighed.

"Yeah, whatever you say. I'm going and check on my daughter." I knew that would get a response.

"Oh, you have a daughter?"

"Yeah, and a son."

"Oh yeah? How old?"

"My son is six, and my daughter is eleven."

"Both by the same mother?"

"Nope."

"Do you still get along with them?"

"Yeah, we cool. I'm just not with either one anymore."

"Why is that?"

"It just didn't work out, that's all."

"You got any pictures?"

"Yeah. I'll show them to you later when I dig them out, Okay? I'll be upstairs if you need me."

"Alright... Wait... What would I be needing you for?"

"Hmmm, if only you knew but you don't." I gave her a taste of her own medicine and I walked away like she meant nothing. The truth was, I was starting to feel Reecee for real. She was everything I thought her sister should be, but in a vanilla flavor. I love me some chocolate girls, but don't get me wrong and it's no secret that I'll do a vanilla girl just as fast.

It didn't help the cause at all seeing her with those tight jeans on, and she had just he right amount of ass too. It wasn't all fat and funky or flat like some of the white girls I knew growing up that we teased all the time, saying they suffered from a disease called 'No-ass- at-tall'.

Hers was nice and plump, but neat with a three finger gap like she rode horses all her life. That shit just turned me on, but I had to keep in mind that most of my mistakes were made by moving too fast. Now I just take my time and let it come to me.

On another note, I had much more important shit on my mind, like how I was going to get ten thousand dollars to pay this boy. I had twelve ounces and didn't know who to sell it to until Sharice saved the day.

Reecee must have took creeping lessons or something because she walked so light I never heard her come up the steps.

"Dee. Dee."

"Yeah. What's up?" I said through the door.

"Can I come in?" I had taken one of the sandwich bags of coke out of the shoe box to bag up a little so I can take with me tonight and was putting it away when she walked in.

"Oh, I'm sorry. Am I interrupting something?"

"If you was, you already interrupted now."

"I can come back..."

"Nah, you're cool." As I said the word cool, she sat right on the bed, inches from the coke that I hid under the covers.

"Dee, you are somethin' else. I was listening to you on the phone talking like an Indian guy while we were over Mel's. You sound just like 'em. Like you lived in India or something. So where did you learn to talk like that?"

"It's just natural. If I hear somebody talk, I can imitate them. I've been doing it since I was a kid."

"Boy, Mel gone love you. You just don't know.."

When she moved her hand she felt the bulge in the cover and asked me what it was and started squeezing it.

I grabbed her hand, saying, "Damn, you noossey."

She asked again in a concerned voice, "But for real, what is it? Weed?"

"Nah."

"Coke?"

"Yeah."

"Can I have some? Is it the same thing you had last night?, 'cause that shit was the bomb. I couldn't get to sleep. I tossed and turned until I fell to sleep. That's the kind of coke I need before I go to the club."

I pulled the bag out from under the cover where I had rushed to hide it. As soon as Reecee saw it she began asking more questions.

"How much is that?"

"What do you mean how much is it?"

"I mean I've seen an eight ball before and that looks like a lot more than an eight ball."

"Oh. I thought you were talking about price." I mumbled with my head down, taking a twenty dollar bill out of my pocket to put some coke on it for Reecee. "It's an ounce."

"Ain't that a lot?"

"Not really."

"So what, are you sellin' it?"

"Shit... I don't know who to sell it to."

"Something told me to ask you last night did you have some more because I figured if you were hanging out with Lil Kev, then you were probably a dealer too."

"Oh, just because I hang out with somebody I gotta do what they do." I said handing her the bill with the coke in it.

"I ain't saying... Thank you... I'm not saying you have to be. I'm just saying that the odds are that you probably are. See you wasn't listening, I said probably."

Reecee used her pinky finger nail and scooped a small mound of coke and sniffed it.

"Mmh. This shit is good. I got a drain already. I could get you some sales too because we usually cop from my little cousin Larry and his shit got a lot of cut on it. You could tell because it burns like hell when we sniff it. My girlfriends will love this."

"Oh yeah?"

"Yeah. Shiiit, my cousin might want to buy some weight from you, or you could get him to sell some for you like I did when I got my taxes back."

"How old is your cousin?"

"He seventeen, but he think he's grown and he's a big young boy. He look like he's around twenty five though. I'ma introduce you to 'em whenever he comes through. He'll probably stop by today because the girl next door owes him money and she gets paid today."

We both heard a car door slam outside. Reecee went to the window and saw that it was her sister, Candice.

"That's Candy, Dee. Please don't tell her you gave me no coke 'cause she'll swear I'm trying to take her man."

"Why do you keep saying that? I told you your sister is just a tease. She's not tryin' to give me none and you ain't either."

"You don't know what I'm trying do, so don't speak for me."

After she put my twenty-dollar bill in her pocket, I asked, "Oh, so you're gone take my money, huh?"

"No, I'll give it back..."

"Nah, I'm just kidding. You can keep it..."

By this time, Candice had entered the house and closed the door behind her. Sharice went into her room, I guess to make it look like she wasn't just in my room flirting with me. 'Some girls ain't worth two pennies to rub together'. That's what my grandmother used to say about Ms. Gladys, the lady who lived down the street that became the talk of the block because she kept different men coming and going. a lot of times, just missing each other. If you ask me, I think them old ladies were jealous.

I went downstairs to greet Candy, and there she was, in a sexy taupe two piece skirt set that I later found out was Ann Taylor. You could tell something was on her mind though.

"So what did you do today?" She asked with a curious look on her face.

"Sharice took me...,"

Reecee cut me off as she entered the kitchen, "I took him to meet Mel and we stayed over there for a few hours and just got back a few minutes ago. Probably fifteen minutes before you came.

"Oh yeah? What Mel have to say?"

"He said Dee was just what the doctor ordered. You should've seen him girl. He was on the phone sounding like Indian people, and Africans. Huh, girl he took all them names that nobody could pronounce and started pronouncing 'em and talking like 'em."

"Shhhiiit. I know Mel was happy as shit then. I know if he turned that dead pile into money, that's big."

They were talking like I had just won American Idol or Star Search or some shit. I guess my acting impressed them.

"So how was your day, Candice?" I asked her to break the cycle and get the focus off of me.

"My day was cool except for this lady getting' on my last nerve..."

I cut her off asking, "What lady?"

"My client that I'm redecorating for. She just purchased an old Victorian house in the Palisades near San Pedro. I think she said it was her aunt's, now she's re-doing the whole interior. New wall paper, new chandeliers, new carpet, and a new furniture in some of the rooms. But this bitch is sooo meticulous. She just gets on my nerves. First, she loves my ideas. Then two days later, after I start decorating around that theme, she tells me she changed her mind, which makes me have to start all over again and that shit gives me a headache. I could use me a drink."

Damn, she gave me a whole earful of drama. But I guess I asked for that shit.

"Oh yeah. We still got a couple Heinekens in the refrigerator from last night."

She leaned back in her chair, raising the chair on only two legs, grabbed the door to the refrigerator, and tried to reach the beers, when suddenly her chair hit the floor with her on it. "Oh shit. Oouch."

I quickly ran over and grabbed her, lifting her from the floor. She looked up and her eyes locked onto mine. It was almost like she did it on purpose, just to get some intimate attention. "You aw' right?"

"Mmhmm. That's what your ass get for being lazy. You know you couldn't reach them beers. So I don't know why you tried that shit." Reecee laughed as she picked up the chair. The jealousy factor was definitely emanating from Reecee's voice.

"Damn girl, I really hurt myself and you laughing. I hit my back on that damn chair." I started to massage her back. "Uh Mmh. Damn that feels good."

"Damn. Look at the look on your face. You look like you're in another world... Damn."

"Damn, is right. Girl I feel like I'm at a spa..."

I knew Reecee was coming with something. I could tell by the way she looked at Candice that she felt like it should be her getting a massage.

"Dee, are you a massage therapist or something?"

"As matter fact. I am... I went to school for two years for massage therapy, but I never made it a career. I use it when I need it."

"Shhhit. By the look on her face, you got it goin on." Sharice just keeps pouring it on. Like one day she's just gonna come right out and tell me exactly what she wants and how she wants it.

I broke the ice by going in to the refrigerator and grabbing the only two beers that were left.

"It's only two," I said, taking the two Heinekens out of the six pack carton, "but y'all can have 'em. I'm cool."

Reecee beat Candy to the punch. "You can have half of mine Dee." There she goes throwing them innuendos at me again.

"Nah y'all go ahead, I'm cool. I'm going to take me a nap. I gotta take care of some business later on with Kev. Can somebody wake me up around six o'clock?"

Chapter 15

Brishette and I arrived at the Manns Chinese Theater shortly after 8:30. I did not expect for there to be valet parking at a movie theater, but this was a DreamWorks and Paramount Pictures collaboration and some of the heaviest movers in the movie industry were there this night. Brishette tried to fill me in on the way but all of this kind of stuff was foreign to me. All I know is, I looked like a million dollars with this tuxedo on. We entered, we were met by a tall, slender distinguished caucasian man with an after-five shadowed beard. He wore a black tuxedo with a paisley print, silk lapel. That shit was sharp. He stood behind the burgundy valet ropes and unlatched the dog-chain like clasp. As Brishette and I approached, "Good evening. Right this way." Pointing his skinny, well manicured finger towards the gentleman standing by a table, "That gentleman will take your coats."

"Thank you." Brishette purred in her sexy, seductive voice.

I was like Damn. She's sexy even when she's talking to the doorman, and probably the same at the checkout counter at the super market. I guess that's natural for a Parisian woman since Paris is for lovers.

This spot was off the Chain, the Chinese chain at that. Everywhere you looked it was some Chinese dragon statue or Chinese hut, miniaturized to display size. We walked up to the coat check, I removed her full length, chocolate brown sable mink, looking like it was a part of a Liz Taylor's collection. It was all of that and a bag of chips, like my sister used to say.

For some reason, I kept thinking about what Reecee said as I was leaving. She fucked me up with her statement. If I recall correctly, she said, "Damn you look good. What ever business you taking care of is gonna end in you sweeping somebody off their feet." It seemed like everything she said to me had a message in it, and Candice obviously was a bit oblivious to what was going on or maybe she wasn't and was just playing naive to see what I was going to do.

Anyway I was with a princess from Paris, and she was feeling me just as much or more than I was feeling her. I checked in my coat, now revealing my tuxedo that I purchased for three hundred fifty dollars, with a one thousand fifty dollar price tag on it, from a booster who worked for Nieman Marcus.

As we walked over to the escalators, Brishette must have felt the breeze on her exposed back. Showcased by her St. Johns, midnight black silk and sequent gown, revealing the perky shape of her now braless titties, which seemed to be getting hard in response to the cool theater air, and they weren't the only thing that were hard.

This dress was so seductive, her beauty-mark saturated, back was out all the way down to her lower back. It was so silky; it hugged and highlighted every curve of her beautiful shape. She had the perfect ass, and you could tell that she either wore no panties, or the best hiding thong was being modeled tonight and I was proud to be her date.

We found our way to the reserved theater. She introduced me as Dejohn. It was her French accent that made me sound like a celebrity. I could feel the jealousy in the air from the guys she introduced me to and I couldn't blame them. I couldn't help but notice the way she looked at the daughter, Mayleng, of one of the producers, Jack Chow, as she seemed to massage my hand as she greeted me. Maybe it was just being friendly in the Chinese culture, but that was flirting in America.

Brishette said, "C'mon baby. Let's take our seats. I think they are ready to start." Baby? Was she just saying that for the Lil China girl or did she just reveal her true intentions for us?

It was colder in the quaint theater than out in the hallway, so I offered my jacket.

"You look like you're cold."

"It's a little cool in here, but I'm okay."

Shiiit, I was even a little chilly, so I know she was cold with her back out.

"Here." I wrapped her in my jacket and rubbed her arms up and down to warm her. We took our seats and watched the movie. Just as it got close to the climax, there was a scene where the woman gave in to the stockbroker she had avoided for months, but he never gave up. It was the perfect love story. She started to sniffle and even my eyes began a water filled experience. I put my arm around her and held her.

"Oh shit." I was startled by my cell phone in my pocket. It vibrated, so unexpectedly it scared me.

I excused myself to go to the restroom, stepping over the couple that occupied the two seats that separated me from the isle. It was as call from the house. It was probably Candy. I took the call because I didn't want to be wondering for two hours whether there was an emergency or something and I certainly didn't want to ignore my new landlord.

"Hello."

Much to my surprise, it was Reecee. "Dee, remember I was tellin' you about my Lil cousin? He's here and he wants to speak to you."

"Put him on."

"Hello, whaz up?"

"Not a whole lot right this minute. Listen, uhm... How long are you going to be over there?"

"I'll be..."

I cut him off, "Nah, you know what. Let's get together tomorrow around twelve o'clock; lunch time and we'll talk then."

"Awight, that's cool. I'll see you then."

"Put Reecee back on the phone."

He called Reecee with his raspy voice that so obviously gave away his being high, probably off that weed which I will never smoke again. I had a real bad experience with weed when I was younger. That shit tripped me out.

"Hello. I know you don't talk on the phone, but he said he's ready to do something. Anyway, he'll wait on you till tomorrow."

"Awight, that's cool."

"What time are you coming home so I can try to wait up for you because Candy is in the tub and she'll be knocked out within thirty minutes of getting out and you don't have a key."

"Damn, that's right. So.. Uhm, I don't know yet. I know it's gonna be late though."

"Well... I tell you what. Just call me on my cell when you're on your way. I'll just keep it by my pillow. Okay? Let me give you the number. You got something to write with?"

"I'll remember it, what is it?"

She gave me the number and I returned to my seat. The movie only been on for a while but I didn't miss a lot. But I could tell that Brishette was uncomfortable with my leaving, almost like we were married or something.

"You missed a real good love scene." She whispered in my ear as I put my arm back around her.

The way she said it reminded me of her pillow talk. I could tell she was ready to do the damn thing when we left and I loved the way she made that tiger noise when we made love. That shit was sexy as hell.

She took me to her house, and gave me the best head I'd had in a long time. I couldn't make love to her because she was on her period. Afterwards I took a taxi home and was met at the door by Reecee wearing a long t-shirt or nightshirt, just covering her ass. I could tell she wasn't wearing a bra.

"Thank you for waiting up for me. Is Candy up?"

"I told you she's knocked out with her door closed." Damn, that was a strong hint. "I made some lamb chops if you're hungry."

"I ain't got a taste for no lamb chops, but I'll tell you what I do have a taste for though."

"What's that?"

"You know what I want to taste."

I put my arms around her waist, pulling her back in to me as she walked towards the kitchen. Her ass was as soft as two industrial sized rolls of Charmin. Damn. She grabbed my hands and led them to her breast and turned her head towards me. Our lips pressed against one another. She then turned around facing me and asked did I have a condom. I told her no, then she grabbed my hand, turned out the kitchen light, and guided me through the darkness up the stairs to her room where the flicker from the television provided the only light we needed. I quickly took off my tuxedo jacket, slipped off my shoes, and Reecee began unbuttoning my shirt, then my pants. I lifted her shirt over her head, exposing her perfect sized light caramel breast, and a red with black lace trimmed thong. She had no scars, stretch marks or discoloration, her skin was evenly toned. Her naked shadow was reflected on the wall by the light of the t.v.

"Is this door locked?" I asked her.

"Yeah, it's locked. Plus my sister is dead sleep. If we had a party, she still wouldn't wake up. Trust me, she is dead to the world.

She pulled the cover back, and laid on the bed. I crawled onto the bed and started licking on her leg, nibbling as I ascended towards my tender goal, she began to sigh. As I got closer to it she parted her legs like the Red Sea. It was moist and ready to enter. I licked around the lips, inserted two fingers inside of her as I sucked her clit like it was a Jolly Rancher. She moaned and as she got closer to climaxing, she grabbed my head as if to tell me don't stop. That was my cue to stop cold in my tracks. My uncle Arnold always told me to deny them and they will crave it, please them too much and they become board with you.

"Please don't stop baby. Oh my god. I was almost there." She whispered to me.

I cut her off, "Shhhh... I got chu."

I moved in and she grabbed my swollen love stick and shoved it all the way into her sugar walls. I gave her a few long stokes in and out, then I pulled out and assumed the sixty-nine position. She took me into her mouth, it felt like heaven. The more she sucked, the more I licked.

She exploded into a convulsion like tremor, that's when I felt teeth. She was sucking too hard as a result of her new found pleasure. I decide to give her a treat and let her feel how I work the magic stick inside.

I turned her over on her stomach, spread her legs, and entered her from behind. I grabbed her arms and spread them out to each side of the bed to get a good hold, and began banging away. The bed started squeaking, I slowed down and Reecee moaned into the pillow, trying not to make too much noise because even though Candy slept like a log, she still might get up to go to the bathroom.

"Let... Me geett on top..." She managed by turning her face to the side.

I let her roll over, she went down and began sucking my balls. I spread my legs and felt her tongue descending, touching my asshole. That sent a tingly feeling up my spine, then she licked up and down the shaft. That's when it hit me. We had forgotten all about the condom. It was a little late now though. She sucked my dick so good my eyes rolled up in my head. Then she climbed on top and began to slowly ride me then she went faster. I grabbed her hips to slow her down so I wouldn't cum so fast, but that pussy was too good. I shot my load inside of her and she went even faster until she let out a shriek and started shivering. While I was still inside of her, getting soft, she just leaned into me and kissed me. We just laid there, holding each other, it was beautiful. The next morning she acted like nothing even happened.

Chapter 16

Reecee woke me up around 7:43am and told me I needed to be ready in fifteen minutes, because Mel would be by to get us around 8:00. I took a quick shower, like the one you were forced to take in jail. A five minute 'wash your ass and get out; no playing or making love to the water shower'. Obviously Candy had gone early because when I got dressed and went down stairs, I saw no one except Reecee.

"You want a quick sandwich?"

"What kind of sandwich?" I asked, grabbing my coat from the hallway closet near the door.

"A egg and cheese on toast."

"Yeah, that'll be nice."

Moments later we both heard the horn blow. I was tired, but my adrenaline quickly overrode my fatigue.

"So what's up youngster?"

"What's up Mel?" I got in first. Reecee had not come out of the house yet.

"You ready to work?"

"Hell, yeah."

Reecee got in, they said their greetings. She had fixed him a sandwich also. Our first stop was a coffee shop about a half mile from the UPS hub. Mel went in, and grabbed two coffees because I declined.

While he was inside I asked Reecee, "Why are we sitting here? Are we meeting somebody?"

"No. We sit here and watch the trucks go by to see if the regular drivers are by themselves. Because sometimes the drivers have their supervisors with them and that means..." She stopped as Mel came back, "I'll tell you later."

We must have sat there for thirty minutes and I must've seen six tractor trailers come and go. Then suddenly it went down. This shit was like something you see in the movies. Like a 'Stakeout'.

Mel opened the glove compartment and pulled out some miniature binoculars and began looking at the truck drivers as they came out the hub.

"Okay, number one is by his self. Youngster, this is how you see trouble before trouble sees you."

"Okay. I'm feeling that."

Mel counted out one thru four and then he pulled off. I didn't fully understand why we were driving a Pinto and waiting for trucks to leave their base, but all this was answered later that day when Mel got a call that one of his boys got locked up. We found out it was because he walked up to an Airborne Express truck and there were two guys first of all, and neither one of them was the regular driver. As it turned out, they were police on a sting operation and stung his dumb ass. Mel said it was probably greed because this guy gambles a lot and he was going to make around four hundred dollars commission off the sale of that computer from IBM.

I was catching on fast. You didn't have to tell me twice, that was safety lesson number one. Never approach a truck to get a box unless it's safe.

We chased trucks all that morning and picked up eight boxes. How those eight boxes fit in that little assed Pinto is beyond me. But we dropped them off and went and got some more. When we finally made it back to Mel's apartment the second time, we had picked up a total of fourteen boxes. Four of them were computers from IBM. At that time, computers like those were running about forty-five hundred to six thousand dollars, depending on what you got in it. Before now, I knew nothing about computers, but I quickly learned because Mel had me write down the specs on each computer. Two Gigabyte hard drive, six Megs of memory, Pentium 4 processor.

Shhhit, when he got finished with me I felt like I worked in Best Buys or Service Merchandise or something, especially when he sent me on my first mission. He told Reecee to ride with me to the car rental spot and drop off a computer to the owner and pick up another car.

"So you want me to get money from him too?"

"Naw, I'll take care of all of that. You just pick out another car, and don't get that brown Pinto with the Raiders bumper sticker in the window. She'll show you what to get. You should be back by 12:30."

On the way over there I remembered the meeting with Reecee's cousin. "Reecee, can you get in touch with your cousin and tell him that we might be late. Tell 'em to come around ten o'clock."

"He lives two or three blocks from the car rental spot. We can meet 'em while we're over there."

"Alright, call him. See what's up."

Reecee picked up her cell and called her cousin, told him we were gonna stop by his house. We dropped off the computer, picked up this old assed Pinto. I asked Reecee how much these cars rent for 'because they looked like they belong in a junk yard or an old assed movie from the sixties.

"They rent the Pintos for sixteen dollars a day to Mel because he always rents from them. Mel is a smart dude.

He gets these cheap cars, that don't attract any attention, makes him look broke. He got the owner on his payroll. So if anything happens and he gotta leave the car and they come back to the car spot, the names are always bogus and so is the description of the renter. So he got that part covered."

Now it was starting to make sense. He knew the drivers of the trucks, he knew the owner of the car rental spot, and he even knew the bail bondsman, Buddy's Bails Bonds West. I found out this was an East Coast bails bondsman who expanded to the West Coast. I wondered if the car rental dude was from the East Coast too. I noticed that most of the people he had around him was East Coast. I was really starting to like this dude Mel. He was sharp and was a hell of a chess player. I could never beat him.

Chapter 17

We arrived at this big, three story, weather beaten shingled house in the middle of the block. Reecee doubled parked and threw her flashers on and I followed suit. She must have called from her cell because I could see her with the phone up to her ear. Moments after she got off, a tall kind of goofy looking young boy with a white tee, sagging jeans and some timbs came out the white muti-paned glass door. His braids needed a re-up 'because they looked frazzled like he had a wild night with some freaks last night. The dog next door began barking almost like he was saying, 'I don't like yo ass. You the mutha fucker that used to throw shit at me and tease me and if I ever catch yo ass I'ma bite the shit out of you.'

He went to Reecee's car first and spoke briefly to her through the window. Then she pointed back to my car behind her. As he approached the car I reached over and unlocked the door and waived him in.

"Waz up? So both of yaw got the Pinto hook up huh?"

"Yeah, this is what it's hittin' for, you gotta stay on the D.L. you feel me?"

"Yeah, so my cuz say you tryin' get rid of some coke..."

I cut him off, "Check this out. I don't have a lot of time. I gotta take care of some shit right now, but she said you was ready to cop something. What was you trying to cop?"

"A half."

"How much you pay for a half?"

"I pay three seventy-five to four hundred dollars. Depending on who I get it from, and my cuz say your shit like that! Fish scale."

"Awight, this what I'ma do. I'ma sell you a half at four hundred, and front you a half at five hundred. So that's cool with you?"

"Hell yeah. I'll be done all that by tomorrow."

"Awight so what time you gone be ready?"

"Shhht, I'm ready now."

"Awight, meet me at your cousin house in a hour. Naw naw, let's do this another way. Reecee will call you when she got it in her hand."

"Awight, well just drop me off on the other side so I'll be there when she call. Hold up, let me get a jacket."

"Awight, I'ma follow you. You can ride with her 'cause she know where to take you."

While he went in the house, I pulled on the side of Reecee, blocking the street, rolled my window down, "When you drop him off let's stop by the house real fast." We dropped him off and stopped by the house. I picked up the coke, gave it to Reecee along with my price, minus fifty dollars for her troubles.

When we got back to Mel's, there were boxes everywhere. Obviously the fourteen boxes we picked up together were only the beginning.

"So what car did y'all get youngster?"

"A baby blue Pinto. Ha-ha."

"Why you laughing youngster? That Pinto will keep your ass out of jail and keep the jealousy down. It's a work car and the hatchback makes it easy to transport your boxes, and boxes mean money youngster. The more boxes the more money."

I was feeling that, he was right. When you hustling you don't need to be flashy because flashy will get you locked up, robbed, or even killed on the streets.

"Youngster, I hope you didn't have nothing to do tonight because I need you to hang out with me."

"What time tonight?"

"Around ten o'clock I guess, and wear some old clothes because we might get dirty."

"Awight, that's cool." I didn't have any old clothes with me but I'll wear what I got. Shhht, I'll get some new shit and the clothes I got will be old.

Mel grabbed two piles of about ten index cards with information on them and handed a stack to me and a stack to Reecee.

"Did y'all eat anything?"

"No, not yet. Why? You gone order a pizza?"

"Y'all want a pizza youngster?"

"I don't care?"

Reecee called Domino's and ordered pizza and Pepsi's for pick up because they were scared to deliver to this area. While she was out, she served Larry the ounce of coke and picked up the four hundred dollars.

We ate pizza and placed orders until almost 4:30 p.m., then Mel told me and Reecee to take the baby blue Pinto and he'll see me at ten o'clock. Normally, I would've never been caught dead in a baby blue Pinto or any color Pinto, but this was different. I was proud to be driving a Pinto because it was all about the money and staying on the D.L. Speaking of the D.L., Mel mashed me with four one hundred dollar bills on our way out. I wasn't expecting that, nor was I expecting Reecee to ask me "What do you think?"

"I told you dude is cool. I told you that yes..."

She cut me off, "I'm not talking about him. I'm talking about me and you last night. Now do you think I'm like my sister?"

"Ohhh... So that's what this is about."

"What do you mean, that's what this is about? What is it about?"

"You and your sister competing against..."

She cut me off, "Hold up. This ain't about me and my sister. This is about me and you. I mentioned my sister because you said my sister was a tease and that I was just like her. So what I'm saying is do you still think I'm a tease like my sister?"

"No. I don't"

"And please, don't even give my sister a hint that we slept with each other."

"Why not? She might want to join us."

"Seriously. She will put both of us out."

"So what if I'm leaving anyway, what I get for keeping my mouth shut? Can I hit it whenever I want to?"

"Stop playing."

"I ain't playing."

We both got out of the car. Candy's car was there so she was in the house. I was thinking to myself. 'Damn. Now I got two people to hide this from. Mel and Candy'. So I thought I'd make Reecee jealous, I called Candy.

"Candy. Honey I'm home." Reecee gave me this dirty look and just smiled.

"Hey Dee. What's up?" Candy came down the steps.

"What's up Caaannndy girl? You are my world." I started singing the old New Edition song.

"Yo, your man's a trip. He got us rollin' in a Pinto."

"Oh. Y'all been with Mel all day? I called here a couple times and ain't get no answer."

"Yeah. He came at eight o'clock and picked us up. We've been working every since and just got finished. So what are you doin' for dinner? You want to go somewhere and eat?"

My cell phone rang and my daughter's mother number popped up.

"Excuse me." I took the call, walking into the living room.

"Hey, what's up Rissa?"

"Dee, what you gone do about this boy...?" I cut her off.

"What boy..?"

"He called here..."

"What?"

He called and told me to tell you to call him. It was too late to call you, so I called Splizzy and he told me who this boy was."

"What do you mean, he told you who he was? What did he tell you?"

"He told me that you owed the boy money and that's why you went to California to get... the money."

"Well the next time he call there, tell him don't call you, call me and give him my number. Awight?"

"Okay. So what am I supposed to tell your daughter who keeps asking when you're coming home?"

"Just tell her sooner than she thinks. Tell her it's a surprise. So where is she now?"

"She's over my mother's house with my Lil sister Nahjay."

"Oh, yeah. That's my Lil buddy, Lil Nah Nah."

"So is everything going okay?"

"Yeah, its fine. Everything is going fine. I'm working on the money."

"Please get that boy's money Dee so you can come home. Everybody miss you and I don't want nothing to happen to any of us."

"Yo, everything is cool, Awight. I'll call y'all tomorrow. Let me call this boy up Awight. I love you, hear."

"Awight. I love you too."

I called 'L' and got his voice mail. I left a message, "Yo 'L', I'm working on yours as we speak. I will call you when I'm ready and if you need to talk to me sooner, give me a call. My cell number is 410-482-1717. Awight peace." Three or four minutes later, I'm talking to Candy and my phone rang.

"Hello." I knew it was him because it was a 410 number.

"Yo, what's up Dee? What kind of games you playin' man?"

"What do you mean, what kind of game I'm playing? This ain't no game."

"Good answer." He said in a real sneaky voice.

"Listen man..."

"No you listen. I ain't heard from you in a few days, and you ain't even tried to get no money to me."

"Hold, hold, hold up. Did you get my message man?"

"Aye. Check this out. I don't want no messages, no excuses, none of that. I just want my money. Awight, that's enough talking. You need to see me and soon. I'll be waiting for your call." The phone went dead. I don't know who he thought he was talking to, but I know a couple people who will pull that trigger. Don't get it twisted.

Candy could tell by the look on my face that that call was a disturbing call.

"Everything alright?"

"Yeah. Everything is cool. Call Reecee, let's go get something to eat. Better yet, let's go somewhere for happy hour."

Candy called up the stairs to ask Reecee did she want to go. Reecee declined, probably guilt and probably she just didn't want to be around Candy while she was flirting with me. Anyway, I went up stairs and on my way to my room I stopped by her room.

"Yo, what's up? You going with us to have some drinks or what?"

"Naw. Y'all go ahead, I'ma chill."

"You sure?"

"Yeah, I'm straight." Reecee said with a look of disappointment that I was with her sister instead of her.

"You want the keys to the Pinto?" I said, laughing.

"Naw. I'll be here. I ain't goin' nowhere."

I didn't trust her ass, so I moved my coke. I put it in my tote bag and took it out to the baby blue Pinto, made sure nobody was looking and stashed it in the glove compartment and locked it. My grandfather always said, 'An ounce of prevention beats a pound of cure', and just in case she did have some idea to steal from me, it would be gone.

So I took Candy out to the Marriott, around a mixed crowd. We had drinks and she started to open up.

I asked her, "So what do you want from me?"

"What do you mean?" frowning her face all up.

"I mean, do you want to be just friends or more than friends?"

"Why are you asking me this?"

"Because I wanna know. Look, I know that when a woman meets a man, she knows immediately what she wants to where she wants to go with that man. So you know exactly what you want, and I need to know so I know how to treat you."

"What do you want?"

"It's not my choice. It's lady's choice. It always has been." I was enjoying this conversation because every time she tried to shift the question I pushed it right back in her court.

"Look, I already told you that I wanted you. Don't you remember when I whispered in your ear while we were in the closet?"

"Hmph, do I? Like it was yesterday.. That shit keeps running in my head."

"What?"

"What you said?"

"Do you really remember what I said."

"Yeah."

"Then tell me what I said."

"You said you wanted to fuck me right there but you were on your period and even if you weren't, you'd make me wait because you're worth it."

"So you do remember, that's good." Candy said smiling at the fact that I remembered.

"So how long do I have to wait?"

"Not long, just until I'm comfortable with. I don't want to give you my goodies and you turn out to be a jealous serial killer."

"Could it possibly be tonight?"

"Could I learn everything I need to know about you tonight?"

"You must have had some bad experiences."

"Trust me, I have." She began telling me about her past and how she's had three abortions because she didn't want to have children by these dudes because their true character defects started showing. She told me about her mother, how her father killed her because he thought she was cheating on him, but she wasn't. She also told me about her uncle, who they were forced to live with, forced her and her sister to have sex with him. Shit, my emotions went from horny to feeling sorry for her ass. Plus if the pussy was as good as she had me thinking, it was worth waiting for.

We had a couple of drinks and decided to leave. I called Mel at 9:23 p.m., and he was ready early and picked me up. This was the first night I truly learned the meaning of 'One mans trash is another mans treasure'. We must have found over two hundred credit card numbers in the trash cans and dumpsters outside of the stores he took us to. He said we were looking for the "Throw Away". He explained that that means a store does its accounting and inventory and goes through its files and throw away all the old paperwork or scans it into the computer and throw away the paper records.

This went on every night. We had so many credit card numbers that we took the next two years, that means if this year was, lets say, 1992, we would take 1993 and 1994's expiration dates and put them up in storage until we ran out of '92's.

Within three weeks I was in my own apartment. Mel made sure of that, probably his most compelling reason was Reecee. If I didn't live with the girls I wouldn't have the convenience of just walking in her room and fucking her, or maybe he was genuinely concerned. Anyway, whatever the reason was it was cool with me, plus I was up to ten ounces profit with the young boy Larry.

I sent eight ounces to Splizzy so he could hit the boy "L". He said "L" ain't like it but he didn't say no. At least he knew I was trying, but trying is the same thing that made his cousin come up dead.

The girls came over and helped me decorate my apartment. Brishette had gone to San Francisco to see her mother. A week later I got locked up for possession of cocaine. A petty charge but I got off with a cool plea for six months, and you do a third in the county. I'll never forget the lessons I learned in the L.A. County Jail. There were gang fights, rapes, and fatally brutal attacks from the guards. So staying alive and out of harms way was the mission. I was able to make calls to Mel and get him to hook me up with credit card numbers and call stores all over to place orders while I was in jail. So in essence, I was making money while I was locked up. The money I made came to me in money orders in my account. I was able to pay for services, like hot sandwiches from the officer's dining hall. Back then there were six men to a cell and one phone in the cell. The only thing I was missing was a real girl. Some of the gay guys tried to offer their pleasures, but I didn't do guys. They always said even if you let a guy give you head, you were just as gay as he was. So I'd have to have life or something to even consider it and I didn't, in fact, I only had six months to do and with good time I could get out in two months.

Brishette, Candy, and Sharice visited me at least twice a week. Visiting was seven days a week, but only one hour. I even met girls over the phone who became workers. They would return some of the clothing items or jewelry that I'd ordered from Nordstrom and had sent to them or someone they knew.

Nordstrom was known for its no questions asked return policy. It was the sweetest place anyone could ever shop. Women could buy expensive clothing, wear it to an affair, then return it the next day and get their money back as long as the price tag was still on it. It was their policy all over the country and they had a hundred forty-four stores.

I had a ball. I would call one store in the L.A. area and get them to transfer me to any store in the country. I would order gift cards or gift certificates in amounts of four hundred or six hundred dollars and I might call eight to ten stores in a given day. One day I made eight thousand dollars while in prison. Some people didn't make eight grand in four months.

Needless to say I had made a lot of friends, because when I bought commissary everyone in the cell ate, and so did the trustees, they called them. These were the guys that were fortunate enough to move around freely. While the other inmates were locked down, confined to their cells, they were chosen to clean up so they got special privileges. They passed out cold sandwiches and cups of juice, so they ate well and they could watch t.v. until late.

The best thing about my stay at L.A. County Jail was meeting Stephan Green. He was one of my "Cellies". A tall, dark skinned dude that play basketball, he must have been 6ft 7in. with a bald head. Not a bad looking dude, most guys his size were, or looked goofy. Dude was in pretty good shape too. He inspired me to start doing push ups because he was doing about five hundred a day. He just came out of nowhere one day and said, "Yo Dee. You a cool mutha fucka man... You would be good for my girl's cousin, plus she looks like Halle Berry. No bullshit."

"C'mon man. Stop the bullshit... Like Halle?"

"Man. Ay Dee, I bullshit you not. that Lil. broad look just like Halle. She just a little bit lighter, same body, same hair style. I'm tellin' you man... Wait till you see a picture of her. I'ma tell my girl to send me a picture so you can see her. As a matter of fact, when I call, if she's there, 'cause she lives with my girl, I'll get my girl to put her on the phone."

Shhht, he got me all excited and shit. C'mon, he could have said anybody but Halley Berry. That's my baby.

"So what's up with her? Is she single or what?"

"Yeah, she be in the house all the time. She's studying to become a court reporter."

"Yeah?"

"Man I'm tellin' you. Y'all would be perfect for each other."

"Why you say that?"

"Because she is spoiled, and you can make shit happen and ain't gotta pay for it, so you be a perfect match."

Later that night I spoke to her. Her name was Vanessa. She was from Houston, Texas, and had come here to go to school after being in the Navy for four years and was staying with her cousin. We hit it off immediately because she was down to earth, and it didn't hurt that I was getting out soon and would be able to meet her in person. I got her address and phone number at home and work. I sent her combination roses, half peach and half red, and she sent me a poem that I just have to share with you.

"Sunshine comes through any window you leave open.

I left my window open today at work and the rays of sunshine from your thoughtfulness came shining through to make my day more pleasant. The roses made the air more fragrant, your follow up call was a desert and I am thankfully full."

When Stephan saw the poem, he said, "I told you. See what I'm saying. Hmm. I know what I be talkin' about. I bet you can hit that."

"Yeah... You think so?"

He was pumping my head up. "Hell yeah... Man you got her sending you poems and shit"

She and I talked on the phone quite a bit. I sent her flowers, bought her outfits from Nordstrom's and even sent her and my secretary, or my celly's sister on a cruise for new years, all from jail.

When I got home, we met and went to the Santa Monica Pier. They were having a carnival, so we did the carnival thing together. Her U.S. Navy training paid off because she was a sharp shooter. She even beat me shooting the rotating tin ducks and I thought I was the shit when it came to shooting those B.B.'s at the tin ducks, but I never got all of them in a row. But she killed it, all I heard was "ping, ping, and ping".

Even the carnival worker behind the counter said in his country voice, "Damn Miss. You're the first lady that ever hit all the ducks in a row. You must go to target practice or somethin'."

"I used to be special forces marksman in the Navy." Vanessa said pointing to the biggest brown teddy bear they had. "Let me get that one please."

"You'd better not piss 'er off 'cause if she can shoot that good buddy, I'd sure hate for you to be her enemy." We both started laughing as we walked away.

"So do you normally scare your men away when you tell them you can fight and shoot?"

"Well, not all the time, but some men probably feel like they shouldn't be with me because they're not gonna do right and I might be vindictive. And they're right because I don't like people to play games with my heart."

"I need to ask you a question that I never asked because it didn't matter as much as it does now that I'm out."

"Okay."

"Are you seeing anyone right now?"

"Well, I guess you could say that. Do you know of the boxer Kevin "the Bomber" Wilson who lives in Palm Beach?"

"No, I can't say that I do."

"Well, we've gone out a few times and he's wanting to be with me, but I don't know. He's a nice guy and everything, but he's kind of possessive though."

"So how often do you see him?"

"Ahh... Probably two or three times a week."

"That sounds like a relationship to me."

"Well, that's what he calls it."

I said to myself, 'this is a problem waiting to happen'. She's the kind of girl that leads you on, go out with you, and might even have sex with you, knowing all the time that she don't want you. So you know what I did right? I stopped calling her pretty ass.

As soon as my man Stephan got out about two or three weeks after me, we hooked up and he showed me everything about makeup and costumes. This dude had went to school for make up and costumes and got a job in the film industry when he was nineteen years old, and been doing it every since. He is twenty-seven now.

Chapter 18

Mel had kept my apartment for me while I was away. It was only $750 a month and I was still making money while I was in jail. Candice and Sharice kept an eye on my apartment the whole two and a half months I was gone, they were real troopers. I owed them big time.

I also got the surprise of my life when Brishette got back from Canada, where she spent two months writing a Canadian movie script. I'll never forget that night she came to my apartment.

"Dee, we need to talk."

I always think that when somebody says that, they are either dumping you or they have some disease or something. never in a million years did I think some freak shit like this would happen to me.

"I'm pregnant with your baby."

"You're what?"

"You heard me. I'm pregnant." She said it this time with this serious look on her face, so I asked the obvious question.

"How many months are you?"

"I'm three months pregnant, and you're the only one I've been with."

That was about right because I was two months on a six month sentence and got out early on work release, so that is about right.

"So are you going to have the baby?"

"Do you want me to have the baby Dee?"

"Of course I want you to have the baby."

"The question is, are you going to be here for our baby?"

That was a very good question she just asked and I didn't know how long I was gonna stay in California, but I couldn't let her know that. Besides, even if I stayed on the East Coast when I went back we'd always have a bond because of the baby.

"Listen, Brishette I am crazy about you and I will assure you that if you have this baby I will be here for you."

"Do you mean that?"

"Yes I mean it. If I didn't I wouldn't have said it."

"What about your daughter in Baltimore?"

"What about her? She'll spend the summers with me or she comes here for school and spend the summers with her mother, but whatever we decide, it will work itself out. You have to trust me. Do you trust me?"

"Yes..."

"Come here."

She came closer and we began the best foreplay I'd ever experienced with her. We both missed each other a lot and it showed in the love we made that night. I woke up around 7:20 a.m., she was still asleep, looking so beautiful and peaceful. I gently lifted her arm and slipped out of the bed, thinking that I would let her sleep. I got into the shower and ten or fifteen minutes later I heard the phone ring then stop. That's when I heard her open the bathroom door.

"Dee, someone named Mel is on the phone. He says it's urgent."

"Tell 'em I'll call him back in five minutes, I'm in the shower."

"He wants to know does he have to come and get you. If so, you need be ready at eight o'clock."

"Can you take me to meet him?"

"Sure, no problem."

"Awight, ask him does he want me to meet him."

"He said the coffee shop at 8:30."

"Tell him..." She cut me off.

"He's gone baby." Brishette joined me in the shower and wanted to get a quickie in, but I told her we didn't have time because I need to be on time.

"Who is this Mel guy?" She asked as I got out of the shower.

"Another time. Not now."

We both got dressed and were out of the house by 8:05. I knew I was pushing it with the early morning traffic but we made it just in time.

"Okay, I'll call you later okay." I reached over and kissed her.

"I love you Dee."

"Yeah, I love you too." She pulled off, sending a couple of rocks from the graveled parking lot flying.

Mel had the look of approval on his face. Maybe he was impressed by the youngster having a dime piece that drove the big bodied BMW 745i.

"Okay youngster, I see ya. Mannn she was bad. Were you find her at?"

"I met her on the plane on the way out here."

"What, is she in real estate or something?" He asked, putting the binoculars up to his face.

"Naw, she's..." He cut me off.

"Youngster, check this out." He gave me the binoculars.

"You see what I see?"

"What, two people on truck number two?"

"Thaaat's it. Now you're catchin' on."

That meant we do not approach truck two at all today: Whatever they have, they can keep. You should've seen his face. He had a big Kool Aid smile on his face, as if he had just taught me to ride a bike with no hands or something. He was a funny dude. What he didn't know is that I was about to take this thing to another level. Especially when I put the mansion shit in effect that Stephan is showing me.

That day we picked up around fifteen boxes. That was not counting the boxes we had sent to the East Coast or to Candy and Reecee's cousins in Louisiana. I had three computers of my own that day. It was no longer just about him, I was starting to really make some money. He could feel me getting bigger than he ever expected, but one thing is for sure, he'll never have to worry about me crossing him or being disloyal, because I was always taught to never turn and bite the hand that feeds you. Plus, if it wasn't for him I would be depending on the young boy Larry to make me rich selling crack, which by the way, wasn't doing too bad.

We were up to a half a key, for those who don't know, that means a half of kilo of coke. After we flip this, then I could afford to take about ten ounces and send to Baltimore, then I'd be finished paying "L" and not have to worry about a war. This would set us back but at least I'd have this crazy dude out of the way.

I got a call from Stephan, telling me to meet him at Roscoe's near Sunset. Anybody who knows L.A. knows that Roscoe's is the spot.

Chapter 19

I met Stephan at Roscoe's Chicken and Waffles, the location near Sunset Blvd. It was about 6:00 p.m. when I got there. Mel dropped me off because I didn't want to be driving no blue Pinto, or any Pinto for that matter. The only reason I hadn't got a car yet is because Stephan was telling me he was going to introduce me to the boy who worked at TRW who could add lines to my credit report. I'd be able to walk into the dealership and ride out with whatever I wanted, no money down. Shhht, that was worth waiting for.

When he pulled up in a XJ6 Jaguar, green with beige leather with the top down, he made me a believer. In Cali, your car was like your receptionist or calling card because it represented you. It was your first line of communication so to speak. This dude was so tall, he had to duck coming in the door.

"Yo... What's up my man?" I stood up, shook his right hand and tried to give him the second half of the greeting where you give the half hug but even when he bent down it was hard to do because he was so damn tall.

"What's up Steph? I see you pushin' the shit out of that Jag out there.'

"Awh man, that ain't nothing. I got a few cars man."

"So when you gone hook your boy up?"

"I gotchu, just be patient. I talked to..."

We were cut off by the gorgeous young waitress that came to our table.

"Can I take your order please?" With her sexy ass.

"You can take anything I got." Steph quickly returned with a smile.

She started grinning, "How about I take your order right now and we can talk about the rest later."

That amazed me. Damn, you mean it's that easy. You pull up in something nice, with a little bit of jewelry on and they fall in your lap. Man I couldn't wait. She took our order and was back in less than twenty minutes with our food. This dude could eat. He ate three huge chicken breasts and two whole waffles, one waffle was enough to share and I had a hard time finishing one breast and a whole waffle. We paid the check and the girl slipped Steph her number. He showed it to me as we were walking out the door.

"So where did you park?" Steph asked me, chirping his alarm to the Jag across the street.

"I didn't, somebody dropped me off man. Remember I'm waiting for you to help get a car."

"Oh yeah. Damn, that's right you did tell me you ain't have no car. Awight, I gotchu. Come on get in, you hangin' out with me. I'ma show you around a lil bit, then I'ma show you how I'm living and how you gonna be living."

We stopped about six blocks away, in front of a store called The Costume Gallery, it was about to close. But we made it to the door as the Greek man was about to turn the lock. The man noticed it was Steph and opened the door for us.

"Hello my friend. What can I do for you?" Obviously the man knew Steph real well because he acted like the president had come by. "We had some new compound come in today. It's darker than anything we've had before."

"Let me see it. Let's see what it looks like."

While the man went into the back, Steph showed me a fat mans body costume, a fake beard and mustache and he showed me an old mans costume with a hump in the back.

"Yo Dee, this is the spot right here. Once you learn this thing, boy the sky is the limit. You can look like almost anything you want to look like partner." All this shit was new to me, this was some shit you see on t.v., like, what the pretender does. He wears masks and costumes and different identifications.

The man returned with a pint sized tin can full of some brown gooey stuff.

"How many cans do you want?"

"I'll take just this one right now. Let me see how it works first."

As we walked to the counter Steph showed me all sorts of stuff. Fake blood then they had these pills in the case that he said made you foam from the mouth like you were having a seizure. He told me the brown stuff, mixed with another compound made fake skin. He said this is what the characters on Star Trek used to make themselves look like aliens.

We left there and went to a strip club called Exotica. When we walked in, the smell of stale pussy, cigarette smoke, and alcohol smacked me in the face. The girls immediately came over to talk to him as if he was a regular. He told them all at one time, "You see this dude right here, this is my partner Dee and he just came home from jail. So take care of him, give him anything he wants."

"Oh yeah, he just came home huh." This beautiful cocoa brown, petite doll baby looking girl with the most pretty light brown perky breast with darker brown rings around her nipples sat on my lap.

"I'm China Doll, this is my girlfriend Luscious. So how long you been down?"

"Not long, just a few months, but a few months are like years to me. You feel me?"

"Yeah baby..." We were cut off by the waitress.

"What can I get you?"

I ordered a Remy XO and two drinks for the girls. When Luscious got her drink she said she'd be back. China Doll gave a lap dance and got me all hard and ready.

"So how much is the lap dance?"

"Don't worry about it, Kareem will take care of it."

"Kareem? Who is Kareem?"

"Oh, what do you call him? We call him Kareem because he's so tall."

"Oh, okay. You're talking about my man. Okay, I was wondering who Kareem was. Yeah okay."

"You been to any of his mansion parties yet?"

"Naw, not yet, remember I just got out."

"Yeah, that's right. His parties are off the chain, it be all kinds of people there. Shaq and A.I. was at his last party. Oh yeah, so was Ice Cube."

"Oh yeah?"

"So I know you've gotten your nuts out of the sand since you've been home." Shhhit that sounded like funkin' words to me.

"So why you ask me that? You tryin' to help a brotha out?"

"You are kinda cute." She really started grinding on my lap. My dick was as hard as penitentiary steel.

"I don't know, we might be able to work something out."

Steph came walking over to our little corner table in the dark, "Dee, I gotta run. You staying, or you going with me? As a matter of fact, I need you to go with me."

If I would have stayed, I would've had to fuck something 'cause she had pre-cum coming out of my dick. I was ready, I could've pulled that thong over and slid right in her pretty pussy, raw, and you know that shit ain't cool. I decided I'd better go.

"Boy, this China Doll is something else."

"Oh you ain't gotta tell me. Shhit, she's about her work."

"Let me give you my cell number Dee, hold up." She left the table briefly to grab a napkin and a pen from the bar, wrote her number and handed it to me, "You look a lil swollen down there. You might need to put some ice on it or some warm, moist, heat to bring the swelling down." Of course she was licking her lips standing there. Man, California was treating me real good. Shit, I might not go back to Baltimore if it keeps going like this.

"Yeah, okay, maybe you can help me when I call you."

She just smiled and I turned to walk out. Steph had pulled the car up to the door, it had just gotten dark while we were inside. The street lights really set that money green paint job off. It was about eighty degrees so he had the top down.

"What's up Steph. What, you got V.I.P. status in the town?" The girl asked me have I been to one of your parties. No, she said 'Mansion Parties''. You ain't tell me 'bout the mansion parties... What's..." Steph cut me off.

"We gone stop by my house. I'ma show you something, that's why we left because I got a call from my young girl. She's locked out. She said the remote to the gate is not working."

"To the gate? Don't you mean garage?"

"Naw, the gate. You'll see, we're almost there."

We turned left off Sunset headed towards Los Felix and went up a steep hill. Then we made another turn and started going up a spiral mountain, it seemed like we passed a few huge houses partially hidden by the trees. That's when he pulled behind a black Mercedes CLK 500, the little female sports car.

This bad assed young girl got out of the car and walked back to the Jag, "Hey baby. Oh... Hi." She couldn't see me until she got to the car because it was dark. "I don't know what's wrong with my key card. I swiped it against the thing and the gate won't open."

"Here, try mine." He handed her a thin white card. She walked over to the gate and tried it and quickly returned.

"Yours doesn't work either."

"What? What do you mean mine doesn't work? Hold up. Watch out... Let me out." He exited the car and walked over to the well lit gate, illuminated by the cars bright halogen lights. He tried it and suddenly the gate opened.

"Why did it work for you and not for me?"

"Probably because you weren't doing it right. Show me how you were doin' it." She showed him how she swiped the card, "That's why, you are going too fast. Look. You have to hold it over the contact for three seconds."

The gate opened again. Once we were inside both cars followed the circular cobblestone drive that led to the front of this mega structure that reminded me of the mansion owned by the Carrington's on the T.V. series 'Dallas'. I couldn't help but notice what looked like a hundred thousand dollar landscaping job. The palm trees in front stood in formation as would soldiers on the front line. The bushes were expertly manicured, and the photograph-quality lighting showcased the front of the property as if it were on display in an outdoor museum. The three or four steps leading to the foyer were marble as was the floor of the octagon shaped foyer. We walked through the huge Red Oak double doors with brass handles, and what I saw, I could not believe. It felt like I had just walked into a scene of the movie 'Scarface'. You would definitely remember the inside of his mansion where the stairs ascended on both sides, meeting at the balcony.

Man, this shit reminded me of when I was a kid in the sixth grade. We went on a field trip to the White House. There were so many rooms we didn't get to see them all. All I could think of was the stripper China Doll asking me had I been to one of the mansion parties. I could imagine a party up in this big mutha fucka, with naked strippers running around everywhere. Champaign campaign and getting lost in one of the many rooms.

"Yo, Steph this crib is like that! So this is how you living huh?"

"Ahy Dee, don't even trip. In a minute you gone have your own. This shit come and go man. All you gotta do is stick with your boy."

My mind was running a hundred thousand miles an hour thinking about how long it'll take and what I had to do to be living like this. It was like Steph read my mind.

"Yo Dee. Stop thinking so hard. I could hear yo ass thinking. Relax, make yourself at home. I got some Heineken in the refrigerator and all kinds of liquor in the bar back there.." He said pointing towards the kitchen and den area. "Oh yeah, if you look behind the bar you'll see a ummn, a burgundy leather-like box. That's my private stock. I don't share that with just anybody, that's my Louis XIII. But chu' my man Dee, so go ahead, get yourself a shot or two. Awight. It'll put you where you wanna be. I'm fittin' to holla at my shortie and make a few calls. I'll get with you in a minute."

"Where your bathroom at?"

"They're all over. As a matter of fact there's one right behind you." He walked up the stairs and disappeared.

While I was using the bathroom it hit me. He never even introduced me to the girl. I wonder what that's about. What he think, I'ma steal his girl or something. Shhhit, I had enough problems of my own, Brishette worrying about whether I was gonna stay in Cali to be with her and the baby, I was fucking Reecee, and trying to keep it away from Candy and Mel because we were getting money together. I didn't want to hurt Candy and I sure don't want to fuck it up with Steph trying to fuck his girl. If he gonna have me living like this. Shit, and now with broads like China Doll coming at me, my plate is full.

It seemed like as soon as I poured my shot of Louis, my cell phone rang.

"Hello. Damn girl, I was just thinking about you. Is everything aw'right? You need something Brishette?"

"No. I just miss you and I just wanted to know if you were coming over or do you want me to come over your house?"

"Uhmm, what time are you talking about because I'm over my mans' house taking care of some business. Naw, you know what, I should be here in no more than an hour but I'll call you as soon as I'm done and ill get him to drop me off over your house. Did you cook?"

"No. I had some shrimp and broccoli from the Chinese restaurant in China Town, but you could pick up some butter pecan ice cream on your way."

"Oh, the baby want some ice cream already?"

She laughed, "I guess it's the baby talking to me. You know I'm eating for two."

"Awight. I'll call you when I'm leaving."

"Okay, I love you."

"Awight. I love you too."

As I began sipping my extra fine cognac Steph and this bad assed young girl that was locked out of the gate entered the den where I was. He introduced her fine ass, "Dee, this is my shortie Lashanda. Lashanda this is Dee."

"Good to me you." I shook her hand. Her hand was soft as a mutha fucka. I could imagine what it was like him punishing that. But what always fucked me up was how these little assed girls always go for these giant dudes. She must be no more than 5ft 3m and about twenty-two or twenty three years old. She looked like a lil girl compared to his almost 7ft ass. She left the room and Steph pulled out some real estate magazines with these mansions on the cover.

"Hold up Dee." He walked over to a desk, opened the drawer and pulled out a burgundy leather organizer, opened it and pulled out an envelope with some papers in it.

In forty-five minutes I learned some game that changed my life forever, and when you hear what's about to go down you will definitely agree with me.

Chapter 20

Steph opened the magazine and showed me the same mansion that we were in. The price on it was $2,489,000, reduced to $1,899,000. "Check this out. Once you pick the ones you want, and you have to pick a few, and try to deal directly with a owner instead of an agent."

I'm looking at him like he was crazy. Where was I going to get enough money to put a down payment on a mansion. I cut him off, "So where is the money comin' from?"

"What money? You don't need much money. Just a few hundred for your expenses and five grand to pay the credit boy at TRW. Just listen Dee. So like I was saying, you pick a few of them because you're gonna have to go through a few of them before you find the one that works."

"What do you mean, that works?"

"Look, you gotta find a owner who either lives out of town and shows the property by appointment or somebody who is going away on vacation or to their summer home or something. They will tell you to rush you to make your decision, and you tell them you'll get back to them. As soon as they are gone and won't be coming back for months, you take out an add in the newspaper's real estate section." He pulled out a clipping of a newspaper ad which had an add to lease or buy the property we were in.

"This is what it will look like. You do this so you can show how you stumbled up on the properties. You take out the ad and you give them a name and number to a voicemail. Next, you go to Office Depot or Staples and get a payment receipt book and a pack of blank lease with option to buy forms."

"So. . ." He cut me off.

"Just listen. You get a real estate calculator from Best Buy, or you can use mine. It will show you what the mortgage payment would be if you were paying the mortgage. For example, a property selling for $1,500,000, your payment would be $4,824.93 a month. So you'd add a few percent for a lease, say $5,300 per month. So six months in advance would be $31,800. You would fill out the receipt as if you paid it to the name of the person you used in the ad."

"So let me get this straight. I'm really not paying nobody?"

"Right... You just look like you did everything right, on paper. Now remember, you're gonna fill out the lease, type it as if the owner did it himself because the owner's name must be on the lease and he is leasing it to you with an option to buy. Then you take the lease and your birth certificate and Social Security Card to DMV and get your license with your new address on it to the mansion. Now it's time for the TRW boy to do his thing, and the alarm boy will disable the alarm. Then you call the locksmith, tell 'em you're locked out."

"Hold up. Let me make sure I got it all...".

Steph cut me off again. "I'm not finished. Stop cuttin me off, just listen before you miss something real important. So like I was saying, the TRW boy add a couple of lines of credit to your credit report, he add the house at 2.4 million, a yacht paid for at 1.6 million and a few other things. Then you set up an office, which is easy. You find one of those companies that rent these huge prestigious offices that rent virtual offices where they have you use their address, their receptionist, and you could rent a small office or just use the conference room when you need it. It only cost a few hundred a month, but you will be a commercial real estate broker with a salary and commissions upward of three million a year. So you will look like platinum on paper."

"Damn, this shit sounds sweet. So that's how you got this spot?"

"Yeah, and the best part of this is that the boy, if he trust you, he'll let you pay him his five grand when you get it because you guaranteed to get your car and everything else you want, most of the time with no money down. So like I told you, you can get anything you want. Once you got this hook up working for you, you can cop you a S600 Benz or Range Rover or whatever, and it's yours. You can make money off the mansion parties, two hundred dollars a head, and rent a few rooms out to the strippers so you'll be living like a star and making money."

"So how soon can we get started?"

"I gotta go out of town tomorrow and I won't be back for three days, but as soon as I get back we'll start looking for you a spot. Awight?"

"Hell yeah."

"Finish your drink so we can get out of here."

"So do you stay here every night?"

"Not all the time. Sometimes I stay at my house in West L.A. I got a house in Culver City too."

"Oh yeah?"

"Oh, and I almost forgot. Don't ever get attached to the mansion because until you're making enough money, these shits is temporary because when the owner comes back he's gonna want you out. But with all the paper work you got, the law is going to be on your side and then it becomes civil and it takes almost six months to get you out. You got from the time you move in until three or four months after they find out, but you never stay long enough to get put out. When the owner finds out, you got a couple months."

"So how you get all this furniture, and what do you do with it when you gotta move?"

"Oh, that easy. You just rent, plus your car will have the mansions' address so if they come looking for it because you missed a payment, but you'll be making money so you'll pay your car payments. Plus I got somebody on the inside of the bank that approves loans once you get the credit right. So you'll never be broke."

As we left, we passed by a green Toyota Corolla with two girls inside. Steph stopped and they backed up until the two cars were side by side. Steph hit the window on my side. "What's up girls."

"Hey Kareem."

"Hey Rhonda. What's up China."

"Hey Reem, you coming back?"

"Yeah, I'ma drop my man off real quick, I'll be back."

I quickly asked, "They live with you Steph?"

"Yeah. Ay Rhonda, did you meet Dee?"

"I didn't but China did. How you doing." She spoke

"I'm good, what's up?" I responded giving China that look.

"Oh yeah, that's right you did meet China. Awight, I'm out. I'll see y'all later."

Steph took me to 7-11 on Lacienega. I grabbed the butter pecan and he dropped me off.

I twisted and turned almost all night thinking about this mansion shit., Imagine living like a star, having mansion parties and strippers as roommates and instead of you paying for anything, everything is paying you. The only thing about it is the better you live, the more drama you have in your life. For example, I got to figure out how I'm going to be living in a mansion with strippers, while Brishette wants me to be with her and the baby every night. Then I got to deal with Reecee wanting to sneak behind her sister Candy's back and sex me. Then her sister is starting to open up and I think she's ready to do the damned thing too. But I want a taste of this mansion life. The question is, is it worth it and how do you keep all this shit separate.

Then I got this drug shit on my mind, I owe the boy in Baltimore ten ounces of coke. I'm scared to send it because it might not get there. If I take it, I might not get there. Then I got this young boy Larry selling coke for me. I don't know what he might do if he get caught and they ask him who he is selling for. That could turn into me getting locked up for a conspiracy. Plus I still don't know whether I'm involved in a conspiracy with Jay, and he's hot as a mutha fucka because he shot that FBI agent and is on the run, and I'm getting the coke from his brother. I don't know if they were watching him and got pictures of me meeting him, or what? Shit... I gotta figure all this shit out.

Chapter 21

I woke up next to Brishette again. This shit was starting to become a beautiful habit, a model from Paris, a man's dream next to me every morning but something was missing, that lifestyle. I had to have it.

The phone rang. It was 7:28 am, 10:28 on the East Coast. The 'caller I.D. on the nightstand next to my black V-tech cordless phone showed Splizzy's cell phone number. I wondered was he needing his twenty-five hundred dollars he lent me cause I sure didn't have it yet.

I picked up the phone, "Hello... .Yeah I'm up. Yo Splizz, I'm glad you called yo. I need to talk to you. I need to get your opinion on some shit."

I felt Brishette moving in the bed probably awakened by the phone so I got up off the bed and went into the living room to talk in private. Splizz started telling me what was going on, "Yo Dee, Lil Stevie got killed in front of his mother's house and his girl was in the car. They must ain't see her."

"When this happen?"

"Four-thirty this morning. They were coming from the club, he stopped by his mothers for something and they must of followed him. Yo, they shot him eleven times all in his face and chest."

"How you find out?"

"His girl called me 'cause my number is programmed in his cell phone. But she said she was tryin' to contact you but she couldn't get you or she got your voice mail or something."

"Why tha fuck she ain't leave a message?"

"I don't know, what da fuck you asking me for? Ask her."

"Damn yo, that was my mutha fuckin' man. Out of all my cousins he was the coolest one. Yo, find out who did that shit Splizz."

"Awight, so you going to the funeral right?"

"Yeah… 1 can't miss that. That was my man. I'ma call my aunt and them and find out did they know anything and when the funeral is. I'ma have to fly in there and show my respects. Oh yeah, I need to talk to you about some important shit yo, but I gotta get ready to get out of here. So I'll call you back when I get a chance."

"Awight, if I don't answer the cell it's because I'm not getting no reception in the studio. So just call the studio number direct. Awight, luv you yo."

"Luv you too yo."

I dialed Mel's number next, "Yo, Mel what's up?"

"Hey youngster, what's going on?"

"Ain't nothing, what time you want to meet?"

"You know what time. I'm getting ready now. I'll see you at the spot youngster." He hung up.

I got Brishette to drop me off, this time I beat Mel there so I got two coffees and sat at the table by the window. Mel came in, pulled up a chair and pulled out his binoculars. We checked out each truck, then followed them.

Today was big for some reason. Maybe because we worked extra hard on the phone, but twenty-six boxes wasn't bad at all. All I could think about was $300 per box, average that is, because sometimes its more, but twenty-six times $300 equals $7,800. Shhhit, eight g's ain't bad for a days work, that is forty grand for the week. Five weeks would be $200,000, fifty-two weeks would be one million sixteen thousand. Fuck what you heard, that's living!

Anyway, I made three grand out of those boxes and I had some money coming Western Union for some of the boxes we has sent to Baton Rouge, Louisiana to Candy and Reecee's cousins. And of course, that made Candy and Reecee eligible for a treat, of a finder's fee.

We all went out to Benny Hanna's and enjoyed the dinner theatrics, watching the chef throw shrimp in the air, not to mention the flaming food. This was their first time, even for Mel. You would have thought that Mel would have been all over, but he confessed that he was just a homebody and loved his T-Bone steaks which he kept a deep freezer full of.

"Dee, what's wrong? You look like you lost your best friend. You not enjoying yourself?" Candy asked with her mouth full with food.

"I'm cool, but I do feel like I lost my best friend. My lil cousin got killed last night, right in front of his mother's house."

"Damn, I'm sorry to hear that youngster." Mel responded.

"Yeah me too. Ahhh... . Baby. He was real close to you huh?" Candy put her arm around my shoulder.

"Yeah. That was my favorite cousin."

"So when is the funeral?" Reecee asked, putting her arm around my shoulder, consoling me.

"I think its gonna be Friday."

"He's from Baltimore too?"

"Yeah."

"I could get some airline tickets cheap."

"Nah, I'm good. I have a friend who owns a travel agency. He called me when he found out and we made reservations already."

"Awight, I'll take you to the airport."

"I already got someone to take me, I'm good. And I appreciate ya'll being there for me." My cell phone rang.

"Excuse me y'all." I answered my cell, it was Steph. I got up from the table and walked away.

"Yo, what's up Steph? Where you at?"

"Dee I'm at the airport, and this fuckin' girl ain't here man. I don't know where this girl at. Mannn."

"So what, you need somebody to come get you?"

"Hold up, this look like her car. Nah, that ain't her. Yess it is. Awight Dee I'm on my way in, I'll call you tomorrow."

"Naw, I need to talk to you tonight. It's important, I need your help."

"Well, what's up?"

"Where can you meet me at? I'll get somebody to bring me to you."

"Awight, do you remember the street we turned on off of Sunset?"

"Naw, not really."

"Well, just come straight down Sunset like you going to Los Felix. Whoever is bringing you should know where Los Felix is if they live in L.A. Anyway, once you pass the strip you'll see a Denny's on the left, keep going until you get to a residential area, then start looking to your left and you'll see a pool hall. Meet me at the pool hall."

"Awight, I'll find it. I'll be there as soon as we get finished eating. I'm at Benny Hanna's."

"Awight, peace." I returned to the table.

"Is everything okay?" Candy asked with this sincere look of concern, like she would give me some pussy tonight if I just asked. But I had business on my mind.

"Yeah, I'm good. Thanks."

Chapter 22

Mel and the girls dropped me off at the pool hall. Steph was already there playing pool with some girl that looked like Tyra Banks with short hair dyed blonde. Now every time I see him I expect him to be with a stripper. He spotted me and waived me over to the table.

"What's up Dee?" He put the pool stick down and we shook hands and embraced. "Dee, this is Shalamar, Shalamar this is my main man Dee."

"How are you doing?" She sounded all proper and shit, like she was a Harvard Graduate. But you'd be surprised how many good girls, good wholesome girls, are taking off their clothes and making a decent living.

"I'm fine. It's good to meet you. Anybody ever tell you you look like Tyra Banks?"

"Ha ha. It's funny you said that because that's what my girlfriends call me sometimes."

"Hold up Dee, let me finish her off. I only got three balls on the table and she's got seven. I'ma end this real quick. Watch my moves. Who's go is it, is it my shot?"

We finally got to talk at the bar where we ordered drinks. "So what's on your mind Dee?"

"Check this out Steph. Awight, I originally came out here to pick up some coke because some coke came up missing in the mail, and my connect said he was not sending nothing else in the mail, so I had to come and get it. So I came out to get what was left in hopes of flippin' it from six ounces to eighteen and pay the boy back who paid me in advance for the product."

"So what's the problem?"

"The problem is this, I got a young boy selling the ounces for me and I already sent eight of the eighteen to the boy back in Baltimore now I owe him ten more. Right now the boy is back up to eighteen, so I got enough to pay him but my connect is on the run."

"Who you talking about, Big Jay? I seen that shit on t.v. That's my man, we used to go to the same high school."

"Yeah. It's a small world. So you know my man Jay?"

"Everybody knows Jay. Dee, he been in the game a long time. He been ducking the law for a long time."

"So look, I need somebody to fly back to Baltimore with me and carry the coke because I don't know what's gonna happen in the airport. They might stop me because the FBI agent that Jay shot was his girls' sister. And she was with him when we met, so she saw me and she knows I came to get coke from him. And they might have my picture and stop me. So I need somebody to carry the coke."

"Awight, so all you need is one of the girls to carry the shit on the plane. That's nothing. As a matter of fact, do you remember the girl China Doll that you met at the strip club?"

"Yeah what about her?"

"She rents a room in the mansion, and she be going out of town a lot right. So one night I'm talking to my shortie Lashanda and she tells me China Doll be making trips for this boy Duncan, a big drug boy. So I asked her why she tellin' me that. She says she was just tellin' me now because she's gonna be gone for a week and when she comes back she'll have her $1,200 for her rent so I won't think she's playing games."

"So she cool like that huh?"

"Yeah, shortie is down for hers."

"So you fuck her yet?"

"Hell naw. That's my shortie's best friend and although she's a stripper, she's a classy lil broad. So she probably ain't gone go out like that, you know what I'm saying?"

"So you think she messing with the drug boy Duncan?"

"Naw, I don't think so, but ah, there was this dude that used to come by the mansion sometimes, but he don't come around no more. She must of got rid of his ass, but you gotta talk to her."

"Where you think she at now?"

"She's either at the Exotica or at the mansion. Hold up, let me call..." Steph dialed the number at the mansion.

"What's up baby? Where everybody at? Is China Doll around? She is... Awight, tell her that I said don't go nowhere, me and Dee on our way, tell her Dee need to talk to her about something important Awight. Awight baby." He hung up the phone, "Come on man let's get out of here. China is at the house."

"Oh yeah?"

"Yeah, I told my shortie to tell China you need to holla at her so don't go no where."

It was 8:26pm when we arrived at the mansion. This fuckin' house was so big, Steph had to call upstairs from his cell to Lashanda and have her tell China I was there. She told him to tell me come up because she was doing her toenails.

"Dee, just go up to the top of the stairs and make a right and go all the way down almost to the end of the hall. You'll see a picture on the wall of some roses, her room is next door to the picture, to the left of the picture. If you pass the picture you went too far."

"Awight." I got to the top of the stairs and was met by Lashanda, who pointed down the hall in the direction of China's room. I located the picture and knocked.

"Come in." I heard through the door, "Hey Dee. What's up? I see you found me."

"Yeah, you ain't tell me you lived with my man Steph."

"You mean, rent from."

"Same thing."

"No, it's not the same thing because he's hardly here. Me and Lashanda run this, that's my girl."

"I see you're jamming. that's my song you're listening to." I began to sing along, "Somebody rockin' knockin' your boots! Come on and rock my body! Rock my body".

"Oh, you sing a lil bit huh?"

She was turning me on, giving me shots of her perky lil breast by leaning forward in the chair, painting her toes as her pretty feet rested on the brown leather ottoman. Her toes were separated by little form fitting pieces of foam sponge. Her black silk robe was only held together by the matching belt which appeared to loosen each time she bent forward to reach another toe after returning the nail polish brush to it's dipping position. I had always heard guys saying 'I'd suck her toes', talking about celebrities like Toni Braxton or Halle Berry, hell China's feet were pretty enough for me to try that toe sucking thing.

She sounded like a little girl when she said, "So what's up? What you wanna talk about?"

"I wanna talk about you helping me to get this swelling down." I started smiling and we both laughed.

"Ha ha, you're a trip boy." She had the biggest grin on her face.

"Girl you're like a sex magnet. I bet every guy who sees your beautiful body wants some."

"You'd be surprised, a lot of guys think I'm too much for them. Do you think I'm too much for you too?"

"Naw, I think you're just right for me. When I think of you, I think of classy sex appeal with a lil hint of a freak, but only for the right one."

She paused the painting of her nails and bit down on her bottom lip and her eyes peered up at me with this seductive look like I just unlocked a treasure chest of possibilities in her mind. "I see you like to play with words."

"No, actually I'd like to play with you. Rub your body down in some warm oil, lick you all over, and touch every hole you got with my tongue. Then go on a G-Spot excursion till you reach your explosion."

"Okay. I hear you talkin', but everybody talks a good game. Can you hand me that fan over there?" China pointed to a small personal sized fan that she probably used for her nails, "Thank you."

"Anything for you."

"Watch what you say around me because I take things literally. Most people don't be serious when they say 'I'll do anything for you', it's mostly talk."

"Well let me share something with you. My father always taught me to say what you mean and mean what you say. So when I say something, nine times out of ten, that's exactly what I mean."

"Okay, if you'll do anything for me, would you go downstairs and get me something to drink while my nails dry?"

"Sure, only if you stay like that and don't move because I was imagining me doing something to you in that position. But I don't want to mess up your nails so I'll wait till they dry."

"What were you thinking about doing?" Damn, she looked sexy as hell licking her lips real slow while she said that.

"Something you like."

"How do you know what I like?"

"Every woman likes what I'm thinking about doing to you, and you're dressed perfectly for the occasion."

"Oh am I?"

I reached down and kissed her soft lips. I tasted the strawberry or raspberry lip-gloss. She surprised me and grabbed hold of the bulge in my pants, I was hard as hell. "Yeah." I gently grabbed her right breast and began squeezing her softly. "Sssss!!! Ummmph ummp." She sighed as I caressed her titties. I reached down her robe between her legs, she was wearing panties but I noticed they were moist when I started rubbing her pussy. Then I remembered the 'Art of Seduction' and I pulled away.

"Let me get that drink, and I'll be right back. Okay?"

"O...kaay..." You could tell by her raspy voice that she was ready.

"Oh yeah. Remember when you told me at the club I look a little swollen down there and should get some ice to put it on, or something warm and moist to take down the swelling.?"

"Yeah I remember."

"Well, I think you're a little swollen down there too and instead of you having to choose between cold and heat, I'ma give you a treat. When I come back I'ma give you both."

"Hurry up please." Damn, I didn't know I had this kind of effect on these girls, but obviously something I have is working for me because I didn't have no problems getting pussy at all.

I went down stairs to get the drinks but only I grabbed the whole bottle from the bar, and a Pepsi and put ice in two glasses, and headed back upstairs. When I walked in I noticed China had taken the sponges out from between her toes, so her feet must have dried. Damn she was sexy. The second thing I saw was the Trojan condoms on the night stand. She had changed the music selection to my favorite Sade' cut 'No Ordinary Love'. Shhhit, that was enough to set the mood right there, but we didn't need no mood setters because we had chemistry. She wanted me just as much as I wanted her.

"You moved."

"So, you just tell me where you want me because I've been thinking about what you said since you left and you've got me curious.

"What are you curious about?"

"About whether you are all talk or can you deliver like you turn me on."

"First of all, I need some hot water."

"Hot water? For what?"

"You'll see, just give me something to put the hot water in." She looked so good laying across the bed I wanted to dive on her ass and fuck the shit out of her. But instead I wanted to take my time and put it on her so she'll never forget me. Ever! 'Cause I know ain't nobody doing it like I do it. Not bragging, but I took it to another level.

"Damn China, I almost forgot about the drink." I grabbed the bottle off the dresser and almost filled the tall glass with Remy, then added a little of the Pepsi. "Here you go." I wanted to get her ass drunk as a mutha fucka."

"Thank you." I went back to grab the empty glass filled with ice so I could put water in it.

"What about this cup right here on your dresser, can I use this?"

"Yeah, it's clean. Just rinse it out."

Aw shit, it's on now. I walked into her personal bathroom to the left of her bed, I ran the hot water until it was too hot to stick my fingers under. I filed the coffee mug then I filled the glass of ice with cold water.

"What are you doing? Playing in the water?"

"Yeah, so I can play in you. You got something to put over the bed so your sheets won't get wet?"

"I got a mattress cover on my mattress that's plastic coated. You're not going to pour water on me, are you?"

"Just give me a towel." She had me laughing, she was fine as hell.

"There's a towel on the chair right there."

"Is it clean?"

"Yeah it's clean. I was getting ready to dry my hair with it but I used a darker towel just in case some of the die got on it."

I had on a green and white polo shirt, some jeans and a pair of all white Reebok Classics. As I pulled off my polo shirt, China scooted to the end of the bed and started to unbuckle my belt and unfasten my pants. My dick was so hard it was hurting. If you are a guy, you know exactly what I'm talking about, and if you're a woman you know the kind of hard I'm talking about too. It's the kind you crave to last all night.

Anyway, there I was, standing there in my wife beater and my boxers. I kicked off my Reeboks and lifted my leg as China helped me take my jeans off. Then she went for my wife beater, pulled it over my head and began kissing my chest. Damn that shit felt good. She kissed and licked down to my stomach. As she lowered her tongue, teasing moist mouth closer to my manhood, she lowered my boxers all in the same motion. I knew if I let her start sucking me off it would be too good to stop. So I grabbed her shoulders and pushed her back on the bed. Her feet wee almost touching the floor. I pulled her panties off, put the towel under her so any liquid that ran between her legs would get on the towel.

I took a sip of the hot water which warmed my tongue and I started my licking campaign. I started at her inner thighs just above her knees. I nibbled and licked one side upwards, then the other side.

"That feels good. I never had..." I cut her off.

"Shhh... I want you to enjoy this. Just save your energy for your climax 'cause I'm getting ready to take you there."

"Uhhhmm. Okay." Her breathing had become heavy. I grabbed the glass with the ice water, drank some of the water, and allowed a piece of ice to enter my mouth. As soon as my cold tongue touched her inner thighs, just inches from her moist, lump and waiting pussy lips, I parted her lips with my two index fingers, right at the beginning, exposing her clit. It was a rosy red color, I let my cold tongue touch it, and she jerked.

"Ooh, that's cold."

So as I began sucking, the little piece of ice dissolved in my mouth. I ran my tongue all the way down, touched her asshole and then went back to work on the clit. I reached with my left hand for the glass of hot water. This time I kept some of the warm water in my mouth, and once I had her clit back under my tongues submission, I swished around the warm water on her clit and let some run down her pussy then I stuck my warm tongue inside her pussy. I gotta tell you, this was some bold assed shit I was doing, sucking a strippers' pussy, but something told me that I was making the right move. Plus her pussy smelled like roses or some enchanting aroma. Plus she was too classy to be a victim of that thang. What the fuck was I thinking. Anyway I said fuck it, if I catch something from sucking her pussy, I pray that it wouldn't be AIDS.

"Ooh baby... Ooh Dee... Suck my pussy baby. Suck it. Ooh ye..Ah. . .Ummp, ummph ummph." That's when I ran my tongue down to her asshole. Then I inserted two fingers inside her juicy, sugary walls while I tried to suck the shit out of her pussy, and had her trying to run from my head.

"Ooooh Dee. Ooh ba...aaby. . I'm cuming, I'm cuming baby. Oh shit." She grabbed my head and held it while she convulsed like she was having a seizure or something. "Oh my Goohhhd. Shit. Damn Dee. What you tryin' do, give me a heart attack?"

She grabbed my hands and pulled me on top of the bed. She wiped herself with the towel then she returned the favor. She started with the entree. She noticed my dick was oozing with pre-cum readiness. She licked around the head, then down the side. She took my balls into her mouth and sucked them softly. Damn the head was the bomb! She deep throated me and all I felt was warm moistness deep at the beginning of the shaft. I felt her tongue doing tricks in her mouth.

"Ohh. Ohhh. Ummph. That's right. China, that's it baby, you almost got it baby. Play with the balls baby." As soon as she started stroking my balls with her fingertips and her nails, I shot my warm cum in her mouth. She swallowed every drop and licked around the head. I had to push her head away because my dick was so sensitive.

We laid there for a minute, then she started stroking my dick, getting me hard. Then she got on top of me and put the condom on me and started riding my dick like a wild cowgirl riding a Bronco. Damn she was doing some stripper gymnastics with her pussy. She dropped down twice like a low rider on Crenshaw on hydraulics, making sure every inch of my dick was inside of her, then when she'd raise up she flexed her pussy muscles and clamped down on my dick. That shit felt a little like head. I flipped her over, put her in the buck and began a triangle rotation. First I hit the right wall, then the left wall, then I pumped twice in the middle. I had her head against the headboard so there was no where to go. I was all in the pussy like I owned it and lived there. We came about the same time. That shit was remarkable. We laid there for about thirty minutes. I felt myself falling to sleep so I got up and took a shower. She joined me and I hit it again in the shower, the pussy was even more exciting standing up.

I finally took a drink. My tongue was hurting because I licked her pussy like I was in a competition. Right under my tongue was hurting like somebody tried to pull my tongue out my mouth with pliers. Man, the shit we do to ourselves.

"China you up?"

"Yeah, I was just restin' my eyes, I wasn't sleep."

"Yes you was, it's okay. You can admit that I put you to sleep." We both laughed.

"Yeah, whatever."

"On a serious note, China. I gotta proposition for you." She cut me off.

"Oh my God, don't tell me it was that good that you wanna marry me. Hahaha.."

"How about it was that good, but I ain't tryin' to get married. Nah seriously, I need your help. I did my homework on you and I found out you're a soldier girl."

"So what you need me to do?"

"Strap up and fly to Baltimore with me, all expenses paid, plus $1,500 for you. We get to hang out, get familiar and we can fuck like crazy in the hotel. You can even scream 'cause I know you wanted to scream but you didn't want your girl to know you got it put on you."

"Yeah, whatever. So when do we leave, so I can let the club know? Plus I could use a little breather, this shit was right on time."

"Awight, I'll make reservations for Thursday because the wake is Friday the funeral is Saturday, so we'll get in there Thursday night and stay 'till Saturday night and get back Sunday morning. That's cool?"

"What, what funeral?"

"My lil cousin got killed the other night."

"Umm, I'm sorry to hear that. So this trip is business and personal?"

"Yeah, I guess you could say that. So you in or what?"

"Yeah."

"Awight, I'll call you."

"Okay... Oh, Dee." She stopped me as I was leaving out the door.

"Yeah..."

"I enjoyed tonight."

"Yeah, me too, and it gets better."

"I hope so."

"Awight, I'll call you tomorrow."

Chapter 23

It was 10:40pm, I hadn't answered my cell the entire time I was with China. I had six missed calls on my cell. Three of them were from Brishette, two from Reecee, and one from Candy. Just as I was getting into the car, my cell rang and Steph thought it was his until I answered.

"Hello. Aye baby."

"I've been trying to get you for a couple hours." Brishette seemed irritated.

"Oh yeah?" I acted as if I was just finding out, "Yeah, the area where I was, got no reception." I couldn't tell her I saw the missed calls because that would mean I received the calls.

"I'm on my way home now. I'll call you back when I get home."

"Are you coming over?"

"I got a couple of things to do at home, like washing and stuff so I might have you come over instead."

"I'ma take a bath and I'll be over. Okay?"

"Awight, I'll see you then."

I had been home only thirty minutes and the buzzer rang, "Who is it?" I knew who it was, but I still had to maintain my security. "Okay." I buzzed Brishette in the downstairs door and timed her just right, as she approached the door to my apartment, I opened the door.

"Damn you smell good. What is that?" That scent was alluring as she walked through the door. I closed the door and locked it.

"Cocoa, by Channel. You like it?"

"Come here." I took her hands and put them around my waist and I put my arms around her neck and began kissing her like I hadn't seen her in months. She loves when I do that. Her lips were so soft that each time I kissed her it felt like I got a little closet to heaven.

"You look tired baby. You want me to run you some bath water?" Damn she be spoiling the shit out of me, and I could really get used to this.

"That would be nice, I'd appreciate that."

"So, did you find out when the funeral is, or what happened to your cousin?"

"Yeah, I found out what happened but not who did it, but we got an idea."

"Was he a drug dealer?"

"Why you ask me that? Everybody that gets killed gotta be a drug dealer?"

"No, I'm not saying that. I asked because I know that a lot of young people today that are involved in the drug trade and they are getting killed. And while we're on the subject, I've noticed that you've been out here in California for over a month and I noticed you go out everyday like you have a job, but you've never mentioned getting a job to me. I didn't ask you any question because I didn't want to seem like I was all up in your business, but you seem to get money from somewhere..." I cut her off.

"Hold up, what is your point Brishette? Where are you going with all this?"

"Okay. I need you to be honest with me, and tell me whether or not you sell drugs."

"Why didn't you just ask the question instead of going through all that?"

"I don't know... Do you?"

"Not anymore."

"What does that mean?"

"Just what I said, not any more. I used to..." She cut me off.

"So when did you stop, today? Yesterday? Last week?" Brishette hissed with her hands on her hips.

"Actually, when I go back home for the funeral, I'm gonna take care of this guy that I owe and close that chapter of my life, because I wanna be here for you when our baby comes."

"Look Dejohn, I've been in a few relationships where the guys were selling drugs and none of them turned out good..."

"We don't have to keep talking about this. I told you when I take care of this situation, I'm out."

"Dejohn, I just don't want to lose you, okay. I love you and I want you to be around when this baby arrives. If not, its no use of having a baby and..."

"I'ma be here for you, okay."   I interrupted reassuring her I would be there.

"Oh my God, the water!" I watched her lil ass jiggle as she made her distressed sprint to the bathroom.

My cell vibrated in my pocket, "Hello."

"Hey Dee. What's up? Do you know who this is?"

"What's up Candy?"

"I've been tryin' to call you..." I cut her off.

"The area I was in wasn't getting' a signal. I was gonna call you but right now I'm getting' ready to get in the tub, so I'ma have to call you back."

"Okay, I'll be up for a while, call me back."

Brishette came back and sat down on the couch next to me, "Your water is ready. It almost ran over."

"Thank you." I kissed her on her forehead and went into my bedroom. I took my bath, expecting to be so tired after freaking China Doll that I'd want to just cuddle with Brishette until we fell asleep. But you know what happened, that's right, I got a second wind. I gently played in her pregnant juicy pussy until we both came and fell asleep.

I woke up around 6:40am, thinking about all that I had to do this day. Time is money and opportunity, or at least that's what my grandfather used to say before he died. They may have thought that I wasn't listening but I absorbed everything I heard and saw.

I thought I'd get Candy out of the way first, so I called her, "Hello. Hey, what's going on? I figured you'd be up getting ready for work."

"Yeah, I'm just about to take a shower and get ready, you're right. So what happened to you callin' me back last night?"

"I fell asleep, but damn I wish I was there. 'I'd help you get ready."

"I bet you would. I just bet you would."

"Candy, check this out. You know I'm leaving today right?"

"Yeah, Reecee told me. So what time..." I interrupted her.

"So you know I'm tryin' to see you before I go, right?"

"What time does your flight leave?"

"My flight leaves at six, but you know you gotta be there an hour and a half before your flight is scheduled to leave. So I'ma be there around 4:30."

"So how are you gonna see me when I don't get off until four?"

"That's easy. You go in a half a day, and we make it happen."

"What if I can't leave early, then what?"

"Then I'll see you when I get back, that's all."

I heard Brishette go into the bathroom, so she was awake and that meant I need to wrap it up so we could do our morning ritual. I guess they want to catch us men as soon as we wake up because it's gonna stay hard until we use the bathroom.

"So when will you know whether you can get a half a day off? Just call me as soon as you know, Awight. I gotta go. I got a lot of shit to do."

"I'll call you and let you know."

"Awight." I hung up just as Brishette walked into the room.

There was something about her in these Victoria Secret nighties. She always got me hard just looking at her. Her perfect sized brown nipples stood at attention under the black, see-through negligee. She came over to the couch, released my now throbbing hard manhood from my boxers and straddled me, guiding it inside of her. That look on her face was like she was conquering a savage beast or something and she was, because even though I hadn't took my first piss yet, and was rock hard, no hard-on could last with Brishette's pussy, it was too good. She got hers, I got mine and all of the sudden she started crying.

"What's wrong?" I thought the dick was that good and was just magnified by her pregnant emotions.

"Nothing, I'll be fine." She said, sniffling and wiping tears. I didn't know what to think.

"Tell me what's wrong baby. You don't just start crying because it's in style."

"I... Just got too used to waking up next to you and I'm scared that you might not come back when you go to Baltimore. . . Because you got your daughter and family there."

"Hold up, Brishette listen to me. I told you, you have nothing to worry about because if God doesn't take me away from here, I'll be here with you and the baby. That's the only way I won't be here."

"What about your daughter? I know she misses you."

"I told you we are going to work this out. Maybe you don't understand because I haven't told you, but you're everything I've even wanted so it's my choice to stay with you in California. Not just because of the baby, but also because I love you and I don't love easy." Damn, that shit even sounded good to me.

"I love you too Dejohn and I just don't want to lose you. I never told you this, but I think my father killed my last boyfriend."

"What made you think that? Better yet, what made you say that?"

"Well, when they met for the first time, my father told him that if he ever hurt me he'd kill him, and it just makes so much sense. My father was in town around the same time that Steve and I got into a fight. He hit me, I fell and hit my head on the edge of the table and had to go to the hospital to get stitches. Then about two or three days later Steve went missing and to this day no one ever found him."

I thought, 'Shit, what the hell did I get myself into and was her father just overly protective of her or was she a victim of incest and her father is in love with her ass because her pussy is like that, for real'.

I knew this shit was too good to be true. But the guy shouldn't have put his hands on her though. She ain't gotta worry about me putting my hands on her because I don't hit women. I love 'em or leave 'em alone.

"So where's your father now?"

"Who knows? He might be in another country."

"So what does he do?"

"I don't know. He never told my mother or me."

"Are you serious?"

"Yeah, my mother thinks he's a hit man."

"Why does she think that?"

"Well, a similar thing happened to my mother in Paris. There was this guy she used to date and the guy was very, very jealous. You may have heard this name before he was a famous artist Jean Dejure."

"No, I've never heard of him, but go ahead, continue."

"My mother worked for the French Embassy as an interpreter, and met my father while he was in France on a business trip. This old boyfriend of hers didn't want to accept the breakup and..." I cut her off after looking at my watch and noticing it was 7:45 and Mel was picking me up at 8:00.

"Hold that thought, we are gonna talk about this when I get back from Baltimore because I gotta go baby. Mel's gonna be outside in ten minutes and I'm not ready."

Chapter 24

THE TRIP

10:48 am Mel and I had picked up seventeen boxes, three of which were clothes for my trip. I had ordered two for China Doll, a pair of Gebeau jeans and a polo shirt and a pair of Capri pants, and a lime green Ann Taylor twin set, the cashmere short sleeve sweater with another long sleeve to cover it. I thought this would be a nice comfortable wardrobe for our trip since she was staying around the hotel while I went to the funeral.

My phone vibrated in my pocket. I answered, it was China Doll.

"Hello."

"Hey Dee, what's up?"

"Danm girl..." She cut me off before I could finish my statement.

"What?"

"This shit is crazy, while I was thinking about you, you must have been thinking about me at the same time. How coincidental is that?"

"Yeah right, you wasn't thinking about me. Y'all men always tryin' to come up with a fast line to flatter a sista, cut the bullshit mannn."

"Girl, you a funny mutha fucka. Why y'all always think that a brotha be on some bullshit? My father was right, you tell 'em truth, they think it's a lie, you yell 'em a lie and they eat that shit up."

"Yeah whatever, so why was you thinking about me?" China quizzed.

"It wasn't 'cause I'm whipped and tryin' put a ring on your finger, but I did think about you when I went shopping and I copped you a couple outfits."

"Oooh, for real? You thought about me? That was sweet, thank you."

"That was me looking out for you like you looking out for me. One hand washes the other. So I'll see you in a little while, Awight?"

"So what time are you picking me up, or how are we gonna do this?"

"Our flight leaves at six o'clock, we're gonna be at the airport around 4:30, so I'll see you around 2:30 or 3:00 'cause I'ma meet the boy around two o'clock and then I'm coming straight over there to you."

"Awight, well I'll see you when you get here. I'm going to my hair appointment at 12:15, I'll be back by 1:30."

"Awight, I'll see ya. Peace."

Mel and I went back to his house and took inventory. We had six computers at $2,000 a piece. That was $12,000, I was to get half and he was to get half, especially since I placed all the orders. But because only one buyer had paid in advance and I didn't have time to wait until later to get paid, Mel gave me $5,100 because that's all he had at the time and promised to wire me that rest Western Union.

"Awight youngster, we had a good day. So how long you gonna be gone again?"

"Just two days. The wake is tomorrow night, the funeral is Saturday, and I'll be back on Sunday."

"Awight, so you'll be ready for work Monday morning."

"Yeah."

"Cause we got some boxes coming slow that'll be here around Monday or Tuesday."

"Yeah, I remember."

"Plus when you get back, I'm gone take you to a new spot where we get Macy's account numbers and Nordstrom accounts."

"Now that's what's happening 'cause they got that bomb shit."

"I figured you would like that cause that's right up your alley, 'cause you like to stay fly for the girls."

"I need to use one of them cars so I can go meet the boy Larry."

"You need to watch him because that kid is out of control."

"What do you mean?"

"What I mean? Let me tell you about this kid. He set up his best friend to get robbed because he took the girl he liked to the prom. So whatever you doin' with him, watch yourself and if you don't need to mess with him I suggest you leave him alone. I'm just warning you." Mel had a very serious look on his face when he told me to leave the boy Larry alone.

Chapter 25

I felt like Michael Jackson or Tupac, 'All eyes on me', as I walked through the airport a close distance behind China Doll. The only thing that helped my nervousness was focusing on China's ass jiggling in front of me. She had the perfect body, compliments of her gymnasty stripping career.

We made it to the plane without incident and we acted as if we didn't know each other the whole six-hour flight to Baltimore. We got through the Baltimore Washington Airport and checked into the Marriot near the airport.

I called Splizz to let him know I made it. Obviously I was just paranoid because apparently the feds were not looking for me, at least not at the airport, or not at that time.

"Yo Splizz, where you at?"

"I'm on my way home, I'm at Hammer Jacks downtown right here by BWI Pkwy across from Camden Yards."

"Awight, I'll see you when you get here tomorrow."

I helped China remove the tape and eleven ounces of coke from her body. We unpacked and China took a shower, I joined her and got the head of my life. Damn, she got on her knees and took me into her mouth. Awwh man, it felt good to have the water running down my body and China's tongue running up and down my dick at the same time.

We had wild sex that night and woke up about 8:30 am, took a shower and went down to the hotel's restaurant for breakfast. China wore one of the outfits I bought her, she hooked it up with accessories. She had the lime green Ann Taylor twin set on with the Brooks Brothers khaki Capri pants. She had a pair of lime Muels with her pretty feet half covered. She also had on some Jade Bangles with the matching earrings and her hair was in like a bun with a long ponytail coming out of it, it was probably an extension but that pull back hairstyle showed off her little Chinese looking face. You just had to see this girl, she was eye candy to the fullest.

"Can I order what I want?" I said, talking to China.

"Yeah, you order whatever your heart desires, as long as you got money to pay for it."

"I thought you were treatin'."

"How did you think that? You're the big baller." She had the cutest smile on her face saying that. I was really feeling China Doll, but I just couldn't let her know that shit. She already knew her sex was the bomb.

The waitress walked over, asked for our order, "I'm gonna have the blueberry pancakes, the turkey sausage and orange juice. What are you getting China?"

"Let me have the Steak-n-Eggs, and a Belgian Waffle please." The waitress walked away.

"You're not gonna eat all of that."

"Yes I am too, I'm hungry. I know I lost about two pounds last night or this morning rather, messing with you. Acting like you ain't had none in years, or you had something to prove."

"I can't help it if your pussy is the bomb. I just can't get enough of you and you should consider yourself fortunate because I'm really picky and it's been a while since I could say that about anybody."

I felt my cell vibrating in my pocket again, "Hello... Yo what's going on Splizz?"

"What time you gonna be ready?"

"I'm just getting up and having breakfast with my girl China. I should be ready around ten or ten thirty."

"Awight, I'm leaving in a few minutes. Did you talk to the boy yet to find out what time you gone meet him?"

"Naw, I'ma call 'em now, I'll see you when you get here."

Obviously 'L' must have been sleep or something because he didn't answer until the fifth ring, just as I was about to hang up, "Hello..."

"Ay, what's going on 'L'?"

"Who is this?"

"It's Dee mann.

"Oh, oh, oh... What's up Dee, what's going on? I was just getting up yo."

"What time you wanna meet so I can take care of the rest of that?"

"Ahh, I tell you what, you can meet me at ahh, at ahh... Let's make it the McDonalds right there by the race track on Park Heights at 1:15."

"Awight, I'll see you there, peace."

"Peace." I called Splizz back and gave him the meeting place and the waiter showed up with our food.

"You're right Dee, I'm not gonna eat all of this. I didn't know the waffle was this big." China happily confessed.

"I told you, you couldn't eat all of that."

"So what time you coming back, and what am I supposed to do until you come back?"

"I don't know what time I'm coming back yet, but I will be calling and checking on you. We can go out later if you want, meanwhile you can get some rest and watch some movies or something. If you want me to, I'll send somebody to pick you up and take you to the mall or something."

We finished our meals and went back to the room, "I'm okay, I'ma just chill because I feel like I got jet lag and my body is all jittery and shit."

"I know why your body is jittery."

"Why?" She fell right in my trap.

"Because it's excited 'cause it knows I'ma put you on your ass when I come back, beat that thing up like you stole something."

"You ain't beatin' up nothin' with your three minute ass 'cause you know this pussy is too good for you to last any longer."

"Yeah awight. I hear you talking all that Tuff Tony shit now. You just wait till I get back, I got something for yo ass..." My cell vibrated.

"Yo…"

"Come on yo, I'm out in front of the lobby."

"Awight, here I come." I kissed China on her forehead and told her to lock the door as I exited.

We got to the McDonalds around 1:00 and watched for 'L'. Splizz went inside and got a fish fillet with cheese and an order of super sized fries. I had just finished eating so I stayed in the car, besides I don't' eat that greasy shit anyway. All I ever get is the apple pie from McDonalds.

"Splizz. I keep thinking about my girl's sister Lil Kim, and whether 'L' had anything to do with her kidnapping and rape because that was some foul assed shit. I wish I had a way to find out right now because if he had anything to do with that shit, I wouldn't give him shit except some hot slugs in his ass."

"Yo, I told you, it's whatever because I don't like that nigga anyway. He think he can't be touched."

"Yo, anybody can be touched. I don't give a fuck who it is."

"So what's up then Dee."

It seemed like as soon as Splizz asked me what's up, I recognized 'L' or Larry White pull into McDonalds parking lot in a candy blue Mustang convertible with two dudes in the car with him. I was so eager to put this shit behind me I opened the passenger side door.

"Yo Dee, hold da fuck up yo. You don't know what's up with this dude. Mann wait a minute, let me get ready."

He really don't have a reason, that I could think of, to kill me especially that I got his shit and we were gonna be even. But Splizz had a point, so I waited until he parked three spaces away in the only spot available and one of the guys went inside, evening the playing field.

"Yo, watch my back." I got out of the car and walked towards 'L's' car. I ain't gone lie, I did not trust this dude and it was obvious, at least to me, that he didn't trust me either because he had two dudes with him. But we talked for a few minutes, then I asked him did he hear about my girl's sister getting raped, he convinced me that he didn't have anything to do with it by his expression. He seemed like he was really shocked.

Anyway, I gave him the ten ounces I owed him and that was the last time I saw him before going back to California the next evening. I guess we were cool but I wasn't fucking with him no more on the drug tip, unless I really needed some money.

Chapter 26

THE WAKE

It was 6:17 pm, we arrived at March's Funeral Home on North Ave and Asquith streets. I got there a little late as usual. I was greeted by Ms. Catherine, the lady that used to live next door to my aunt. We used to call her the cat lady cause she ain't miss shit. She'd be up three in the morning looking out the window, watching people creeping, and telling the next day.

She was showing everybody to their seats. As I walked into the gloomily lit room, everybody started turning around being nosey. Miss Cat told me go ahead up because the Pastor was about to do the ceremony. Splizz and I walked up to the body, and I silently told my lil cuz that I loved him and whoever did this shit I'm gonna get their ass. I had a flash back about him playing on the phone, sometimes he'd answer the phone, "Hello, March Funeral Home, you stab 'em, we slab 'em, Can I help you?", now look at him. My mother used to cuss his ass out too, when he did that shit when she'd be calling for my aunt. I used to laugh my ass off He was a stupid lil mutha fucka, but that was my Lil Man though.

I stood there, shaking my head, Splizz had walked away to give me time alone with Lil Steve and it seemed like the fucking flood gates broke inside of me and tears started rolling down my face. That's when my cousin Na-Na, short for Natasha, came over and put her arm around me.

"Come on D.J., he's gone baby." Why the fuck she say some dumb assed shit like that to me. Bitch I know he's gone unless he was faking, and I ain't got that being the case, 'cause he look dead as they get. It looked like they got a pound of makeup on my lil man though.

"I'm cool. I'ma go holla at Auntie and Grandma and them." Damn she smelled good as a mutha fucka. I remember when we were kids, I used to want to fuck my own cousin but when you're thirteen years old, you'll fuck anybody you can get your dick in, and one night I did get the coochie. She played sleep but her ass wasn't sleep 'cause she pumped back. What the hell is wrong with me? Here I am at my cousin's funeral and I'm thinking about how my cousin NaNa's coochie felt when we were little and we shouldn't have been doin that shit anyway.

I hugged my aunt and my grandmother, and who the fuck was this pretty assed girl sitting next to my grandmother. This little chick look like Chilli from TLC a lil bit. I reached out for her hand and she pulled me in closer for a hug. So I kept the line thing going until I got to the isle, then I went and sat down next to sexy assed Carolyn, this girl who was like a big sister to Lil Steve. He used to go over her house and bag up pounds of weed. I always liked her but she wanted me to sweat her and I ain't with that shit. So I never got to hit it, but she was cool as shit, down for whatever and she made my day when she said,

"Dejohn, I'm so mad right now, you just don't know. I was just with him an hour before this shit happened. He said he was going to see some girl."

"Oh yeah, what girl? Let's go out in the hall."

We walked out together, I gave Splizz the nod to come on and he followed us out. When we got out in the hall she told us that Steve was talking about some girl he met at Choices Night Club on North and Charles streets. "He said they went out a couple times and that they had..." I cut Carolyn off.

"Have you ever seen her or know where she live?"

"No, but he did say they took some pictures down Clay Street downtown."

"Yo I know that dude. He be buying shit from boosters all the time. That's Robin's baby's father. They keep the negatives to their pictures too, so he got copies. I'll just get Robin to get them."

"Are they open tomorrow?"

"I'll check it out, 'cause we ain't gonna have time tomorrow because after the funeral, you know they gonna want to see you at the reception, then you gotta get to the airport at least a couple hours before your flight leave."

"Yeah, you're right Splizz."

"I'll check around to see if any of the guys on the block know anything."

"Take my number and call me if you find out anything." Splizz handed her a peace of paper with his number on it.

We caught the closing of the ceremony. I saw so many people in there faking tears that I thought I was at an audition for a crying part in a movie. Especially my grandmothers' boyfriend, he couldn't stand Lil Steve. That's why we used to go over there all the time, just to irritate his old ass. He pulled his gun out one time when we told him we'd beat his old ass.

I saw a few of Steve's homeboys getting ready to leave and pulled them up, What's up main man? You remember me?"

"Yeah, you Steve's cousin. I remember you yo."

"What's your name?"

"Ronald, and this is my brother Scoop and my cousin Wayne." I see why they called his ass Scoop, he was tall as Shaq. I know they was scared of his ass on the block.

"Yo, shortie, I wanna know who did this shit man." The look on my face said it all.

"Don't even sweat it, we gone find out who did this shit." The smallest one spoke out.

"Y'all exchange numbers with my man so we can stay in touch. If you find out something, call immediately." Splizz cut me off.

"Yeah, I don't care about what time it is, just call and let me know something. Awight shortie?"

"Awight, that's a bet." Replied the funny looking light skinned boy with the Charlie Brown freckles.

If you asked me, all these niggas was suspects until I find out what was up and who did this shit to my lil cousin. One thing about Baltimore mutha fuckas they be running their mouths so somebody gone hear something. You just gotta keep your ears to the streets with all that noise.

I noticed people were starting to come out so I slipped into the men's room and called to check on China at the hotel.

"Hello…Aahhhh…I'm sorry for yawning in your ear."

"What, are you sleep?"

"I had just dosed off watching this movie… Ohhh."

"Damn, you sound like you're tired."

"I don't know why. I took a nap earlier, it's probably because I had just took a nice, hot bath."

"Oh yeah… You got the coochie all clean for me."

"What time are you comm' back? I'm lonely." She sounded so cute, like she was whining a lil bit. Sounds like she's ready for whatever when I get back.

"I'm just getting ready to leave the funeral home, then I'ma stop by my daughter's house and surprise her. Spend a few minutes with her then I'm on my way."

"Dee can you bring me some vanilla ice cream and some Hershey's chocolate syrup when you come?"

"You want some whipped cream with that too?"

"Uh Uhh, just the ice cream."

"Yes you do, I'ma get you some anyway. You might need it."

"Boy get you mind out of the gutter."

"I'll see you when I get there."

I had to hang up because it was getting loud in the bathroom because it seemed like all the dudes in there all of the sudden had to go to the bathroom. Nosey mutha fuckas.

Splizz doubled parked while I went to see if anybody was home, because I didn't see any lights on and it was just a quarter till eight. No telling where Rissa might be, but I rang the doorbell anyway. I listened a little closer because it seemed like I heard music. I turned to see if it was coming from the car and noticed Splizz was on his cell, so that was out. I rang the bell again, no answer. Then just as I was turning to walk away, I noticed the curtain move so I rang the bell again. Rissa comes to the door in a flowery robe and her birdie slippers, hair all over her head like somebody was banging her back out, fuckin' freak.

"Yo why the fuck it take you so long to come to the door? Never mind, I don't even want to know."

"Mutha Fucka why didn't you call first. You don't just pop up like that."

"What da fuck you mean, this my daughter's house."

"Correction, this is my mutha fuckin house. Your daughter just lives here."

"Why you blocking the fuckin' door like you don't want me to come in? I don't give a fuck about you having no company man, that's..." She cut me off.

"I keep tellin' you stop fuckin' callin' me man. Save that shit for your homeboys."

"Girl move out the way so I can see my daughter."

"She ain't here."

"What do you mean, she ain't here? Where she at then?"

"She's over my sista's house."

"The same sista that got kidnapped and raped? Are you out of your fuckin' mind?"

"Not that sister, my oldest sister Karen. The one who's a Pharmacist at the hospital that live out Randlestown."

"So when is she coming home?"

"Tomorrow, I was gonna bring her to the funeral 'cause I knew you were comin in town for the funeral."

"How you know?"

"Please, I know everything, and plus you couldn't miss his funeral, 'cause yaw was real tight. Don't forget I was your fucking girl for eight years."

"Man, that's fucked up. I wanted to surprise my daughter and you sent her over somebody else's house so you could get some dick. What kind of shit is that?"

"Look, I gotta go. I'll see you tomorrow at the funeral."

"Yeah, awight... I'm out."

"Yo, what happened?"

"Man, fuck that bitch. She fuckin' sent my daughter out Randlestown. Why she got some Nigga over there. Take me back to the hotel, I got some good assed pussy waiting for me. Oh yeah, I gotta take some..." My phone vibrated in my pocket and scared the shit out of me. You'd think I would've gotten used to it by now but I'll never get used to the surprise. "Vanilla ice cream, oatmeal cookies, chocolate syrup, and whipped cream back with me." I didn't get the call in time and missed the call from Brishette.

"Damn yo, you must got a live one."

"Man, this girl pussy good as a mutha fucka, boy and she know it too."

"She got any girl friends?'"

"Hell yeah. Yo, it's on when I get back. We getting ready to take living to another level yo. As soon as I get back to Cali I'ma start looking for a mansion yo."

"What da fuck you talking about yo? What you do, bump your fuckin' head or something?"

"Yo Splizz, no bullshit. I'm serious as a mutha fucka, that's on my daughter yo. Nigga we getting ready to start living in a fuckin' mansion yo. With strippers as our roommates and having big ass mansion parties and shit. Yo, shit gone be crazy yo, you watch."

"Yo, what the fuck you been smokin'?"

I couldn't believe this mutha fucka still didn't believe me. Yes I could, because this ain't some shit you hear everyday. So it would be hard to believe because I didn't believe Steph until he showed me, "Yo, you ain't gotta believe me. I'ma show your ass." I reached over and turned the radio down.

"Yo, what da fuck you doing? That's my song." Splizzy said in disbelief that I turned his shit down. We had a rule, don't touch my radio while you're in my car.

"I gotta call her back."

"Who? The girl at the hotel? Man you gone be there..." I cut him off.

"Naw, this is the movie girl in California."

"Hello."

"Heyyy... What are you doing? Is everything okay?" Brishette sounded so sweet with her French accent.

"Yeah, I'm good. Just missing you."

"Awwh... That's sweet. I'm just sitting here finishing my script for the 'Tahitian Heist'."

"Yeah, I've been thinking about you all day. I just left the funeral home, from seeing the body. They did a pretty good job. But he'd be mad if he only knew how much makeup they caked on his face though." She could tell I was hurting.

"I was just calling to check on you, make sure my sweetie was okay."

"Yeah, I'm good. Nothing was too bad, everybody seemed to be holding up, but tomorrow is a different story. There might be some people falling out when they put him in the ground. I'm getting ready to go get some sleep now and get ready for tomorrow."

"Okay, I love you Dejohn."

"Yeah, I love you too."

Splizz dropped me off with the ice cream and stuff. Splizz wanted to meet China, but I told him he could meet her tomorrow because she was sleep. I got on the elevator and was immediately slapped in the face by the foul smell of cigars and cheap liquor that emanated from the overweight, grey haired man who kept coughing. I couldn't wait until one of us was off the elevator. Thank God he got off on the sixth floor.

I stuck my key card in the door and turned to open it, but the chain blocked my entry. Before I could call out for her, she had rushed to the door and taken the chain off. The rooms' only lighting was the light that peered from bathroom and the flickering from the Panasonic television, decorated with all sorts of advertisement for movies and room service. When she turned to walk back over to the bed, I noticed she was wearing a red super sheer see through nightie that came down just far enough to cover the top of her beautiful, perfectly proportioned, caramel ass that the matching thong so seductively showcased. She layed back down.

Damn, I got hard instantly. If I ever thought about marrying a stripper, she would definitely be my first choice. Her body alone would keep me coming home at night. She just had the perfect shape, a shape that she wouldn't have to worry about when she gets older, she'd be sexy through her sixties.

"I got your ice cream and chocolate syrup."

She sat up slowly, turning towards me, supporting herself with her elbows and forearm looking at me, and her dark eyes where like twin entrances to a soul called possibilities. There were definitely possibilities with China, her real name was Zen Morritz. What a name right? Well she was living up to her name. She was beautiful, smart, sexy, and even reserved with a hint of naive for those who didn't know any better. I knew better, there was nothing naive about her and I knew to treat her as a worthy opponent in a chess match, this way I'd watch her every move and stay a few steps ahead of the game.

I walked over to the bed, handing her the ice cream and placing the syrup, the oatmeal cookies and whipped cream on the nightstand.

"Thannnk youuuu... No spoon?"

"Oh yeah, here you go. It was in the bottom of the bag."

"Why did you buy whipped cream? You ain't got no apple pie."

"Cause you're the apple pie."

"Mmmph... Well okay."

"I told you I had a treat for you when I came back."

"I like treats, especially if they last long." She did that thing with her tongue, licking around her lips, then she'd bite on her bottom lip. She didn't know, but I read a couple of books on body language and that whole thing she does can be summed up as 'You turn me on so let me give it to you'.

I was always subconscious about lasting long enough, so I'd always ask them "Are you cuming, then let me know when you're cuming". Her bringing up that "lasting" subject up made me want to really put it on her, so I let her know.

"I'm glad you mentioned that because I always think about what my partner wants, and a lot of the time the woman never gets to cum because the man never lasts long enough and a part of that..." She cut me off.

"The problem is you cum too fast, that's it right there."

"Hold up, it's not about that, the problem is communicating with each other."

"What's communicating gotta do with it?"

"A whole lot, check this out, just listen for a minute."

"Awight, I'm listening."

"I got a concept that might help us to end that problem."

"What's that."

"Just let me finish." China now opened the ice cram and started digging in with the spoon. It was time, I had her attention and now I had to lay down my plan, 'The rules of the game when you want satisfaction without frustration'.

"Okay, this will be our own lingo, and we're gonna call it R.S.G. or 'Read-Set-Go', that's the woman's worst nightmare, because as soon as the guy who has anticipated getting in the pussy, and is dripping with pre-cum gets in, he's cuming minutes later unless he has taken something. So I came up with the Let's get the R.S.G. out of the way so we can really do the damn thing. In other words, if you make me cum first, by sucking me off, I'll last longer. Long enough for you to cum every time. So this way you won't be disappointed and you wouldn't have to make men feel inadequate when you say something about lasting, at least that's how it is with me.."

"You got a point. That might work. Come here, let me put some ice cream on your dick and suck it off. I never tried that before." Shittt, she didn't have to say that twice. I got naked and got on the bed.

"Lay back, let me pour the melted part on you. Wait... Hold up, let me get a towel first." China scooted to the edge of the bed, got up and got the towel and returned. "Get up for a minute, let me put the towel right here."

I thought she was just saying that she wanted to put ice cream on me because she was eating ice cream and it sounded good. But she was serious about that shit because she grabbed the pint sized Ben and Jerry's, vanilla bean ice cream, put a spoonful in her mouth and began pouring the excess ice cream on my now throbbing love pole. That shit was cold, but was quickly neutralized by the warmth and maneuvering of her mouth and tongue. It made me just close my eyes and try to enjoy the feeling without reaching for her hand full-of-titties or even trying to rub her pussy as I would usually do. So instead, I just interlocked my fingers behind my head as if I was ordered by a police and tried to truly enjoy this feeling until China guided her tongue down my shaft to my balls. She took one, then the other into her mouth, then I felt her warm, moist tongue touch my asshole.

"Whoaa... Mmmph..." That shit caught me off guard because I wasn't expecting that, but it felt good.

China started licking in a circular motion on the inside of my thighs, then she licked my balls one at a time, just like I liked it. Damn, that shit felt like a dream, especially when she deep throated my hard member until it was completely covered, almost like a sword swallower.

I started to coach her, "China lick the sides baby.. Yeahhh, that's right, Ahhh, mmmmm. Yeahhh just nibble while you lick up and down. Damnnn, China, that's it baby."

She took me into her mouth and did this swirling thing around the head of my dick with her tongue. I felt it deep down in my loins, I was about to cum, but she was sucking too fast, trying too hard.

"Slow down baby...Yeahhh, oh shit. Mmmh. It's cuming China, just slow it down baby. Yeah, real sloowwww...Ooohhh... Yeahhh, that's it baby. Yeahhh, Mmmhhh. I'm cumin China... Uuuhhh."

I grabbed her head, slowing her motion and shot my warm liquid protein into her mouth, down her throat. She swallowed every drop. Damn, why do they always want you to approvingly kiss them when they are done.

"Kiss me." She said with traces of my glue like cum around her mouth, but I had no problem kissing China, cum on her mouth and all.

The head was out of this world, and I was obliged to show my gratitude. I laid there for a minute to savor the feeling as long as I could, but I didn't want her to think that I had selfishly manipulated her into giving me mine first because it wasn't like that. I really wanted to last longer, one, because I've heard too many women say they gave a guy some pussy to see what they were working with, and if they cum too fast or only worry about themselves, they did not get anymore pussy. I know I did alright last time, but I want to keep it up.

Call me the panty bandit or whatever, but I like to remove a woman's panties with my mouth. It sends a message that I can do great things with my mouth, and they love that shit. Their nipples get all hard and the pussy gets wet at the same time. The trick to it is that my upper lip is touching and caressing areas of her skin that normally aren't touched at every pull of the panty line.

So that's a creative form of foreplay that sets me apart from the rest. When I'm done licking all over the legs and thighs, it's a wrap. They're ready! Can you blame 'em? If the tongue melts ice, and make ice drip, you know it can make the pussy drip.

I simply wanted to be better than last time, last longer and give her something different so I could blow her mind, similar to an old flame Karen from Chicago who's sex was good enough to make me last for four hours. I'll always remember that time because I broke my record. I'm not saying I didn't cum, but between the Ginseng gum, Ginseng power drink, and her young, sexy looking body that she worked out to keep fit, I was like the energizer bunny. I tore the pussy up over and over again. China had the same kind of body to die for.

"Please don't fall asleep on me, 'cause I know my head is da bomb." It seemed like my dick accepted the challenge because it started to grow as if someone inside was inflating it with a pump.

"Fall asleep? You gotta be kidding, girl I'm getting ready to put it on you and you can get your scream on. I don't care if they call the police, we ain't dirty."

"Oh, you're that confident, huh?" Before she could finish, I was down there performing my panty removal with my mouth. You should've seen her squirming as I got half way. I guess it tickled a little and sent all kinds of crazy signals through her body.

Tonight I was gonna do this thing I learned from White boy Bob back in training school. He told me how white boys with little dicks keep their women, by specializing in eating the pussy. I rolled over on the beige sheets, and watched her body convulse like she was having a wild seizure while I tried to catch my breath. The bed was soaked, we had been going at it for about two hours and some change. It felt good to know that I was still large and in charge, especially after all that shit she was talking about me being a three minute man. China cuddled up next to me and we fell asleep holding each other.

Chapter 27

THE FUNERAL

It was 7:15 am, and obviously China was horny as hell when she woke up because I woke up to the beautiful feeling of her warm moist mouth all over my dick. It was the best alarm clock I ever experienced. She got me nice and hard, then mounted and rode me until we both came. We took a shower and I got empowered with my black Hugo Boss single-breasted suit I bought in Georgetown at the Hugo boss store. To accent it, I wore the Brooks Brothers blue cotton button down with the French cuffs. A black Versace silk tie with a print of royal blue diamond shaped designs in the background. Of course, I had to put on my Rolex that I threw bricks at the penitentiary to get. Then to top it all off, I put my black Montagani Crocs on I got from Caesar's Palace mall in Vegas. If they were going to turn this shit into a fashion show, I was ready for the runway, except for one thing, a man that looked this good deserved to show up with a dime piece on his arm. So I decided to take China with me and shit on Rissa's whore ass.

"You sure you going to a funeral looking all good, like a movie star?" China said as she fixed my tie and cufflinks.

"I changed my mind, I want you to go with me."

"I was beginning to feel like I was in the witness protection program or something, hiding from the Mob. So now you want me to go with you to the funeral where I know nobody but you."

"There's gonna be a lot of people there who knows only the person they came with, plus you're going to support me not them, and if I'm looking as good as you say I am, I deserve to have you with me because you make a million dollar man look and feel like ten million."

"All right, what am I gonna wear? I have a dress but it's not black."

"Don't trip, we're gonna stop by the Galleria downtown on the way in." My cell rang, it was Splizzy.

"Yo, I'm outside."

"Just put on something so we can go, our ride is here."

Finally Splizz got to meet China, and later told me she was like that! We stopped at the Galleria across from the Inner Harbor. I took her straight to Brooks Brothers, chose an elegant black gown, and a royal blue scarf, and a Bangle to accent it. She kept the dress on and bagged her clothes. We picked up shoes and sheer black pantyhose on the way out. It took every bit of twenty minutes, which was probably record time for both of us. The Bethel A.M.E. Church was only five minutes away on Druid Hill Ave., so our timing was fine.

Of course there was no parking spaces, so Splizz let us out in front of the enormous, old 19th century architecture, who's property not only occupied the large corner, but it's presence reached throughout the community with it's seven thousand member congregation and outreach affiliates.

It was going to be a scorcher, it was already seventy-eight degrees at 10:03 am. China was looking like a model from heaven, the sun illuminated her long, beautiful jet black hair and her diamond earrings. People were pulling up late as usual as we walked. I noticed my cousin Benji, he had just got out of Hagerstown State joint from doing five years. He was big as shit standing next to Big Mamma, my grandmother. Big Mamma always talked about losing weight, but kept a freshly baked cake or pie on the table, supposedly for company. But everybody knows who really ate them. Benji spotted me and walked towards us.

"Yo, what's up cuz, oh how you doin' miss?"

"Fine." Splizz sat down and China followed, I didn't blame her, Benji's breath smelled like he had just drank a fifth of liquor.

"Yo cuz, who is that?"

"That's my girl. Let me go over here and holler at Big Mamma, I'll see you later." I walked away.

"Hey Big Mama, how you doin'?"

"I guess I'm gone make it baby, I'm tryin' to hold up. You alright?"

"Yes ma'am, I'm okay so far."

I said my hello's to everybody and took my seat as the service began, and suddenly Rissa came in with my daughter. As soon as she spotted me she started running towards me. I picked her up and hugged her.

"Daaddyy. When did you get back?"

"Yesterday baby. I came by your house and your mommy said you were over your aunt's house. Did you have fun?"

"Yesss. Daddy I want a poodle like my auntie. You said no big dogs, a poodle is not big."

I walked back towards the back of the church where Rissa was, "What's up? Who you riding with?"

"Why?"

"Because I want Isha to ride with me."

"I don't care, she can ride with you."

"Awight, I'll just see you at the grave site when I get there." That was way too easy because she always fights me. She was in a good mood or she was up to something.

The pastor Frank Reid allowed several people to come up and speak, so I got up and read my poem I wrote called 'Who Am I, If I'm Not Myself'.

Am I the second hand on the clock?
Swift like that,
Am I my brother's keeper?
When keeping myself is hard enough on the block,
Am I a child at fourteen?
When I can buy my own school clothes and Christmas
presents for everybody,
I am your son, your grandson, your brother, your
homie, your next door neighbor,
door neighbor,
your baby's father, your dynasty,
and travesty all at the same time,
But who am I, if I'm not myself?
Am I you?

The church was filled with the sounds of sniffling and crying. As I walked down the isle people reached out to shake my hand, nodding with approval. Minutes later it was over and everybody headed for their cars to form the procession, to the Woodlawn Cemetery.

It was now 11:53, the sun induced temperature had ascended to 82 degrees, but there was a nice breeze that flirted with the women, successfully lifting their skirts and dresses unexpectedly showing all kinds of legs and ass. The setup was nice; there was a polished brass frame which enclosed the Champagne-tinted casket. Draped in rose and flower arrangements. The well manicured grass swayed back and forth to the shift of the wind.

Big Mama, Aunt Sheila (Stevens mother), Shirl (Steven's oldest sister), Tatyonna (Stevens baby's mother) and his bad assed son, Lil Steven on her lap, everyone else stood while the pastor gave his closing eulogy. The sniffles turned to crying, the more the pastor said, the more crying I heard.

It wasn't until I looked over and saw Rissa all hugged up with some dude that I realized why she gave up Isha so easily at the church. That's when the pastor said something about 'He's gone now to be with our Lord', Big Mama fell out, and we didn't know whether it was a heart attack or whether she just fainted. Anyway, that caused an epidemic, everybody let go. Even my daughter Isha started crying. Rissa found her way over to us to comfort Isha. I couldn't help it; I had to whisper to her, "Why the fuck you bring that country assed dude here? He don't know nobody here."

Rissa blurted out, you got some fucking nerve, and you brought that lil Chinese looking bitch. Who the fuck she know?"

China heard every word she said, "Who you calling a bitch? You don't know me, I will take off my heals and beat your ass out here. Dee you better get her."

"You lucky my daughter is here, so you get a pass this time. If you ever talk about doing something to me again I will lay your ass down." Rissa angrily responded.

It was time for me to intervene, "Awight, that's enough. We're at my cousin's funeral. Have some fuckin' respect. Plus why you come over here anyway."

"Fuck you Dejohn. Come on Isha." Rissa grabbed my daughters left hand, I already had her right hand, and tried to take her from my grasp and tried to walk away angrily causing both arms to be stretched out like she was a rag doll.

"Let her go."

"No, you let her got, she staying with me."

"No she ain't, I'm leaving and my daughter is leaving with me."

"Look... I said she's staying with me." By the look in my eyes and the tone of my voice, she knew I wasn't playing. She let her go. "I'll bring her home after the reception."

"Whatever, you just call first."

Right about now, China was probably feeling real good, like I had just chose her over my daughter's mother. I was merely seeing it as a boxing ring, and China was in her corner next to me, but Rissa was to the left of us in the crowd. So I simply told Rissa to go back over there where she was to keep the drama down at my lil cousin's funeral.

We all left the cemetery and went back to Big Mamma's house for the reception. Her house was bigger, that's why we didn't have it at Steve's house. They had liquor, weed, and it seemed like everybody was cursing up a storm. Everybody kept asking me who China was, even Big Mama said, "You are the cutest thing. Boy you better not mess this one up."

China was blushing, she must have had about three drinks and was starting to get loose, and I didn't want my daughter seeing her too high. Splizz agreed we should leave so we left, dropped off Isha and headed for the airport to catch our return flight to Los Angeles.

Chapter 28

RETURN TO L.A.

It was a warm, but dry 78 degrees at 1:15 pm when we arrived at L.A.X. Airport. As soon as we cleared the gate I called Steph from my cell to let him know we were there.

"Yo Steph, we're here."

"I'm already outside. I called to check the arrival schedule."

"Okay, where are you?"

"Downstairs at ground transportation. You'll see me, I'm double parked."

"Which car are you in?"

"I got the Jag."

"Awight, we're on our way."

"So how was your trip? I take it everything went alright because y'all made it back. Watch... Stupid mutha fukazz, man. He saw me pullin' off and pulled right in front of me, probably tryin' to make me run into the back of him and I would've beat his ass too."

"It was cool, we had a nice time."

"You had a nice time. He left me in the hotel, I thought I would've gotten a chance to go out on the town, have dinner, and hang out at the Inner Harbor. The closest I got to the Inner Harbor was the morning of the funeral; we stopped by the galleria to get an outfit. No, I'm just kidding, we had a nice time."

"Dee, I found a couple of mansions that fit the profile. Are you ready to go to work?"

"Am I? That's all I've been thinking about."

"Okay, we'll see because we're gonna take a trip later on, after you get settled in. Dee I'ma drop you off first."

I didn't even get in the door good, and my phone was ringing. Probably because my cell phone battery needed to be changed. I lifted the receiver from the base and grabbed my Hello Direct cordless headset so I wouldn't be confined.

"Hello."

"Hey Dee, how was your trip? I've been trying to get you on your cell but I didn't get an answer."

"My trip was fine."

"I missed you Dee. You miss me?"

"I've only been gone for two days Reecee and you missed me in two days. So does that mean you're tryin' to see me so you can fuck my brains out? Wait a minute, hold on, somebody's on my other line."

"Hello."

"Hey sweetie."

"Heyyy. What's up baby? Hold on for a minute, let me clear the other line."

"Hello."

"Yeah."

"Let me call you back Reecee, I gotta take this call. You want me to hit you on the cell or the house phone?"

"The cell."

Awight, I'll hit you back." I clicked over.

"What's up Brishette, how's my baby girl?"

"Fine, when did you get back?"

"I just walked in the house."

"Did you get my messages?"

"What messages, wait, wait, I did get one message last night, but it was too late to call you back. So how is your mother?"

"They don't think she's gonna make it Dejohn. She was doing better but now they say her condition has taken a turn for the worst."

"I'm sorry to hear that. So when are you going to see her?"

"I'm making arrangements now, I've just been nauseated the last couple days, throwing up all over the place. This baby got me going man, but anyway, I need to see you. I gotta talk to you about something very important and I don't wanna talk about it over the phone."

"Why don't you come over here 'cause I'm just getting in the door. I was gonna take me a bath, eat something, and take me a nap."

"I'll be over in a little while."

"Awight, I'll see you then."

I called Larry and Mel to let them know I was back in town. I didn't get an answer at Larry's house or cell, and Mel was probably out chasing trucks because he never answered either. So I started my bath water then slouched down on my favorite soft, beige corduroy-like fabric "Play Pin" sectional couch set with the matching end tables and the recliners on each side. I located the remote, hiding in between the cushions and began flipping through the channels. I immediately noticed and became irritated by the blinding ray of sunlight that boldly projected through a misplaced vertical blind.

I later learned that the misplaced blind was only the first of a series of things in my apartment that were out of place. Someone had been in my house while I was gone.

But who? Nothing was missing. Then it hit me, I gave Brishette an emergency key.

Brishette had been to my house, snooping around. I don't like that shit at all, and just as I started contemplating whether what she wanted to talk about had anything to do with something that she might have found on her nosey spree, I heard keys and she slipped in all lit up from her excitement at seeing me. But women who are as sincere looking as Brishette always shocks you when you find out how sneaky and conniving they are.

"Hey, hey. Did everything go okay?"

"What do you mean, did everything go okay?"

"I mean with everything, the funeral, the drug thing you supposed to be ending, your daughter's mother and your daughter, you know... Everything."

"Yeah, everything went fine. I took care of the guy like I said I would, so that's over and now I can move on with my life. I seen a lot of friends and family that I hadn't seen in a long time. I also spent a little time with Isha, and I told her I'm gonna come get her this summer and she can come and stay with us for a few weeks."

"That'll be nice, I'd like to meet Isha and that would give us a chance to bond." Brishette said smiling.

"Okay, that's enough about me and Baltimore, let's talk about you. I thought you said you had something very important to talk to me about."

"Yeah, I do."

"Before we get to that, did you stop by and check on the house for me?"

"That's kind of what I want to talk to you about."

"So what, you been snooping around my house or something?"

"Snooping around, no... I came by to check on the house like you asked me and just so happen I had to use the bathroom real bad so I doubled parked and ran inside. I heard a car blowing, so I looked out the window and it was a car blowing for me, but I had to go, bad."

"Ohh, okay, that explain why my blinds were out of place..."

"I'm sorry, I was in a hurry. This baby got me running back and forth to the bathroom, but I do wanna ask you a question though."

"And what's that Brishette?"

"While I was using your bathroom, your phone rang and that loud machine came on and some guy left you a message, talking about something about a mansion. I didn't get it all but; I do remember him saying at the end, 'I hope you're ready to put in some work'. I mean... I don't mean to be nosey but what does he mean 'Put in some work'?"

"Damn, you don't miss nothing do you?"

"Nooo, I try not to. Remember I write movies so I literally have a working knowledge, literally of what putting in some work means."

"Yeah, well, the guy you're talking about is a developer slash rehabber. He does it all, kitchens, bathrooms, extensions, you name it and he wants me to come and work with him. That's what he was saying on my machine."

"That makes sense then." I was going to watch her because she's sharper than I thought.

"So, does he, like fix up mansions or something?"

"Actually yes. He says that's where the money is and if I do decide to work with him, it will give me a chance to see the inside of mansions because every since I was a kid I always said that one day I'd be living in a mansion and I will. So is that what you wanted to talk about?"

"No. I wanted to tell you that, I'm gonna spend a couple weeks up in San Francisco with my mother because the doctors say that she is not expected to make it, in fact they sssaay, shhsss... Any da...yy!!" Tears began falling form her eyes as if the flood gates broke open to the Panama Canal. I quickly grabbed her, resting her head on my shoulders and she cried with such fervor. I can't say I know what it felt like but I certainly understood, especially that I had just left a funeral days ago.

My cell phone rang so untimely and rudely at that point. I don't know why I even thought about answering it because this was not the time to be apathetic. I let the voice mail pick up.

It seems like emotional loving is the best kind because there's so much passion involved. It seems like there's a different kind of ambiance that surrounds it. Then to top it off, we started in the bath tub and worked our way to the bedroom, it was crazy. Pregnant pussy is the best, it stays nice and juicy.

After about an hour of heated sex, I took a shower, got dressed and called Steph. That's when I learned that it was his call that I missed earlier.

"What's up Steph?"

"Dee what's going on? I called you an hour ago and I got your voice mail. You get my message?"

"Naw, I just got out of the tub."

"Man get ready because I'll be there in about fifteen minutes to get you."

"What time is it now, its 3:25, I'm on my way."

I didn't know exactly where we were going, but I knew I had to look the part so I put on a creme colored raw silk-linen blend double breasted sports jacket by Fred Hayman of Beverly Hills, a cool assed Tommy Bahamas button down short sleeved shirt, beige with burgundy leaves, some creme Zanella slacks and the burgundy Croc slip-ons with the gold classic bit across the top. I was sharp. I put on a serpentine gold bracelet and my gold flat Rolex with the burgundy band. You would have thought by looking at me that I had a team of fashion Gurus dress me.

Chapter 29

We took the scenic route up 101, along the coastal shoreline, nothing but beach for miles, until we started ascending higher into a spiral road into the hills of Santa Barbara. I already knew I wasn't going to like it because it was too far. We had been driving for an hour and twenty minutes and we still weren't there yet.

"How far is it?" I resounded with a hint of frustration.

"That's it right there."

We turned right onto a winding road that led us to an old structure that looked like nothing but money. It was huge. As we pulled up, we were met by an older White woman wearing a navy blue coat dress with large gold buttons down the front, oyster pearls doubled around her neck and a pair of spectacles over which she peered at us as we got out of the Jaguar.

"Follow my lead, and we'll be fine." Steph said with a look of confidence, like he does this shit all the time. I didn't know what he wanted me to do, I just went along.

"Which one of you is Mr. Williams?"

Steph extended his hand, "I am, and this is my associate, Mr. Farnwald."

I shook the lady's hand and noticed she was wearing at least a three carat canary yellow stone set in a platinum band on her freckled, wrinkled hand.

The landscape was breathtaking. Each bush was expertly sculpted in either a pyramid shape or perfectly rounded sphere. In front of the entrance stood a stone figure of some sort of Greek Goddess standing in a ground level pond. To the left were all sorts of roses or tulips, I couldn't tell which without a closer look. Then to the right there was a dash of these cotton-like puffs, protruding from the skinny branches, they were unmistakably pussy willows I knew them because my grandmother had them in her yard.

We walked inside the tall, wooden double doors that had to cost two to three thousand dollars a piece. The floor in the foyer was a beautiful beige marble with lightening streaks of burgundy. Just beyond the foyer the floors were evenly toned shellacked oak wood. You could almost see your face in the floor.

I was expecting the Scarface dual-sided staircase, but this single stairwell was fine because the lady, after showing us the library, the family room, laundry area, pool, theater and the huge outdoor patio adorned with gorgeous tree and rubber plants, led us to the elevator although it was not glass it certainly had a nice touch. Inside it was draped in deep mahogany velvet all the way around. The railing was a professionally polished brass. The elevator took us to the second floor. There seemed to be wings because down one hall was six rooms, down another was five rooms, and obviously the best was saved for last, because the last hallway led to the four rooms leading to the master bedroom. Surprisingly, one of the rooms was a state of the art exercise and massage room.

Then we finally saw the master bedroom. It was enormous. There was a separate his and hers walk-in closet with motion sensors, so the lights came on when you walked in. The bed in the center of the room was round with steps leading to it. There was a theater-like screen on the wall facing the bed, probably for a projection unit.

What really sold me on the bedroom was the hidden wall bed. Someone must have pulled that out when they couldn't sleep together. But I had never seen a bathroom quite as large as this one. It was incredible. There was a huge marble Jacuzzi with a big screen t.v attached in the middle of the floor. The glass enclosed shower was made for two, there was a burgundy couch against the wall, a vanity for her, a barber chair and two toilets with the spray action like the ones you'd see on the t.v. program "Life Styles of the Rich and Famous" hosted by Robin Leech. Then there were two double doors which led to a balcony with sun chairs, and a breakfast table. She showed us everything.

I gave Steph the look and nod of approval. He knew I was feeling this spot.

"So how long do we have to make a decision?" I asked as we walked form the main house to the guest house where the maids and chefs would stay. Even it had six rooms. Wow.

This place had a tennis court, an Olympic sized swimming pool outside, and eight car garage and plenty of acres to get lost on. Just being here made you feel like a celebrity. This was definitely the kind of life I wanted, no mistake about it.

The lady was explaining that she would need to know something before she went back to Palm Springs in three weeks. When I heard her say that, I realized why Steph chose this distant location. This was exactly the kind of situation that we spoke about. I smiled because this could soon be mine.

Chapter 30

My phone vibrated, displaying Brishette's number, "Hey Baby, where you at?"

"I just learned that my sister got me a Buddy Pass on Southwest and the flight leaves in three and a half hours. Should I get someone else to take me, or can you make it here in time?"

"I'm about an hour and forty minutes outside of L.A., we'll be pushing it. Wait, hold on... Steph do you think we could make it to L.A., pick up my girl and make it to the airport in three and a half hours."

Steph replied, "Yeah, that's plenty of time."

It did not surprise me at all that Candy called while I was talking to Brishette, and again I couldn't answer.

"Okay baby, I'm on my way. I'll be there in about an hour and forty-five minutes, and you're only fifteen minutes from the airport. We'll be fine. Okay?"

"Okay, I'll see you when you get here. Let me finish packing."

I called Candy back, only to find myself a participant in the phone tag game as her voice mail picked up, but somehow she was calling again while I was leaving a message.

"Hellooo."

"Hello yourself, Mr. too busy for Candy." She seemed to always find the right combination of words to show her wit.

"Don't even try that Candy, I'm never too busy for you."

"I can't tell, it seems like every since you moved out my house and got your own place you don't have time for me no more..." I cut her off.

"Don't do that... You know I tried to see you before I left and you couldn't get away, remember?"

"So when am I gonna see you?"

"When do you wanna see me Candy?"

"Have you eaten dinner?"

"No, and I'm starving. What do you have in mind?"

"Let's just say it's a surprise. So where do you want me to pick you up? We can come back to my house."

"How about I pick you up and we go to my house?" I took the lead.

"Okay, that's fine."

"Awight, I'll call you when I'm on my way. I got a couple of things to do first, but I'll see you by nine o'clock."

"Nine? Why so late? You know I gotta work tomorrow."

"If I can do it sooner, I will and I will call you."

Steph dropped me off at Brishette's house in Culver City. She left her white BMW 745i with me. We made it to the airport just in time.

Brishette boarded the plane at 8:20 p.m. and I made it to Candy's by 8:45. I called from my cell phone, as I waited in the driveway I saw Reecee come to her upstairs window to see who it was that was picking up her sister. At that same moment my phone vibrated.

"Hello."

"I thought that was you." Reecee said in almost a whisper.

"Come on, she told you it was me."

"She didn't, I swear to God."

"Awight, here she comes, I'll call you later."

"You better call too."

Candy came out looking good as ever. She was wearing a beige two piece outfit with some brown heels and a Channel bag on her arm. She was cute as hell with her sexy self.

"Hey Dee, so this is why no body sees you anymore. You're balling out of control now huh? That is what they call it ain't it?" She reached over and kissed me on my cheek. This was a good start, she was letting me know that she wanted to be close and intimate, or that's what I got from her gesture.

"This ain't mine; someone just lent it to me for a week or so."

"Yeah right, and I'm supposed to believe that?"

"You believe what you want, I'm just telling you what's up so you want think I'm fronting like it's mine. You know what I'm saying?"

"So where are we going?"

"It's your call, we can go out to dinner or we can go to my house and I'll cook you something."

"Like what? Can you cook?"

"Can I? You better ask somebody. I'm one of the best; you'll love my cooking girl."

"Okay, I'm a put you to the test. Let's go to your house... You got wine already?"

"No, but we can stop by the store and get some though."

We arrived at my house around 9:20 p.m.; I couldn't wait to get her upstairs. I had something for her ass. I had waited for almost four months and I only had one time to make my first impression. That's what my mentor taught me, so it was my duty to put it on her ass. Especially with what she said to me when we first met, she would give me some, but she was gonna make me wait because it was worth waiting for. That's a hell of a statement, pussy better be good too.

As soon as we walked in the door, I grabbed the remote to my Bang and Olsen stereo and summoned my favorite songstress, Sade'.

"Make yourself at home. Naw, better yet, come with me so we can wash our hands and you can help me prep. Is that cool with you?"

"Uhmmm hmmm. I see you got a few new pieces of furniture."

"Like a bachelor pad, right?"

"No, that's not what I was gonna say. I was gonna say that it looks cozy now. But I could do wonders with this place." I took her to the bathroom, "I bet you could."

While she was washing her hands, I grabbed a hand towel from the closet, threw it over my shoulder and wrapped my arms around her waist until I was snug against her tempting, plump butt. She smiled as we posed in the mirror cheek to cheek. Then she grabbed my hands, still around her waist and began soaping them up. All the time she's pulling me closer. I rinsed my hands and just as I started to move back, feeling a little embarrassed because of being this close to her, my heart starting racing which obviously sent blood racing through my veins, filling my penis.

She felt it rise, pushing the fabric of her pants against the bottom of her soft ass, I'm sure she felt my heart racing just as I felt hers, when she turned to face me. We looked into each other's eyes, and saw a passion that seemed to be boiling over.

Our lips met with such precision, they were just right. The right amount of moisture, her breath was not offensive; the taste in her mouth, as we swiped tongues was a taste that reminded me of my first real kiss back in the ninth grade. I had just turned fourteen and I kissed the babysitter Karen, who was seventeen at the time. She taught me how to French Kiss, so when I meet someone whose kiss makes me close my eyes, I always think of Karen. She was kind of the standard.

Candy must have enjoyed the kiss also because she softly grabbed the back of my head with both hands and started kissing me with such fervent desire. Her eager hands moved quickly to feverously grabbing my shirt and pulling it out of my pants, giving her access to my strong back. Her hands were all over my back.

Our breathing intensified, I was pumped. By this time, I knew we were not gonna make it to the kitchen, so I hoisted Candy's 145 pounds, and carried her into my bedroom and laid her on the bed. She pulled me on top of her, and I positioned my throbbing penis, now protruding from the confines of my slacks, right between her legs. I felt her softness through the thin fabric. I was so on target that if we were naked I would have slid right inside of her, no problem.

I couldn't take the teasing anymore. I went for her jacket, she started unbuttoning my shirt. It was like we were competing in an "undress 'em" competition. I was having a time getting her jacket off her arm, so I helped her up to her feet and we undressed each other in record time.

It seemed like as soon as she got my wife beater over my head, she started acting like she hadn't had any dick in years. I mean, she started kissing me and grabbing my dick all hard. Whoa, that shit hurt. I was too hard for her to be grabbing my shit like that. I grabbed both of her hands and put them around my neck. Then I grabbed her soft ass with both hands and began to lift her, and it was like she knew exactly what I was thinking because she used her toes and sprang upward and in one motion she wrapped her legs around my waist, just like a little girl jumping up and into her father's arm. but her father would be arrested and shot by a firing squad if he even thought about doing what I was about to do to his daughter.

I balanced myself as she locked her hands around my neck to keep a hold of me. This is exactly why I work out, for times like this. Those shrugs really made my neck strong because she was heavy as shit pulling on my neck. With one hand, I continued to hold her up, while with the other hand I guided my now oozing love muscle into her warm, juicy waiting tight pussy.

I lifted her slightly, making sure I didn't slip out, and let her down on my love pole somewhat quickly. She sighed, "Sssss", and gave me a look, like 'oh shit! You're really inside of me, every inch of you'. Her mouth was wide open; the look reminded me of someone who had forgotten something. That look gave me a jolt of adrenaline, then I went crazy, I leaned her back against the wall and began banging away.

Every time she made this sound, "Uht", it was a sort of grunt, that shit just fed my ego, like spinach does Popeye. I really went wild, then she changed her song, she was going from, "Uht', to "Oh shit", "Yeahhh baby... Ooh, that's it ba...oooh, yeah, fuck me baby."

I tried to ram it up in her stomach. I didn't have a ten-inch dick, but I knew what to do with what I have, "Oh shit... That hurts." She managed to get out.

I turned around, laid her down on the bed slowly to make sure I didn't slip out. I pushed her legs up until they were touching her shoulders, then I delivered every inch inside of her with real slow and long strokes. It felt like heaven inside of her. I see now what she meant when she said she was worth waiting for, but for some reason I couldn't cum, so I kept pumping and she started digging her nails in my back.

I wanted to tell her to get her fucking nails out of my back, but I didn't want to fuck up the groove. So instead I paid her ass back, I started thrusting with all my might, hitting everything inside, and even shit I never felt before. "Stop, stop...Sto...hah ha." She was breathing all crazy and so was I. "Let me get on top...Hhhh huhhh."

I slid out of her and turned over. We were both sweating like we just ran a marathon. She straddled me and pointed my love stick into he pleasure chest and started riding real slow, finding her rhythm. That shit was so sexy, watching her be in control of her own climatic destiny. Her hands were strategically holding my waist as she humped back and forth to Sade's "Your Love is King" emanating from the wireless speakers throughout the apartment.

It was beautiful seeing her head go back, the look on her face as she clinched my waist tightly as she came to a slow stop. Her pussy felt like she was pulsating around my dick. She was convulsing like she was having little, multiple orgasms, so I didn't move. Then she collapsed forward, kissing me and smiling. "Don't move." She said, out of breath, "I want to just keep you inside of me for a while."

I really wanted to get up and wash all this sweat and pussy juice off of me, but I let her have her five minutes of aftermath joy.

But in the next couple of weeks, I would get the shock of my life, which is why I should have taken my time to get a condom.

Chapter 31

"Get your ass up youngster", were the words that emanated from the receiver as I awoke to Mel's morning work call. "Come on youngster, we got a big day today. I'll be at your house by 8:05 a.m."

"What ti... Never mind, I see, its 7:23. Awight let me get up and get ready." I started to tell him I'd meet him because I had the Beemer, and we could ride in style, but I gave it a quick thought that he made enough money to buy any kind of car he wanted but he always used rent-a-wreck to work out of. So that was the good reason not to drive anything flashy.

We went to our normal spot across from UPS, only this day was different. There were two police in the coffee shop when we arrived. So that meant no binoculars. In fact, Mel turned and walked out, I followed.

"Youngster, I've been here for almost two years. Every morning and I have never seen a police in here. Did you see how they looked at us when we came in?" Before I could answer he exclaimed, "Something ain't right, it could be just a coincidence but I just don't believe in coincidences."

I started thinking, maybe somebody recognized us always sitting here with binoculars.

"Come on, get in the car. We're gonna change locations. But today is big, so we gotta know whether it's okay to approach them trucks."

"Didn't we get that one guy's cell number?" It seemed like a pretty fair question to me.

"Oh yeah, that's right youngster. You wrote it down. Do you remember where you wrote it?"

"It should be on the back of the Red Dragon Chinese food menu in the glove compartment. I think that's what I wrote it on." I opened the glove box, since I was closest, located the menu and sure enough there it was, 213-771-9825.

I dialed the number to the UPS truck driver's cell phone number, "Hello."

"Hold on." I passed the phone to Mel, who put him on speaker?

"Hey, partner. What's going on?" Mel set the driver at ease.

"Oh... Hey. I didn't know who that was."

"So what's going on? Everything okay?"

"Not really. There were two guys in suits in the office when I got there."

"So what did they want?"

"They just asked me about my deliveries to the 904 address."

"What about it?"

"You know. Who signed for the packages? I told them sometimes it's an old lady and others it was different people."

"So you got anything for me today?"

"Yeah, I got four boxes for y'all. But the ones for 904 got taken off my truck, and they're probably going to try a sting so I wouldn't mess with 'em."

"Awight, we'll meet you later, before 10:30."

"Okay."

We hung up, Mel had this look on his face like something was wrong. I knew that look oh so well. "What? I know something is wrong. What?"

"You know youngster, something about the way he said that the 904 boxes are gone."

"What do you mean?" I asked as if I didn't understand, but I understood perfectly that maybe this guy is stealing the boxes and telling us that it's hot.

"If I ever find out that that boy is stealing from us, I'll have somebody do something to him. He knows we're not going to call and ask about whether someone took some boxes off his truck. So in other words, you're beat. Get over it, and I ain't feeling that shit if that's the case."

"How long have you been messing with this guy?"

"About two and a half years... He..." I cut him off.

"So has he done this before?"

"He made me feel like this once before. I think it was a laptop that he said they took off his truck. That shit is petty, all he gotta do is ask me and I'll get him anything he wants because he helps me, so I'll help him."

"Yeah, I feel you."

We sat there across the street and one block down from the yard where all the trucks geared up to deliver their morning promises by 10:30 a.m. We pulled off soon after truck 10780 cleared the gate.

"Can't you call and track it with the tracking number?"

"That's right." Mel started smiling, "You're a genious youngster, that's why I fuck with you. Can you reach back there and get my organizer off the back seat? There's a folded piece of notebook paper, probably near the front."

Mel took his eyes off the road, trying to point. He almost ran into the back of the car in front of us as the light changed to red.

"Let me do this, you just keep your eyes on the road." I said, giving him the look.

"Is that it?" I reached over showing him a piece of notebook paper.

"Yeah, call them and see where the package is."

I dialed 1 -800-GO-BROWN, went through a series of automated prompts before an operator came on line and asked for my tracking number. She put me on hold. That was not a good sign. But finally she returned and told me that the package was being held at the station.

"He wasn't lying; they said the package was being held at the station."

I could see the relief on his face as I gave him the news. We made an illegal left turn off of Manchester onto LaCienga and headed for the Jungle where we had four different addresses to pick up boxes from.

I answered my first call of the day, "Hello."

"Hello? Ahhyy, what's up Steph? My man."

"What up, where you at?"

"I'm out and about, doing my thing. Why, what's up?"

"We need to get together so I can walk you through this shit man. This shit ain't no joke Dee, your shit gotta be tight partner."

"What time you think we'll be done?" I asked Mel.

"We should be done around 11:00-11:15 youngster."

"Steph, ahhh...Let's.." Steph interrupted me.

"Man you playing games. I thought you said you'd be ready to work when you got back. We got a lot of shit to do. We gotta take out ads; get licenses, and all kinds of shit."

"I'll be done around 11:15."

"Where you gone be at 11:30? I'll come and get you." Steph impatiently responded.

"Just tell me where to meet you and I'll be there." I returned with a similar tone of disgust.

"Awight, there's a gas station right across the street from the Forum where the Lakers play. You know where it's at right?"

"Yeah, that's close to where I am, so I'll see you at 11:30."

Maybe he didn't realize that I was more anxious than even he was about this whole thing, because this was my childhood fantasy that became a long term goal as an adult.

It didn't matter how I obtained it, my father always said to me, "No pain, no gain", when I'd run in the house crying when I'd hurt myself playing football. I didn't understand back then, but I learned later. The more you get hurt, the more you learn about avoiding getting hurt. Preparing was usually all it took.

Mel and I were supposed to go to Hawthorne to pick up boxes also, and Mel decided to let "Dred" pick up the boxes. Luckily we didn't go because we would have walked into a trap. Dred got locked up. We bailed him out as soon as we got the call. That was our motto, 'Treat your people good, and earn their loyalty. "Treat 'em bad, and earn prison wages.' We lived by it".

It was 10:15am, I was on my way to meet Steph when Splizzy gave me the news I had been waiting for. Just as I expected, the shooter who killed my favorite cousin was one of his workers who he had beaten down, but did not kill, for stealing from him.

"Yo, the boy said it was the same dude that Lil Steve use to take care of, tried to set him up. Lil Steve found out about it and beat his ass real bad and put him in the hospital..."

"I don't even wanna hear no more. I wanna know where he lives, where his girl, his mother, his homies live. I wanna know where he works, where he hustles at. Yo, I want to know everything about this kid."

"Yo Dee, I'm here... I got this."

"Naw, this is personal Splizz. I gotta take care of this on my own. I promised Lil Stevie while I was reviewing the body, so I gotta keep my word."

"What difference do it make, who take care of it?"

"Yo, all I need you to do is find out the where, and I'll do the rest."

"Awight, I'll get all that for you."

"Awight, that's what I'm talking about. In the mean time I'ma be setting shit up so you can come live some of that mansion player life shit. As soon as I get set up, I'm coming in there to take care of that, plus it'll give the boy a chance to think everything is cool. Naw-mean?"

"Awight, yo, if you need me I'll be at the studio, so call that number instead of the cell number."

"Yo, how many times you gone tell me that? All you had to do was say I'll be at the studio."

"I forgot your ass remember everything."

"That's right nigga. Awight, I'll call you later."

"Yeah, awight. Peace."

"Peace."

It was 11:22am when Mel pulled into the Stop & Shop gas station parking lot, which was crowded with lunch time traffic, except for the lonely unoccupied vehicles forming a procession along the wall, waiting to be serviced someday.

"Do you see 'em?"

"Naw, we got here a little early. You want something out of here? I'ma run in here and get some peppermints."

"I'm cool, go ahead. Just hurry up 'cause I gotta get back to the house and take care of some stuff."

As I got out of the car, I was greeted by a combination of smog and gas fumes that made me, in spite of Mel's request, move a little faster. As I stood in line, I noticed through the store's window what looked like Steph's green Jag at the light, trying to make a left into the gas station. The traffic, however, was relentless and unyielding. It all happened in a split second; I heard the beckoning sound of the crash. I turned back to the window, and saw the car speed away being chased by Inglewood police, sirens blazing. Steph luckily was almost clear of the intersection, because the speeding car, which we learned had just robbed Bank of America, hit Steph on the rear driver side panel and spent the car around.

The store's patrons started their expected, nosey gossiping chatter and "Oh my Gods". I ran out, not thinking about the peppermints I had in my hand. As I approached the car, I heard the station attendant's Indian accent, "Hey mister, you forgot to payyy." I threw up my finger, signaling him to hold up. Mel was right on point; he was at the window when I turned around.

Steph was a bit shaken up, but he was angrier than anything, "Man... When I turned, there were no cars coming. Where da fuck he come from? He must have been doing 100 miles an hour..."

"Are you awight?" I asked, cutting him off

"Yeah, I'm awight." Steph looked at his car, "Damn, why the fuck me?"

"Yo just be grateful you ain't hurt because that car was flying, and police cars were flying behind him too."

The ambulance's distant siren was now close, "Let me pull this car out the middle of the street."

"Steph, with one foot outside the door, slowly pulled the car to the curb, cracking the pieces of tale light splattered on the street by the impact.

"Damn, you hear that shit?" Steph got out of the car and walked to the car's injury. The accident had smashed the back fender into the wheel, making the fender rub against the tire. "I can't believe this bullshit, damn!" I felt his pain.

Mel made his way over to the car as the ambulance pulled up with its flashing bright lights that seemed to be masked by the sun's ultraviolet rays. I turned towards Mel as he approached, "That must be your boy, huh youngster?"

"Yeah, that's fucked up Mel. Hold up, let me see if he's gonna go to the hospital." I walked over to Steph where the paramedics tried to convince him to go for observation and let the hospital check him out.

"Naw, I'm straight. I'm awight. I don't need no ambulance. I'm cool."

"Okay, are you sure because you need to get checked out sir?" The ambulance driver pitched as if he was concerned, but everyone know their real motive is to get money for their ride to the hospital, and whatever service they provide along the way.

The Police, who appeared on the scene, advised us that they caught the hit and run, bank robbing driver about a mile away. I convinced Steph to go to the hospital to get checked out and Mel to take us. This gave Mel and Steph a chance to meet.

Steph mentioned something about having one of the girls bring his Range Rover to the hospital so we could keep moving from there because AAA was on it's way to get the Jag and take it to the dealer. I had Steph abort his call for help because I was closer to Brishette's car. So after about twenty minutes of waiting in the emergency room, I had Mel take me to pick up the Beemer.

In route, I got the expected call from China, "Hello."

"You Okay?"

"Am I okay? Why you ask me that?"

"Because I haven't heard from you since we got back and of all people, I expected to hear from you. You make me feel used."

Ah shit, here we go, another sensitive assed woman. What she doesn't realize is tha the Art of Seduction is real. All she had to do was wait me out and she may have gotten an upper hand, but now, I get the upper hand and I liked that.

"China, you trippin', it's only been a day and I was gonna call you. I'm on my way to pick up a car because Steph just got in an accident."

"What? When?"

"About thirty minutes ago. A guy running from the police came out of nowhere and hit him on the driver side back panel, where the gas tank is."

"Oh my God! Is he okay?"

"Yeah... Yeah he's cool."

"What hospital is he at?"

"St. Joseph's over by the race track. Hollywood Park."

"I know where that's at, I'ma stop by there. Is that where you gonna be?"

"Yeah, I'm just gonna pick up a car and I'm on my way back there."

"Awight, I'll wait for you, okay?"

"Awight, I'll see you when I get there."

Chapter 32

The girls loved Steph. He was like their "Captain Save-a-Hoe" because some of them were living with roaches and drug addicts, or staying with a boyfriend because they had no where else to stay, and some were living well but not as well as living in a mansion, and they made more money at the mansion parties than they made sometimes at the strip club.

"Youngster, so what's the deal with this guy Steph?"

"Uhmmm, let's just say he's down with the paper game real heavy, and real estate."

"What'd you mean? He into the checks?"

"Naw, He's gonna show me how to get a mansion for several months with no money down."

"It sounds like some bullshit. You better be careful because ain't nobody giving up no damn mansion for no money. So watch yourself youngster, everything that glitters ain't gold."

We pulled up in front of Brishette's car and I got out, "Awight thanks. I'll call you later."

The strangest shit happened, the phone rang, and it was Brishette. Damn, talk about dejavu, "Hey baby. What's up?"

"I've been thinking about you all day long." Brishette emotionally crooned.

"Oh yeah, what you been thinking about?"

"Just stuff."

"Stuff like what?"

"Like what are we gonna name the baby if it's a girl because I know you probably want to name it after you if it's a boy, right?"

"You know it."

"So where are you?"

"I'm outside my house getting ready to go over to the hospital."

"For what, are you okay?"

"Yeah, I'm fine but my man just got in an accident. You remember the guy, the construction guy that left the message on the machine? Well he was at the light by the Forum and had just made a left towards the gas station and some guy who was running from the police hit his Jag and spent it around."

"Ahh man. So did the ambulance take him? Was it real bad?"

"Naw, me and Mel talked him into goin to the hospital. He wasn't gonna go."

"Oh... Okay. Baby I gotta go, the nurse is calling me, my mother may be awake. I'll call you back."

"Awight, call me back."

"I love you."

"Yeah, I love you too."

At the emergency room, I was met by China. She was looking good as ever. She had on a baby blue, pleated tennis skirt with a white fitted tee shirt, exposing her belly button. The shirt showcased the words, 'DAMN. I'M WORTH IT'. She was wearing a pair of booties with a powder blue fuzzy ball hanging out of her Gucci tennis shoes.

"What's up girl?" I grinned as I reached out for her. I had on a white linen shirt with the matching pants, a brown crocodile belt and he brown crocodile tie-ups to set it off. I didn't have on much jewelry, just my Oyster Rolex.

"You, you're what's up." Obviously happy to see me because she embraced me like she hadn't seen me in months.

"Oh yeah? Shiiit, your shirt say you're what's up. So you're worth it huh?"

"Hell yeah..."

"Worth what?"

"Whatever is out of reach."

"I ain't gone touch that, we'll talk about that another time. So what's up with my man?"

"Oh, they said they were about to release him. He's been in the back for a while. I went back there; he's awight, just a little shook up." China said with a reassuring look.

"Take me back there where he's at."

China led the way and I watched her million dollar walk and couldn't help but think of our trip and how good it felt inside of her. We passed the desk where the nurses were and walked into the room where Steph was.

"Heey, what's up? You awight?"

"Yeah, I'm cool, just waiting for the doctor to come back and release me. He said the x-rays were good. I'm still suing the state if the guy was not insured. We need to take care of this business, its 1:45; we are supposed to meet the guy from DMV at 2:00 at KFC."

The doctor came in, released Steph and the three of us walked out to the parking lot. I hit the car alarm and the lights of the white Beemer started blinking.

"Who's car is that?" Steph asked with a look of curiosity on his bruised faced due to the airbag deployment.

"It's a friend's car. I'm just borrowing it for a week or so."

China looked like she had a revelation and stated, "Oh, so that's why you're wearing white today. Okaay, go ahead with your bad self. You should wear more white Dee because you look good in white." Shaking her hand in apprival

"You can get with that social shit later; we gotta go before we miss this boy." Steph curtly interrupted.

"So when am I going to see you Dee?"

"I'll call you in a lil while and we'll get together later on. Awight?"

"Awight then." We pulled off

The DMV was less than ten minutes away, but the KFC was at least another ten minutes away from the DMV, so Steph called the guy on the cell and apprised him that we were on our way, just running a little behind.

We arrived and Steph introduced me to the tall, skinny, light skinned guy wearing round spectacles, a shirt and tie, with what looked like navy blue pants to a suit.

"Yo Dee this is Rodney, Rodney this is Dee." Before we broke our handshake he got straight down to business. I had mad respect for him for that.

"So you got a name for me, and a picture I can scan, or do you want to come in and take a picture with the computer at the DMV?"

I never told Steph, but I had did this several times already, so I knew exactly what he needed and was ready with a photo taken with a blue background, just like the one at DMV. I retrieved it from the envelope in my pocket and handed it to him. I could tell he was shocked by the look on his face.

"Okay, that's what I'm talking about. Now we can do business." Steph paid him and the guy assured us that he would have the license in his possession and would meet us after five p.m., which was good enough for me.

Our next stop was Staples. Steph's instructions were simple. I went straight to the isle where he directed me, found the Mead brand receipt book and the standard lease agreement form and was out in no time, thanks to the pie-faced, mocha complexioned college student who checked me out. If you asked me, she was the fastest in the store.

When I returned to the car, Steph was arguing with someone on the phone. So I waited until he was done before I pulled off, because I didn't know whether this call he was on would change our plans. He terminated the call.

"Damn..." Steph blurted out in disgust.

"What?"

"Mann, this fuckin' guy Leroy, mannnn. He'll fuck up a wet dream..."

"What happened?"

"This mutha fucka gives me this sob assed story the other day about his gas and electric was getting ready to get cut off, and even showed me a bill. His sister said he took that money and ain't nobody seen him in two days. He's out somewhere getting' high, she said we ain't gonna see him until that money is gone."

"How much did you give him?"

"Shiiit. He ain't gone be gone long. I only gave him two hundred dollars and unless he bought some work and call his self flipping he'll turn up tomorrow. One thing for sure, he's gonna call me 'cause he know I'll cut his ass off. And he know that I got a job for him, so he's gonna call.

I ain't trippin'. Let's go get something to eat, I'm starving."

Steph suggested Aunt Kizzy's in Marina Del Rey. We must have gotten there about 3:05 p.m., it was not crowded like it normally is, probably because of the time, but people were starting to pour in. We got nice seats in the back. The beautiful waitress took our order. I had the Red Snapper and Butterfly Shrimp with French Fries and a side of broccoli with melted cheese and some of that famous lemonade.

Steph had the fried chicken, string beans and mashed potatoes. He had a beer with his meal. It was too early for me to be drinking.

While we were waiting for our food, I returned the two missed calls that came through while we were meeting with the DMV dude. Both calls were from Reecee, she sounded like she was asleep.

"Hello."

"What's up Dee, where you been? I called your phone a couple of times. I even called Mel asking about you. He told me something about an accident. You're not hurt are you?"

"I wasn't in the accident; it was a friend of mine. So what's up?"

"Oh, I was callin' to let you know Larry got locked up and he said his bail is fifty thousand dollars. He said please get him out because he's scared that the feds might pick it up because of the gun."

"So where did they find the gun at? Was it on him?"

"I don't know, he didn't tell me all of that he only had five minutes. I guess they gave him a free call because it wasn't collect, and if you need somebody to sign for him

I'll sign if you take me down there and bring me back. Plus I wanna see you anyway."

"Awight, let me make a few calls and I'll call you right back."

"Awight, if I fall back asleep, just keep callin' till I answer." Reecee said yawning.

"Fall asleep? What are you talking about? I'm going to call you back in five minutes, so don't even lay down. You hear me?"

"Okay, I'll wait for your call."

I knew this shit was coming one day, and I should have been better prepared. But no matter how prepared I was I couldn't risk the boy telling on me. I had too much going on, so a few g's was nothing to the giant I was becoming, at least compared to where I was.

"What's wrong? You look puzzled about something." Steph said, as he sipped some of his Heineken beer.

"This kid got knocked off with a gun and needs me to get him out."

"What kid?"

"He's the cousin of one of the girls I mess with."

"So where his father at? Shit, why he call you?"

"The young boy was doing something for me and..." We were cut off by the beautiful waitress returning with the food. While she sat the plates of mouth watering palate pleasers in front of us, I made a call to my homie, Buddy of Buddy's Bail Bonds in Baltimore to see if he could help get my young boy out.

"Hello. Who is this? Can I speak to Buddy?" I was put on hold.

"This isBuddy, how can I help you?"

"What's up shawty?" I said to him in our native Baltimore tongue.

"Who's this?"

"It's Dee."

"Heyyy, what's happening? Where you at? I hear a lot of noise in the background."

"I'm in California at a restaurant getting ready to have a late lunch. I gotta a little situation that I need your help with."

"Anything for my main man. You know that."

"Listen, my lil man got locked up out here."

"So where' he at? And what's the bail?"

"He's in L.A. County Jail. The bail is $50,000."

"Is he from here, or is he from California?"

"He's from here, but shortie is a good lil dude."

"Ahhy man, you ain't gotta say no more. I'm doing it on the strength of you. You naw-a-mean, if you say he cool, then he cool."

"Awight, so what I need?"

"Just give me $3,500 and a signer."

"Awight, I appreciate that. So how do we do it?"

"Just give me a fax number and I'll fax you the paperwork. You sign it and fax it back and I'll take care of the rest. Awight? I got chu' awight."

"Awight... Look, if I'm not here just... You got something to write with?"

"Steph let me hold that pen."   Steph handed me his pen with a look like 'get your own.'

"Awight, go ahead."

"410-683-2151, you got it?"

"Yeah I got it. So I'll call you right back with a fax..."

Steph interrupted, "Dee if you need a fax number you can use mine."

"Okay, hold up Buddy, I'ma give you the fax number now." Steph wrote the number down on a napkin.

"Awight you ready?"

"Yeah, go ahead."

"213-457-1837."

"Awight Dee, I'll get that right to you. If you got any more questions just call me."

"Awight thanks Buddy."

"No problem. I'll talk to you later."

People always say "It's not all the time what you know, but instead it's who you know". Buddy just lifted an unnecessary burden off my shoulders. Now all I needed to do was get Reecee to sign the papers. I called and told her I would be by to pick her up by 6:30 or 7:00 p.m.

We finished our meal, paid the check and fought with rush hour traffic on our way to meet the boy from DMV and pick up Reecee so I could take her with me to the mansion where Steph's fax was, let her sign for Larry and fax it back to Buddy in Baltimore.

Steph called the DMV connect, and just as he promised, he agreed to meet us on Manchester and LaCienga at 5:30 p.m. We were released from the bondage of the rush hour madness when we took the Manchester exit off the 10 freeway. It was more than perfect timing; we got there at 5:15 p.m. The boy was waiting. Steph spotted him in his silver Acura Legend sitting on the lot of the Exxon gas station on the corner. We pulled next to his car, he got out, walked up to Steph on the passenger side and handed him the new license. I checked it out to make sure everything was correct and we were on our way.

Now the only thing we were missing is the alarm being reset, and the rest we was gonna take care of tomorrow. Like pick up the birth certificate and Social

Security Cards from the Mexicans at the corner of 8th and Figueroa. All the guys - at TRW credit bureau - was waiting for was our name and Social Security Number, and then everything would be complete. I could get me a Benz and get instant credit wherever I wanted as long as they didn't ask for a credit card because it would be about a week before I received one in the mail.

It was getting late for a bail, so I hurried to pick up Reecee. When I got there Reecee was sitting on the porch. She saw me and ran to the door; called Candy telling her she was gone.

Candy came to the door just as Reecee was getting in the back seat, waiving, "Hey Dee call me, okay."

"Awight." I responded through my now lowered window. "I gotta go. I'll call you.

Someone backing out, not paying attention almost hit me. I blew my horn, getting his attention. That's all I needed was for somebody to hit her brand new BMW while it was in my care.

"Hey Dee." Reecee said closing the back door. "What's up Reecee, how you feelin"

"I'm good."

"Oh yeah, Reecee this is my man Steph. Steph that's Sharice."

"How you doing Sharice?"

"I'm fine."

Steph got on the phone and called the mansion and spoke to his shortie Lashawnda, who confirmed that the fax had arrived. I asked Steph to ask was China there and luckily she was not there because I didn't want her and Reecee to meet. This was not the time to induce any drama because I needed both girls.

We got to the mansion around 7:15 p.m., as we pulled up to the entrance, Steph handed me his key card. I swiped it and the tall black iron gate slowly opened, giving us access to the property.

"Whose house is this? I thought we were going downtown to the bail bondsmen. I can get us a discount at Harry O's because we've been dealing with them for a long time." Reecee inquired from the back seat.

"Reecee, chill out. All we got to do is sign some papers and we out. I got this. I got a lot of shit to do and I had to stop what I was doing so I could take care of this, so work with me. Awight baby?"

"Awight. I was just asking 'cause I thought we were going downtown, that's all."

"We don't have to go downtown. Everything is being done over the phone. I got somebody taking care of everything."

"Okay big baller. So you just make a call and all your problems go away, huh?"

"Naw, it ain't all of that, I just know a few people who do a few things, that's all."

"Y'all can make yourself at home. Dee you know where everything at, fix the lady a drink or something." Steph said as he walked out of the den, leaving us alone.

"You want something to drink Reecee?" I asked going behind the bar.

"Like what?"

"Like whatever you want. Come over here; let me show you what's back here."

Reecee came behind the bar and pointed to the Hennessey, "I'll take a Hennessy and Coke please, with a lil ice."

As I started to pour, using both my hands I felt Reecee's hand grab my manhood through my jeans and whispered, "I wanna drink some of this." Giving me a seductive look that would've melted an ice sculpture and licking her lips. As she walked away with her drink, I got a quick feel of her soft ass, before Steph walked back into the room with the fax in his hand.

"Here you go Dee; this was the only thing that was in the fax machine."

Steph handed me three pieces of paper. I sat down on the plush black leather couch next to Reecee and leaned over to the glass table and began filling out the bail forms.

"What's the correct spelling of his name Reecee?"

"L-A-R-R-Y, his last name is Miller."

"What's his middle name Reecee? As a matter of fact why don't you fill this out because you know all the information like his mothers' info, last known employer and all that?"

Reecee filled out the forms and signed as co-signer. Steph faxed it to the number at the top and gave it back to me. I had to go because I needed to go home to get the $3,500 and then Western Union, then drop Reecee off.

"Yo Steph I'm out of here man, I'll see you tomorrow. What time you want to get together?"

"I'll call you when I get up around eight o'clock. Oh yea, it was nice meeting you Miss Lady. What was your name again?"

"Sharice. It was nice meeting you too."

We arrived at my house around ten of nine; I double parked and put on the flashers. "I gotta run in the house for a second and grab some money awight. I'll be right back."

Reecee asked me, "Can I use your bathroom real quick?"

"Come on."

We both went upstairs; I showed Reecee the bathroom and went to my room and into the closet to get my money from a Reebok shoe box. There was approximately $5,600, give or take a few dollars. As I sat on the bed and counted out thirty six one hundred dollar bills, Reecee called out my name.

"Dee where you at?"

"I'm back here Reecee; I'll be right out..."

I looked up and she was walking into my bedroom. Reecee sat on the bed asking, "Do you need any help?"

"Nah, I'm finished now and we gotta get out of here before the Western Union close."

"I know where one is open all night." She started unzipping my pants. I got hard as penitentiary steel and began throbbing with anticipation. We didn't have time, but I couldn't say no to a pro. She really knew how to do it.

She pulled my pants down to my knees, releasing my love stick from my pants, now a little moist from the pre-cum. She pushed me back on the bed and began a serious swirling around the head, slowly licking it like it was a Mr. Softee Ice Cream cone. It turned me on to see the look of pure dedication on her face; she was really enjoying giving me pleasure. I tried to hold it, I grabbed her head to have her hold still and that's when she realized she had me and went wild licking up and down the shaft, and it seemed like no soon as she popped it in her mouth I came within seconds. Reecee smiled and swallowed every drop as if it my salt water liquid taffy were a reward. I was now ready for the pussy. I pulled her up from her knees and started to unfasten her pants and she stopped me.

"I'm on my period. I just wanted to do you, so are you good now?"

"Am I? Shiiit, I'm better than good, I came."

She started laughing, "We better get out of here and get downtown because I know he's having a fit in there wondering what's up. How long after you send the money will they let him out? And are we gonna pick him up?"

"Naw he gone catch a cab. Here go the money for him."

We went to Western Union and took care of the $3,500 and I then dropped Reecee off, and headed back to my house. Because I hadn't heard from China I called her cell phone. Her voice mail picked up and I left a message to call me. It seemed like while I was leaving a message she was calling me back.

"Hey what's up? Where you at?" China managed to speak up over the noise of club music in the background.

"I'm on my way to my house." She cut me off.

"And where is your house, is it the place where we dropped you off the other day?"

"Yeah, that's right you were there when Steph dropped me off So what's up, you comm' to see me or what?"

"Yeah I can do that, but it'll be a little late. Around 11:30 or 12:00, is that cool?"

"Just get here as soon as possible because I gotta get up tomorrow."

"Awight if I can get there sooner I will. Okay I'll call you when I'm on my way."

China came by around 11:30pm just like she said and surprisingly she had no intention of sexing me. She just wanted to spend the night in my arms. Some real emotional shit, but it was cool with me because I was feeling her too. We just couldn't make a habit of it because Brishette would be home in another week. One night was cool though.

We woke up around 6:45 a.m. I fixed us some scrambled eggs with cheese and turkey bacon, and some Pillsbury croissants. We had some orange juice mixed with cranberry juice on ice.

I walked in the room with the Tiffany serving tray, looking like it was catered. The plate was decorated with orange slice wedges, the eggs were a pretty yellow, and the bacon was cooked just right.

"Damn, for me?"

"Yeah, aren't you worth it?"

"Of course I'm worth it. It's just that it's not everyday that someone brings you breakfast in the bed. A girl could get used to this. My grandmother used to always say, 'Never start something unless you're gone keep it up'.

"So what are you saying?"

"I'm saying, don't start spoiling me if you not gonna keep spoiling me."

"I have no intentions on starting anything that I'm not planning to finish, that's just not how I do things."

"Well if that's the case, I should be able to look forward to this being repeated... And three peated and all the other peateds." China said with a cool-aid smile on her face.

"Well that all depends."

"On what?"

"On whether you're in it for the long haul."

"Whoa... What are you asking me?"

"Don't even flatter yourself. I'm not asking you to marry me, or no shit like that. In my world flattery gets you nowhere, but loyalty gets you everywhere. And what I'm asking is for you to consider being my partner 'cause I'm getting ready to get my own mansion and I know you can run it just like your girlfriend Lashawnda does with Steph."

"So you think you got me all figured out, huh?"

"Nah, I just know a good woman when I see her, and I can appreciate your talent. Besides, you can't shine if you're in the shade of someone else's shine, and at Steph's mansion that's Lashawnda's shine. I want you to have your own."

"So why all of the sudden you're interested in me shining?"

"Because I'm ready to take this thing to another level, and with you right there next to me. And like I said, I ain't tryin' to get married and shit but I do want to keep you in my life and my offer is a good way of showing you that. So what's up, you in or not?"

She wore a slight grin as she sassily shook her head from side to side, "You know I'm not gonna pass this up for nothing in the world. As a matter of fact, I'ma show Lashawnda how it's supposed to be done."

Chapter 33

10:30 the next morning, I finished with Mel and he took me to Brishette's pearl white BMW filled with thoughts of a beautiful family of three. Our new baby in the car seat. I almost wanted to start buying baby clothes but it was much too soon.

I had to focus on the task at hand because that statement made by Steph that I needed to pay attention resonated in my head. Like a new tenant in a low income townhouse. Mel was starting to feel the distance growing between the credit card business and my new hustle.

I had always hung out with Mel in the evening as we plotted on where we would go to dive in search of credit card numbers or how we would recruit someone who appeared to be cool upon meeting them at one of the car rental lots, or a department stores.

No matter how successful I was to become I made a promise to myself that I would always look out for Mel because he kept me under his wing and made sure I had the craft that I'd be able to eat with for the rest of my life or until the wheels fell off of the hustle.

Steph was waiting as I pulled up in front of the Airport Sheraton where he had stayed with his snow bunny Jessica, a tall blonde with high check bones of a Paris runway model, with a black girl butt and the perfect C-cup implanted breast that Steph gave her for her 23rd birthday.

"Heyy what's up Dee?" Jessica said, swinging her long hair to the side before getting into her silver Mercedes

CLK 320, and graciously putting on her Channel sunglasses.

"Hey, what's going on Jess?" I returned before she pulled off.

"Dee I got good news and bad news. Which one you want first?" Steph said, reclining his seat to a -I just want to fall out- position. Probably drained from being sucked dry by his man-eater white girl that he always talked about while we were briefly in that horrible cell together in L.A. County jail.

I knew exactly who she was when I saw her for the first time at the Beverly Hills Hotel. I knew it was something that made him pick there to have lunch that day.

"Give me the bad news first." I thought uh oh. Here comes the bullshit. I knew this was too good to be true. "Somebody else got the mansion on Miller Drive?"

"No, everything is cool with the mansion. I'm talking about my car, it won't be ready until three o'clock and Lashawnda is driving my Range Rover. She had to pick up stuff for the party."

"So what's the good news, because that wasn't the end of the world?"

"The good news is we don't have to meet the boy from TRW. I gave him the name on your new license and now all you need to do is go get you some credit in that name, and the alarm boy called me looking for money to buy more drugs last night. I gave him the address and he went out there and did his thing and I got the new code to the alarm system." He said, handing me a business card with the code on the back. "In other words, all you gotta do now is go up there and call the lock smith. Tell him you're locked out and the rest is baller history."

Damn, for some reason I gotta slight case of butterflies in my stomach from anxiety, and a touch of fear. But what was there to be afraid of? That is what I've been dreaming about not just lately but since I was a kid, but it just seemed too easy.

"Don't you want your keys?"

"Hell yeah." And just that instant, I had a flash back about junior high school where Splizzy and I hooked school over his house and we had two girls we just had sex with and I came out of one room and he came out of the other. Briefly exchanged words before taking a piss and I remember him saying 'You wanna switch?' I said hell yeah, and went into the opposite room and it didn't go as well for me as it did for him.

"So what are you waiting for? Why are we still sitting here? Let's go."

China's sex goddess body, Candy's amazing head, Brishette's silk and velvet skin and perfectly round stomach carrying my child, Reecee's wild, exciting and kinky slut sex all kept running through my mind. I would have to become the perfect juggler, or leave it all along for Brishette, but could I do it? Am I built like that?

All of this went through my mind as we drove.

Chapter 34

Kevin's voice said it all. "Yo check this out. I'm calling from a pay phone because I don't know about my phone."

"What's wrong?" I asked in a very curious manner.

"Look, I don't know if anybody is following me, so I sent my girl to tell you what's up. Meet her in twenty minutes at Roscoe's; she'll know who you are when you get there."

"Is everything alright with Jay?"

"No, and you either." He said dryly.

Like I said, shit was going too good. I knew something was bound to go wrong, it was time to worry. I played back in my head his instructions before he hung up, over and over again. I decided to let Steph in on it, he advised me to go and check it out. He said that Kevin has a reputation for being a standup guy; he felt it was safe so we headed to Roscoe's., temporarily putting the mansion on hold.

I circled the block to check out the cars then we went inside. Once inside someone waived me over. It was a light skinned girl who looked like Mya a little, but she told me that the feds had been to Kevin's asking about his brother and they showed him pictures of me. They knew my name was Dee, but that's all the information they gave up.

The news was expected but still surprised me. I'd have to drastically change my plans, and go underground because it was not safe to go to Baltimore because the airport would be the only way. I might have got away with it that one time, but I'm not taking that risk again until I know it's safe. My daughter was expecting to see me, I had promised her she could come out to Cali.

I quickly called Splizzy and explained my dilemma. He started talking about a book that he'd read.

"Dee, that book was good. I liked the way it ended when the guy couldn't wait for his partner to get in town because their subject had to go to court and was going to get time. So his partner took care of the guy who killed his main man."

I realized what he was saying. I didn't have to go back. So I asked Splizzy to come out to Cali and bring my daughter. Maybe this was a bad time because the feds were looking for me. To worsen matters, the FBI agent had died and now Jay was wanted for murder. I needed a place to think, so we went to the Miller Dr. mansion, called a locksmith, cut the keys, and ordered Chinese food while I figured out my next move.

I needed to get set up and get out of town for a while, but how, without being seen, the airport, train, or bus stations were out of the question. Then it came to me, there was a Sun Splash Festival in Jamaica and the cruise line was scheduled to sail to Ocho Rios, Jamaica in two and a half weeks. If I could last that long, I'd be good. I booked a trip for two in my assumed name. Now I just needed to make these two weeks count.

I decided that China was the one to take to Jamaica, spend some time with her and explain to her how everything will come full circle. Find out what her goals are and have her back on that following Thursday to prepare for the next weeks mansion party. That way I could get Brishette and my daughter for the weekend and still make money from the mansion parties. At least that's what I thought.

I talked to Mel about my situation and he advised me to lay low. I made my orders while he was out getting boxes, then later that night we did the first party at the mansion.

The lights were turned on, saturating the room with brightness, "Ladies and gentlemen. Please let me have your attention." "Hmmm Hmm." Clearing her throat, "I am your hostess China and I will be making certain that your evening is both a pleasurable and memorable one."

I could hear whispers from the male and female guests alike, probably wanting to know if she personally would make them happy.

"First, on the program will be a fashion show by the pool starting in ten minutes. After the fashion show, those of you who are V.I.P. or V.I.P. members will be escorted to the second level. Those of you who wish to apply for membership see Tiger, and those who wish to upgrade your admission to V.I.P., there will be an additional $150 charge.

I heard one of the guys call out, "What do I get for another hundred and fifty dollars?"

I was impressed with China's answer, "Let me just put it this way, some of us like the best of everything, and in the upper room the V.I.P. get the best of everything from the Champaign to the more relaxed attire —if any at all- and pampering. It's sort of a personal touch. I suggest you ask one of the members."

Out at the pool, the fashion show began. What no one expected was that the clothing was being represented by the actual designers in attendance and they were taking orders. No doubt we would coupe a hefty fifteen percent commission on all sales and the girls got to keep some of the clothing too.

China was proving herself to be a more valuable asset than I had imagined. She sashayed her way across the room to me, "So how do you like the party so far?"

"What's the head count now?"

"The last I checked was a hundred and seventy-four people, thirty-nine of which is V.I.P. Let me check with the laser beam established at the door that does the count. Same thing at the V.I.P. entrance, the guest use one door and the help another so it's easy to keep the count."

"Yeah, that's real sharp of you."

"Thanks."

Steph walked over and shook my hand, congratulating me as it was only 11:15 and 174 weren't bad at all. Of course, if it wasn't for him this night would not have turned out. So I owed him big time.

"See I told you this mansion thing is sweet. So you start collecting your deposits and first month's rent yet?"

"Yeah, a few of them paid already, maybe about four of them."

Steph smiled and said, "Give 'em until tomorrow, you'll see just how profitable this really is. I'm tellin you, if you do this right you gonna be rich in no time. Monday we go cop you a 600 coupe off the showroom floor. I'll take you to see my man, the Armenian at Auto Palace."

Damn, I felt like a celebrity having some kind of release party, and the more Champaign I drank the more I thought about China and our last night together.

I quickly snapped out of it when China returned with a smile on her face, saying, "So far we're at $40,700 and they're still coming in. Did you see Snoop Dog? He's in here somewhere probably in the V.I.P. room. Oh and I saw A.I."

There were Ferrari's, Lamborghini's, Aston Martin's, Porsche's, and even a helicopter on the helipad. Limos were everywhere.

Men came with women, women came with women, and, some men came with one woman and left with two. Almost no one who came alone left alone. I saw some of the most beautiful women in L.A. but my first night I just had to lay back and watch. Besides, I didn't want to turn my most valuable asset into my worst nightmare.

I felt a sudden combination of jealously and possessiveness come over me as I saw a group of guys approach China. Maybe they knew her from the club, or maybe it was her look. She was definitely one of, if not the best dressed in the party. She wore a Versace gold mixed with earth tone sheer dress, which revealed her left shoulder and her pierced belly button. It appeared to be a wrap of material adorning her breast showing just the right amount of cleavage then a small bow on the side at her waist. The bottom was slightly attached and draped around her hips, and just below her thigh showing off her legs and the toes were painted gold with flowers, seen through the gold Stiletto's with the glass cross strap that tied up her legs. She was gorgeous. She's just a dancer, I kept trying to tell myself, but I couldn't fool myself She was growing on me.

Chapter 35

Brishette arrived at 11:15 a.m. at LAX. I was there at the gate waiting as she'd requested. I had Mel sitting in the car so we wouldn't get a ticket.

We spent most of the day together and winded up at my spot. We fell asleep holding each other. When awoke it was 1:05 a.m., Brishette decided she wanted to go home, so I walked her to the door and returned to my bed.

About fifteen minutes later the buzzer rang and I thought Brishette had forgotten something, or changed or mind. So I just buzzed her in and left the door open, and went back into the room.

As I got under the covers, she appeared at the doorway and stood there. "Hey Dee? What, you trying to avoid me?" The voice was not Brishette's, I quickly turned towards the door, and it was Reecee.

"Girl... What are you doing coming by my house without calling? Are you fuckin' crazy?" I looked at the clock on the night stand, "It's 1:30, what da fuck is up with you?"

"You ain't call me back. I thought something happened to you."

"How you get over here?"

"I got my girlfriend to drop me off She thinks this is my cousin's house."

"So how you getting' home?" I asked, knowing I was too tired to go back out.

"You gone take me." She said, removing her coat, revealing a stunning red sheer blouse with the matching red bra, and jeans that gave her body curves like the Tour De France. I mean they were fittin'!

I became instantly aroused as usual. I wanted to say 'Get the hell out my house', because Brishette might just come back but too much time had gone by and I couldn't get the words out.

She walked over, sat on my bed reaching under the cover, groping for my manhood, and found me hard and throbbing. Before I could say anything, she had pulled the covers back and her tongue purred out the Words, "Ahh baabyyy. You must've really missed me. Ahhh." Releasing my swollen member from the confines of it's blue silk prison. She gently started stroking me and massaging my balls through my boxers. My leg involuntarily began to spread like a dog having his stomach massaged, and that fast she had me in her silky, moist heaven. I quickly realized why I couldn't put her out, her head was worthy of an Oscar or Grammy. The phone rang in the middle of my trip to heaven. I couldn't get it so I let it ring, it could only be Brishette letting me know she was home safe. If she really needed me, she'd call back.

And that she did, only this time she left a message, "Dee, baby I'm outside, I left my purse upstairs. Are you sleep that fast?"

I immediately stopped Reecee, telling her she had to go before Brishette came upstairs. I grabbed the phone from its cradle and she had already hung up.

I recalled the last number and she answered, "Dee, I think my key to the door downhere is in my purse, can you buzz me up or meet me at the door down here with my bag."

I cut her off, "I'll bring your bag down baby. Where is it?"

"It's in the living room on the side of the couch."

"Awight, I'll be right down." God was on my side this night.

I told Reecee, "Don't move, and if when I come back I'm not by myself, you know what's up, get in the closet or under the bed or something."

"I ain't getting' under no damn bed." She said with her hands on her hips.

"Check this out, if she comes back up here, do not let her see you, that's all I gotta say. I'ma try to keep her from coming up here."

I retrieved the Coach bag from the living room floor, and made my way to the elevator in the hall. When I reached the door to the lobby I saw the flashers from the white 745i glowing in the night, then Brishette emerged from the car. There was something about her walk that turned me on and the feeling I got whenever she was around let me know she was the one.

"I'm sorry baby, you look tired too."

"Yeah so do you, now go get some rest."

We kissed good bye, and I watched her get back into her car and as she disappeared into the night all I could think about on my way back up stairs, was that I can't let the feds get me. I gotta out think them.

As soon as I entered the apartment, I smelled Reecee's perfume, a dead give-a¬way. I called out, "Reecee it's cool, you can come out."

"So that's wifee huh? She was cute, is that the one you went out with in your tuxedo that time when you were staying with me and my sister?"

"How the fuck you see her and you was supposed to be out of sight?"

"You said, if she come up here not to let her see me, but you never said not to look out the window. So how I'm supposed to know if she was coming or not?"

"If she would of saw you looking out the damn window, she would've came up here."

"Well, she didn't."

"Who da fuck you getting smart with?"

"I ain't getting smart, I'm just sayin'..."

I cut her off, "Plus you know what? Get your coat 'cause I'm callin' you a cab." I hit the number three preset button on the phone and gave the dispatcher my address.

"Oh, so now you puttin' me out right after you got what you want. And you know I can't get my thing off."

"Look Reecee, I'm tired and I gotta lot of shit on my mind and I gotta get up in the morning. You know tomorrow is a big day."

"So why I can't just spend the night?"

"I can't sleep with you around!!"

"What do you mean you can't sleep with me around?"

"Because... All I'll be thinking about all night is sexing you, plus the cab is out there. Here, take this money, I think that's the cab blowing now." I looked out the window, "Matter of fact that is the cab. Damn that was fast. He must have been around the corner."

"Am I gonna see you tomorrow?" She said sounding like a little girl, love struck.

"Yeah, we'll get together tomorrow." I kissed her on the forehead and as she turned to leave I smacked her on her ass. She just turned and smiled.

Chapter 36

I twisted and turned all night, anticipating this particular Monday morning. I was tired but I was also anxious to finally start seeing some of the real life toys that come along with this level of the game.

Mel picked me up at 8:10 a.m. and we rode around chasing UPS and Fed Ex trucks until around 10:45. We split up the boxes, some of which belonged to my daughter who I was expecting to fly in soon.

I phoned Steph to find out what time he wanted to get together, "Hello, what's up Dee. You ready to go do your thing?"

"Hell yeah, I've been thinking about it all night."

"Oh yeah, well I just got off the phone with the dude and he's waiting for us. I told him we'll be there around lunch time. So where you at?"

"I'm in Inglewood on Manchester."

"Meet me at the Bar-B-Q spot, Ah, Ahh..."

"You talking about Umm, Tony Roma's?"

"Yeah, yeah, that's it. Meet me there in fifteen minutes."

"Awight, peace."

We were only two blocks away, so I had Mel drop me off at Tony Roma's. It seemed like as soon as I walked inside my phone vibrated, again catching me off guard.

"Hello, hey what's up Candy?"

"What's up with you? I thought you were coming by here yesterday?"

"My people came in from out of town. I called you but Reecee said you were sleep."

"Reecee wasn't even here."

"Yes she was, she said she was on her way back out, that she had came in to change her shoes or something. So what's up, hold on."

"Hello."

"Where you at Dee?" Steph inquired looking around the restaurant.

"I'm upstairs by the door, the table in the back."

"Awight, I see you."

"Candy, I'm back."

"What's all that noise? Where you at?"

"I'm at Tony Roma's getting ready to have my lunch, then I'm going to pick up my car."

"Oh yeah, what car?"

"I don't know yet. I'm going to pick it out, but it's probably gonna be a Benz."

"Okay, Big Balla..."

"Candy, I gotta go, I'll call you later awight."

"Awight, and don't forget because I got something important to tell you, okay."

"Awight, talk to you later."

"What's up Dee?" Steph said as he pulled up a chair.

"Damn Steph, you gotta hell of a grip. You be squeezing the shit out of my hand."

"They say you can tell if a man is sincere by the firmness of his handshake. So what's good here?"

"That depends on what you like. The Bar-B-Que baby back ribs are supposed to be like that. Well that's what people say, I don't eat beef though. Oh yeah, the beans are excellent. I usually get chicken with a side of beans and I'm straight."

"Mann you and that 'I don't eat pork and I don't eat beef stuff. I eat it all...'"

The waiter took our order, we had a light lunch. On the way to the dealership Steph said something that really made me think, "Dee this is kinda like the pimp game."

You gotta get into… You gotta get into China's head man, and find out what she wants out of life because before you find out you won't be as effective in dealing with her and if you are going to trust her with millions and part of your future, you'd better be on top of your game."

"What do you mean?" I asked puzzled by his statement.

"Look Dee, if you do this right you can be set for life, and never look back. Dee…"

I cut him off, "So you think I made the right move?"

"You couldn't have made a better move. This girl is thorough, she's smart, she beautiful, and she's hungry. Oh, and she ain't no cruddy chick. You feel me.?"

"You need to get her by herself for a few days so you can really get her attention, make her see what you see. Offer her a partnership. Do a contract, whatever it takes but maker her see this thing man. Do you realize that in two months you can buy your own mansion, and rent it out and do parties and it will pay for itself. You drive what you want, buy what you want, man this thing is big Dee. You can let that other shit go. That illegal shit, you don't need it no more after this."

Damn, he had me thinking hard too. I was in a position to become a millionaire within months and have cash money to do what ever. I could buy some properties invest in the stock market and even spend about $200,000 on a home in Jamaica and for that kind of money I could own a mansion in Jamaica too.

We pulled up to this fancy car dealership and was met by the owner, the Armenian, "Heyyy my friend. Stefon, how are youuu, it's been a while. So who's your friend?"

"This is my partner Dee that I was tellin' you about. Oh, Dee this my main man, I call him the smooth Armenian. but his name is Alex."

"Good to meet you Dee." He extended his hand, showing off his pinky rock glistening in the early afternoon sun.

As we walked across the lot to the showroom entrance leading to his office, it seemed like every car I had ever dreamed about was right on this lot right before my eyes, from Double R's to Maybachs, to Bentley's. You name it, it was on this lot and everything on the lot was $80,000 and up. When he saw me looking at the Porsche He turned to me and asked, "You like that?" In his strong Armenian accent.

I felt like I would have embarrassed myself if I asked how much, but I did it anyway because this definitely wasn't a pair of pants or a shirt.

"You want to take it for a spin?"

"Yeah, why not."

"If you like fast cars, this is the one for you my friend. This baby goes from 0-60 in six seconds. Here, why don't you get in?" He opened the door and directed me to the driver's seat. "The seat will automatically adjust to your height. Here let me show you how to put the top up."

He called out to some other Armenians who opened the glass doors and started moving cars around to make room for me to take the beautiful black with burgundy leather, hot wheels for a stroll on the highway.

I couldn't believe it, I was actually driving a Porsche 911 and it felt good. I felt like a movie star, zipping through traffic at speeds that other cars couldn't even reach. Then Steph brought me back to earth.

"Yo Dee, this Porsche look good on you but I thought you wanted something to put your family in."

"Yeah, yeah, yeahhh, you're right, umm damn. Yeah the plan was to get a six."

"Shhhiiit, you can get whatever. You got it! Don't cheat yourself, treat yourself, you only live once Dee. Plus if you gonna be a winner, you gotta act like a winner, talk like a winner, look like a winner, 'cause you definitely fuckin'   with   winners   now."

We pulled back on the lot and the Armenian approached us, "My friend, well how did you like her? Did she feel good to you, was she fast enough?"

"Ha, ha, ha... Ah he's a speed freak and he does not need all that speed with his family in the car."

"Oh... So you are family man? Well I got just the thing for you. You can transport your family in luxury. Let me take you to the Bentley, we just got this two days ago."

It was a platinum color with the peanut butter leather interior, complete with cherry oak wood grain throughout. The TV's, the wet bar in the back, the seat warmers, and the yellow bubbled eyed halogen headlights were all standard. When he finished showing this dream on wheels I was done, and I pulled off the lot on cloud nine. I just took it to another level and got a hell of a deal too. And didn't have to worry about the IRS or none of that because the smooth Armenian would take care of the books on the $75,000 cash I gave him and I'd be making weekly cash payments until it's paid off, all $240,000.

Chapter 37

This was celebrity status and although it was a dream come true, it was also scary because just like the Notorious B.I.G. said, "More money, more problems", and if I was to last in this business I would have to make this operation one hundred percent legal and that would be the theme and topic of discussion with China in Jamaica.

I followed Steph on the freeway until we got to the Manchester exit off 1-10. I called Candy back and had her get ready. While I stopped in front of Mel's house and called him to show him my new investment.

"Mel come to the window." I said into the phone beaming with excitement.

"What's going on youngster, where you at?"

"I'm in the Benz."

"What? Dee what the hell you doin'? Who's car you in? You rented that?"

"Nah, this is me."

"Stop playin' youngster, that car cost over $100,000."

"$240,000."

"What?" Mel said in disbelief.

"You tryin' to go to jail, ain't you?"

"Nah. I just came through so you can see my new hot wheels, and go for a spin with me then I'ma take Candy to Benny Hanna's in Woodland Hills, then I'ma put it up."

"I ain't riding nowhere with you in that thing. I don't need the hassle. Holla at me later when you get finished doing what you're doing 'cause we need to talk."

"Awight, I'll call you."

Heads turned as I turned into Candy's parking lot. The sun was bouncing off of windows and windshields, forcing me to lower the sun visor. My cell vibrated and I picked it up.

"Hello."

"Dee, is that you? Oh my God, boy who car you done stole? Here I come now."

Candy and Reecee came to the door at the same time. Candy came out and got in while Reecee came over to the driver side window. I lowered the window and Reecee leaned in the window exposing her breast, partly covered by her v-neck blouse.

"Oh my God Dee, Who's car is this?"

"It's my car, why? I can't have a nice car? What you think I'm broke or something?" "This is my shit."

"I seen one of these cars on the video with Ashanti and Irv Gotti. This thing cost as much as a house, and you ain't got that kind of money, so where you get this car from?"

"Ohh girl, I am not tryin' to go to jail messing with Dee. For real Dee, is this yours?"

I was starting to get upset so I pulled out my paperwork and Progressive Insurance card to show both of them. "I ain't got no reason to lie to y'all."

"Ummph, go ahead with your bad ass. Y'all have fun, but Dee you gotta let me ride in style too one day."

"Yeah, Awight I got you Reecee. Awight let me get out of here before somebody try to rob me."

Reecee backed away from the car, giving me a shot of her three finger gap up close and personal with her Daisy Dukes cut off shorts exposing her ass cheeks and her slippers.

All the nosey neighbors were out and watching as we made our grand exit. Candy was smiling and looking delicious as usual, especially with her lime green Gucci top, white Capri pants that fit her to a tee and her lime and cream leather mules with the gold Channel ankle bracelet. We listened to Maxwell on the Alpine system as we floated to our destination.

We arrived at Benny Hanna's as the sun sat right before the evening rush, and although we had to wait briefly at the bar until our table was ready, it was nothing like the circus it became within an hour after our arrival. The place was packed and people had to wait up to two hours for a table.

We were seated in front of a grill that was not yet attended. So I thought it was a good time to ask Candy what was so important.

"Have you ever been here Candy?"

"No, not this one, but I've been to another location though."

"So what did you have to tell me?"

"Dee do you remember when we made love?"

"Of course I remember. Why you ask me that?"

"Do you remember what day it was?"

"Not exactly."

"What do you mean, not exactly?"

"What, am I supposed to mark it on my calendar or make a diary of every time I..." She cut me off.

"I remember it, so why don't you remember it?"

"I do, I just don't remember the date, that's all. So what's your point? Where are you going with all of this?"

"Dee, I haven't had my period since we made love and it's been almost a month."

"So shouldn't you wait a little while before you jump to conclusions?"

"Dee, I know my body, and my period should have came by now."

"So you think you're pregnant?"

"No, I know I'm pregnant with your baby, Dee."

Awwwh shit, I thought to myself. How could I let that happen? That's crazy. How am I gonna explain this baby to Brishette.

The waiter told us that our chef would be right with us. They were attending a large party table on the other side of the restaurant.

"So why you so quiet, the cat got your tongue?"

"Ain't nobody go my tongue. I'm just thinking that's all."

"What are you thinking about? Whether you want the baby or not? If that's the case I already made that decision and I'm keeping my baby."

"Damn, you said that like it's only your baby. Shhiiit, it's my baby too, if it's my baby."

"What the hell you mean, if it's your baby? I ain't been with nobody but you and if you don't believe me, we can take a blood test."

"Did I say I didn't believe you?"

"You ain't have to say it, but that's what you meant when you said, if it's my baby. Look Dee, I don't know what your plans are but I'm keeping this baby and all I ask is that you do your part."

"Excuse me, my name is David and I'll be your chef this evening. Have you made up your mind on which entree' you'll be having?" He stood there with this look on his face like we should've been ready to order. We hadn't even looked at the menu.

"Ahh, we're gonna need some more time." I said in a irritable tone. He caught the hint.

"No problem, take your time, I'll be right back." He grumbled as he walked away with a look of disgust. He could tell from the looks on both our faces that we were not a happy couple right now.

I beat her to the punch, "Candy, listen... I used to hear this all the time and I'm just numb to it unless there is some proof of a pregnancy, it..."

"You know what..."

"I'm not finished, let me finish! Like I said, it has nothing to do with you. It's just that when I hear those words, I start getting all excited and expecting to enjoy a boy or girl being born into this world so I can spoil and then I hear either their period came or they changed their mind and got an abortion without even talking to me."

"Dee, I'm not really hungry. We can do this another time so you don't waste your money."

"So you don't wanna eat?"

"You can just take me home, 'cause I don't feel good."

I could tell she was mad and just wanted to get away from me, but I felt the same way. If she wasn't tryin' to hear what I had to say or how I felt, then maybe we needed some time to reflect on what just happened and how we're gonna handle it.

I dropped her off and went inside to use the bathroom, only to find Reecee curled up on the couch in front of the TV, wearing a half T-shirt revealing her navel and some Daisy Duke shorts.

"Hey Dee, what's up?"

"What's up with you Reecee?"

"I'm just chillin'. Y'all back so soon?"

"Yeah, Candy ain't feeling good."

"Yeah, she been cranky as I don't know what lately."

"Y'all talk like I ain't even here."

"We didn't say anything bad about you, did we?"

"You have been acting funny lately Candy." Reecee said smiling a guilty grin.

"I'ma use the bathroom so I can get out of here." I walked up the stairs and Candy followed. Before I could get to the bathroom Candy called out to me.

"Hold up Dee. I got a question for you and I want a straight forward answer."

"What's your question Candy? As a matter of fact, can I use the bathroom first? I've been holding this since we got on the highway."

"Go ahead, I'll be in my room, come talk to me before you leave please."

I used the bathroom and made my way to Candy's room. "What's up Candy?"

"Come in and close the door please." I did as she asked and sat on the edge of her bed.

"Dee, what are we gonna do? I'm scared." Her eyes were so brown and beautiful and I saw the sincerity all about her.

"What are you scared of?"

"I want this baby Dee, and I just want you to want it too. Hold up." She said, walking over and opening the door to answer her sister, "What? Reecee why the hell are you screaming like that?"

"Come here, hurry up. Larry got shot."

"What?" Making her way to the stairs, I followed Candy down stairs where we saw the big lanky, acorn complexioned young boy sitting on the edge of the kitchen chair, one leg stretched out covered in crimson liquid, and tears running down his young face.

"Ahhhhhh. It hhhhuurrrts real bad. Dammmmmn" He screamed gasping for air, "It's stinging real bad."

"I know baby, just relax." Reecee said wrapping the soaked wound with a towel.

"Oh my God boy. What happened to you?" Candy cried out.

"These guys tried to rob me and I shot one of 'em and another one came out of nowhere and shot at me. As I was running I got hit in the leg."

"Thank God. So where was you at and what happened to the boy you shot?" Reecee exclaimed while wiping his face with a wash rag.

"I think he might be dead 'cause I think I shot him in his face because when I saw somebody on their knees crawling around from behind the car with a gun, I just started shooting and all I know is he fell on the ground and grabbed his face. That's when the other one came out of nowhere."

"We gotta get him to a hospital."

"Nah, I don't want to go to a hospital. They gonna ask too many questions."

The first thing that came to my mind is I wonder whether anyone saw him come in here or did the shooter follow him. So I went to the small window near the door, I made sure the door was locked and peered out the side of the curtain, nothing but the police riding by. This was not a good time to leave out because there was a chance we could be stopped if anyone left right now. In a way I felt guilt overtake me because he was selling coke for me. I heard him scream and I returned to the kitchen to find out how bad the wound was.

"Did anybody look at it yet?"

"Hold on, let me get another towel because that one is soaked." Candy hurried up the stairs.

"Dee it's bleeding too bad, he need to go to the hospital." Reecee exclaimed.

"No, no. I'm not going to a hospital." The young boy managed to exclaim with a look of pain on his face.

"Let's find out how bad it is first before you say that. Reecee go get me a pair of scissors." I said trying to lift the fabric from the wound.

"Scissors for what, what you gone do with the scissors?" Larry cried out.

Candy arrived with the towel and Larry screamed as I tried to lift his leg a little so I could try to see the under side of his leg. That's when I noticed the exit hole. It was the size of my pinky finger, not as bad as we thought because the guns on the street today would blow half of his leg, if not all of his leg, off. So he was lucky.

"It looks like an exit wound and the hole is not that big." I thought to myself that Mel introduced me to this girl, a client of ours who always buys clothes and stuff from us. She's a nurse and a shop-a-holic, and she spends her husband's money while he works as a doctor at the hospital. Maybe they can help.

"I can't take all this blood, this is too much for me; we gotta get this boy..." I cut her off.

"I got an idea, hold up." I retrieved my cell phone from its holster on my hip and dialed Mel's number. This way I could kill two birds with one stone. I would be keeping my word as I did say I'd get with him when I was finished.

"Hello, what's up Mel? I got a problem."

"What's your problem youngster? If it's about that car..."

"Nah, Reecee and Candy's cousin Larry just got shot, he's sitting right here with a hole in his leg and it looks like the bullet went straight through and the first thing that came to mind was the girl that works at Episcopal Hospital."

"What about her?"

"Ain't her husband a doctor?"

"Yeah, but he might not get to see him, they gonna give him what ever doctor..."

I interrupted saying, "He don't want to go to a hospital, he's scared he might go to jail. Some guys tried to rob him and somebody might of got killed. You understand now?"

"I'ma call them and see what's up. Call me back in ten to fifteen minutes. Nah, better yet why don't you come around here 'cause this talking on the phone is not cool."

I ignored the call beeping on the other line. It was Brishette's number. "Awight I'ma walk around there."

While in route I redialed Brishette and told her I might be at the waiting room all night and that a friend got robbed and shot in the leg and I'd call her tomorrow. When I arrived Mel gave me the blues.

"Youngster, what the hell you tryin' do, get locked up? I told you never break the rules and you break the number one rule and buy a Bentley. You gotta be out of your mind. What the hell are you thinking about?"

"Damn, you act like I killed somebody."

"You don't get it, do you? You'll never last in this business being flashy."

"I got it for this mansion business, not for everyday."

"So what you doing driving it in the projects then? You gonna get yourself killed or locked up if you don't start thinking."

He was right; I should've never came down here driving the Bentley. Now police are everywhere and I need to get my young boy to a doctor before he bleed to death.

"Didn't you say the police might be looking for you?"

"I think they are looking for me. They went to my man's brother's house and showed him pictures of me, asking who I was." I said, thinking about the situation Kevin told me about.

"So why would you be driving a Bentley, getting all this crazy attention? Forget about that, we'll talk tomorrow, for now you need to get that boy to a doctor. I spoke with Darletta, her husband is there and he said he'll help. So what you want to do, go there or have him come down here? Let me know so I can call them back."

Mel persuaded the doctor to come down because moving the youngster was too risky because the police seemed like they were spending the night around there. The doctor came, and did his thing while Larry had to be told, "You have to keep it down before somebody call the police on us."

I winded up spending the night in my old room. Larry couldn't walk so he slept on the floor in the living room with his leg propped up to keep down the swelling. I was awakened around 5:14 a.m. by Larry downstairs moaning. Nobody thought about giving him something to pee in, so either he had a real "wet dream" or he pissed on himself. I woke up Candy and told her I had to leave. I was surprised Reecee didn't come in the room and try to fuck me while everybody was sleep.

I got home just in time to get Brishette's call. She was worried because I didn't call her back last night. I told her they would not allow cell phones in hospital emergency area.

"Are you okay baby?"

"Yeah I'm fine. I was just up half the night, but I gotta get up and get to work. The question is how are you and the baby?"

"We're okay. We're just missing you this morning. So am I gonna see you for lunch? I'll be at Sony Pictures in Culver City, so maybe..."

I cut her off. "I don't know if I can make lunch but we will definitely do dinner. Hold on, let me get this other line."

"Hello."

"Yo Dee, I got some good news and some bad news." Splizzy responded.

"Yo let me call you back. I got my girl on the phone."

"This will only take one minute. Look, I got a guy who owns property in Ocho Rios, Jamaica and he tryin' to sell some, and your baby mother trippin'. She said she ain't tryin' to let your daughter go to California 'cause she don't know what you're doin' out there."

"That fuckin' girl crazy man. Yo, Splizz I'll call you back in a few."

"I'm sorry. I'm back. So listen, tonight I'm gonna cook for you and we're gonna have a nice quiet dinner by candlelight. Just me and you, and the baby. Awight?"

"Okay. What time and where? Over here or over there?" Her voice was extremely seductive.

"Over there."

"You gotta tell me what you're gonna cook so I can make sure I have it."

"I'll bring everything I need, okay. So I'll see you around 5:00 Oh, and wear something sexy." We hung up.

I immediately called Splizz back and learned just what the doctor ordered, that a well hidden safe house in Jamaica already existed. A five bedroom three and a half baths and two pools, one indoor and one outdoor right on the beach. The price was right at $180,000 and Splizz had already negotiated a $30,000 down payment and he would owner finance or hold the note himself Splizz said the guy used to be in the game so he's real cool.

I prepared myself for the drama and then I called Rissa. "Hello."

"What's up with you?" Why you playin' games? You know Naisha got her heart set on coming out here."

"First of all, I ain't playin' no games. I'm not letting my daughter get on no plane and fly clear across the country without me. So please don't ask me to do that 'cause it ain't happening."

"You act like she gone be by herself. Splizz gone be with her, that's her Godfather and he loves her too and you know he ain't gone let nothing happen to Isha."

"Dee, I'm not lettin' her go unless I'm on that plane. So you can save your breath."

"You know I'm seeing somebody out here right?"

"I don't care. We ain't together no more and I gotta friend too. Why you bring that up anyway?"

"Because I don't want you starting no drama if you come out here."

"Well, I'll just bring my friend and we'll have a good time while we out there."

"What friend?"

"You don't know him. He my new friend."

"Yeah, whatever. Splizz will get you a ticket, that nigga gotta get his own ticket. Call me back and let me know what's up. I gotta go."

Chapter 38

I had Mel pick me up in the Pinto. The Bentley was in the undergound parking lot of my building and tonight I could move it to the mansion and put it in the garage until I needed it.

Today was different, Mel was wearing a button down shirt, slacks and his Big Block Crocodile loafers he bought from Caesar's mall in Vegas at the Martigani store.

"Oh shit. It must be getting ready to rain 'cause I ain't never seen you dressed up. So what's the occasion?"

"When we finish picking up boxes we gone meet with Martin. Remember the guy you met at the car lot?"

"Oh yeah, the real cool old head."

"His brother is a cool lawyer and he's giving a seminar on how to set up trusts and move your money. He gone show us a few tricks and his wife work for Fannie Mae in the collections department, so when home loans go into default they come to her. To make a long story short, they gone show us what to do with the money we make. We gone be buying stocks and property."

We did our normal pick ups without incident, except for the one Airborne Express driver who didn't want to give up the Gateway box with the laptop in it. We met with Calvin and Martin and everything I thought I knew about investing and real estate was nothing compared to what I learned. Now it's really on, because the guy is going to help us for a small fee. What the fuck! Its worth it to learn how to prostitute the dollar bill and make each dollar go get money or have babies. I just had to keep the mansion hustle going and make it legit also.

In the two weeks that followed, Splizzy came out, got acclimated to the new environment. Candy hooked him up with "Sizzle"; she seduced his undivided attention when he wasn't handling business for and with me.

China Doll recruited top-notch runway models and secured serious connections in L.A.'s garment district. We made money hand over fist. We amassed a cool $328,475 for only two weekends from the mansions door and commissions from the sales from the fashion shows.

China and I entered in a contract where she would receive fifteen percent of the proceeds before we went legit and twenty percent after. We set a goal of going legit in four months, but what she didn't know is she was being considered for 50 percent partner.

During the next week and a half we met in the attorney's sound proof basement on six occasions, two of which I took China along because not only was she my partner but I had gotten so excited about learning all sorts of trust maneuvers that I had to turn her on.

We opened accounts with T.D. Waterhouse, Dean Witter, and Merrill Lynch.. He taught us day trading like I'd never heard it before. This guy was a financial wizard. We opened offshore holding companies, estates, and even holding trusts in Zurich all from L.A. through a private bank called Banc International, which we learned were linked to Lords of London. They seemed to be involved in almost all the clandestine money transactions either directly or indirectly. I never imagined I would ever meet, let alone be empowered by what I called "the real money boys." It just goes to show it's all about knowing the right people and being in the right place at the right time.

Mel shocked me, I thought he was just a guy happy with making a little cash and getting a few boxes or was he just trying to compete with me somehow.

"Youngster, I told you. I know people too, and we don't have to do it alone. My people gone walk us through it step by step. Why do you think I send computers over there and never ask you to take any payment from him? It's because I know these guys are millionaires. That car lot is only one of many businesses they own, and if you listen and stop being hard headed I can show you how to make everything legal and leave that drug shit alone because that's gonna be your downfall if you don't get out now." I knew he was right about this drug game.

"Youngsta, he's been trying to show me how to invest my money for a while. A lot of the customers I got-people who spend real money-are because of him."

"I've learned more out here in California in months than I've learned all my life in Baltimore. I thought selling drugs was what was happening..."

Mel cut me off. "Speaking of drugs, you better let that boy keep whatever he got and let that drug shit go. You don't need it, unless you trying to go to jail and miss out on this life you can have and plus you will lose that girl you talking about marrying."

Mel had a point. This is a life, up until now, I only dreamed about but now I'm living proof that you can make it from anywhere even the projects, and get rich.

With this attorney walking us through every step we bought a shell corporation, this was just a corporation set up that really never did any business so that another buyer can use is later. Which a general partnership that was established in the 1980's, and we did what was called a "restructuring" that resulted in a Limited Partnership called a trust. We then made the lawyer a trustee of the trust. Now whatever we put in it no one could take it no matter what, not even the IRS or U.S. Attorney's office because a trust is like a person separate from the beneficiary. I always wanted to know how the rich got richer and stayed rich. This financial revelation was a little scary because I've heard of a lot of people, doctors, lawyers and everyday investors losing their life savings, but I was taking a risk getting the money, so why not take a risk trying to keep it.

Chapter 39

China and I met at the Marriot Hotel for breakfast. We enjoyed fresh sliced pineapple, watermelon, beautiful plump green grapes, humongous red strawberries and juicy orange slices along with the custom designed-to-order egg omelet and Belgium waffles. China had whipped cream and strawberries on hers, I had a blueberry syrup over mine. After our meal fit for a king, we shopped at Neiman Marcus on Rodeo Drive. It was a beautiful day; the sun must've made a special appearance through the clouds because it was a hot one. I was glad to be inside out of the sun, so the two hour shop-a-thon was fine with me.

China purchased a beautiful two piece Donna Karen bathing suit and some seductively alluring tropical summer dresses perfect for our trip. I chose linen. I purchased a straw hat with a tropical band around it and the matching Tommy Bahamas short sleeved shirt I saw on display. From there we did Fred Hayman's where I bought two linen suits, one blue and the other off white. Next we stopped at the Versace store, then Victoria Secrets before we split up.

I got an in-flight call from Splizz, "Hello."

"We're here, about to land so everything will be set up when you get here. Let me give you the routing number for a wire transfer. 02-71461283, Bank of America, his name is Myles Langford."

"Awight, I got it. I'll take care of that today because it's still early and I'll see you when I get there. Peace." I had the bank wire the money.

Two days later China and I boarded the Princess Cabriola, the huge cruise liner. We boarded without incident but there was something strange about the way the porter who came to our cabin kept asking questions like he was sent to investigate or something. And I couldn't get comfortable because I have heard of people getting pulled off a cruise ship in the middle of the ocean, in fact, it was better for them because there's no where to run.

I might not have been able to get comfortable, but China's caramel sculpted body modeling the red with black trimmed lace Victoria Secret thong set, her fragrance and the way her apple lip gloss seduced me, I sure didn't have any problem getting hard.

We made love like it would be our last time. It was explosive and exhausting at the same time. Afterwards we talked about everything, what I wanted out of life; what she wanted out of life; our pasts. I told her how I really wanted her to get rich with me and have everything she's always dreamed of. That's when she told me about her parents.

"Dee out of all the guys I've been with and I can count them on my hands, you're the only one who comes even close to the man my mother talked about all the time before she died. My mother used to always say that 'nine out often men will try to hold you back so they can keep you dependant on them, but you will know when a man really cares because he will try to show you how to become independent and have your own and he'll still treat you nice." "I was young but I remember."

Her eyes were glassy as if she was just in her mother's presence and now in mine; the man that her mother may have told her about.

"Damn, I'm sorry to hear about your mother." I said with all sincerity.

"My parents were paying my tuition at Morehouse."

"Oh, so you're a college graduate huh? What was your major?"

"I majored in Business Administration and Marketing."

"Oh yeah? Me too."

"That's the reason I started dancing, to finish paying for my schooling and get my degree. Then after I got my degree I dept dancing so I could pay the rent and keep up my lifestyle."

"So when are you gonna stop?"

"When I save up enough money to buy me some income properties and who knows, I might open a club for dancers myself and call it 'The Melting Hot'. How do y'all get these mansions anyway? Is this shit illegal?"

"That's part of what I wanna talk to you about..."

"What do you mean?" China gave her undivided attention.

"Well, the mansion is illegal, but it ain't. Let me explain, it's like this, all the paperwork I got, is enough to satisfy the law but once the owner finds out we gotta be out within three or four months after that."

"I knew this shit was too good to be true", China said with this look of disappointment.

I cut her off saying, "Hold up before you start jumping to conclusions. First of all this is one of the best hustles I ever ran across. No police, no stick-up boys, no hassle. You just gotta come up real fast and then turn it legit. That's it, it's that simple."

"So you say."

"Listen China if we do this right, I mean make the parties a success every weekend we can make $120,000 a weekend easy. That's $480,000 in a month plus $20,000 in rents, that's $500,000 China for one month. If we can roll for four months straight, not only will this be a millionaire partnership but we can go legit that next month, so any spending we gonna do, we need to do it this first month. All the money we make next month we save, and if we do this right, we're rich for life."

Chapter 40

OCHO RIOS

The ship arrived in Ocho Rios, Jamaica almost a week later and still I was not celebrating an escape unless and until I reach my destination.

"Right this way sir." The heavy Jamaican accented taxi driver pointing to his taxi across the street before wiping the beads of sweat that escaped from his Dreadlocks that apparently captured the blistering heat of the island's tropical sun.

During our fifteen minute ride China and I asked all sorts of questions about where to go shopping, dancing, and the best restaurants. He warned us to stay away from Kingston and Montego Bay but assured us that Ocho Rios was peaceful and it was good living. He even gave us the history on why the area was called Ocho Rios because it means eight rivers and because they all meet at the area so they named it Ocho Rios. We took his card as he dropped us off at a main street where Splizz and Myles were waiting, along with a Jamaican cousin of Myles named Ralph who preferred to be called "Rude Boy".

"What up kid?" Splizz appeared to be happy to see that I made it knowing that under the circumstances I didn't have to. "And the beautiful Ms. China, long time no see."

"How are you doing?" China exclaimed with her cordial, deceiving smile.

"I'm good, let me introduce y'all Myles this is my good friend, I was tellin' you about, Dee. Dee this is Myles."

"Nice to finally meet you sir." His voice did not quite fit his body. This guy was maybe six foot two hundred fifty pounds in pretty good shape for a man his age. You would've expected a deep voice but he sounded like a youngster, as Mel would put it.

I now realized why I paid so much for the international phone. I believe they call it P.D.A or something. It was because I could get my calls all over the world. The phone rang, it was Steph.

"Hello." I looked out the window and spoke in a lowered tone as I leaned towards the window.

"What's going on? Are you there yet?"

"We just got here, I was gonna call you when I got settled in. So how is business?"

"Business is lovely on this end, the girls Sizzle and Millicent, mannn; I'm tellin' you these girls are so sharp. Do you realize that both spots together did $328? You did $146,000, I know you said I could get half for keeping everything going but I'm only taking $25,000 so you still did $121,000. So what do you want to do with the Armenian?"

"Steph, man I really appreciate your help."

"Look, its nothing, I know you'd do it for me; plus you got some real winners in this group you got. Those girls had everybody asking me about them."

"So what did you give them?"

"They each made over $5,000 on V.I.P., the fashion shows, and they bought in a roulette wheel, turned the pool table into a craps table. I never knew Sizzle worked for a casino in Brazil for six years before coming to the states."

"So, I'm sitting on a gold mine, huh?"

"That's right partner."

"Qkay. Well let me get back to you, we just arrived at the house. I'll get back to you. Oh yeah, do twenty to the Armenian, and I'm gonna have you meet the lawyer that sets up the trusts to hide your money. I'll tell you about it later."

China couldn't wait to ask me how did things go over the weekend, so as soon as we got into the house I eased some of her curiosity and shared the good news. She looked of a relieved soul. Now we could enjoy our time left together because we had our heart to heart on the ship. Now we share the same vision to do the damn thing, by any means necessary.

Splizz filled me in on the details; Myles confirmed his wire transfer and we closed the deal. Myles gave China and I a tour of the house. This house was a steal at $180,000 because in America this house on the beach would be well over one million, maybe two or three, and it didn't hurt that two to three miles away was a resort that rented horses by the hour to ride on the beach.

Chapter 41

For times when the phone was our only way to communicate, I knew I would need some of the skills I learned from the drug game, so Mel and I had practiced our own coded language where we could speak about anything and nobody would know what we were talking about. Since Mel and Steph had become friends in my absence, Mel taught Steph the new codes for the money trusts. Steph already knew how to talk in code because we used to practice in L.A. county Jail in that cell. It sometimes amazed me how unique our technique was. For example, Mel and I agreed we would use names of cars, addresses, distances, gambling language to describe transactions for the trust maneuvers.

We first broke the trusts into three categories, Securities Trust which we gave a code name "STS Cadillac" that's one of the trusts used to invest in stocks and securities. For real estate trust we used "IRS" this trust was used only to buy properties and businesses. Finally for family trust I named it "Fam" as if it were a person and for our offshore numbered accounts we gave them nick names of people like Buddy, Slim Slim, Goofball.

The first time I got to actually use my code craft was when I called Steph back with instructions on how I wanted the money I made off the mansion parties, broke down. Steph was a fuckin' genius because he always knew exactly what I was saying so I didn't have to worry about whether the money would go into the right trusts.

He made me a believer when I told him, "Yo Steph don't let nobody else drive the STS. As a matter of fact, take it around to the girl Karen's house and put it in her garage with the car cover over it. You do remember where she live at right?"

"Nah, all I remember is its near a school."

"Yeah that's right; it's in the forty hundred block. I think the address is 4006, it's a couple doors from the corner." That meant put forty thousand in the securities trust.

"Awight, I got you. I'll drive it around there. So what's up with you and China? Y'all go over everything?"

"Everything."

"Everything?" Steph said like he didn't believe me.

"Yo Steph, this girl is so fuckin' cool. Smart as shit, and she's got vision too. Mannn, she told me every since she was a little girl she was crazy about James Bond movies and in a lot of the movies she saw yachts with names on the side and she always wanted one with her name on the side of a yacht."

"That's what I'm talkin' about. I told you, you had a winner. What she say about the partnership?"

"Man she's lovin' it and I told her about Brishette too."

"You did what? What the fuck you do that for?"

"She knows."

"She knows what?"

"She said she know I got baby mothers and she knows I'm fucking somebody in L.A., but as long as I respect her and don't let our relationship interfere with our business she's cool."

"Did she sign the contract?"

"Yeah she signed it, plus you got to see this house, it's not a mansion but it's beautiful. It's down the beach, that's right, I said beach not street, from a resort. The resort's got horse back riding and they have a glass sliding board that goes into the pool. I'm going to take China there tomorrow..."

"Awight let me get back to what I was doing. I'll take care of everything here. You heard anything from your peoples?"

"Nah, nothing yet. Awight I'm out." China came into the den. The light from the nosey sun peeking through the multi-pained windows seemed to spotlight her well proportioned beauty in the multi-colored well fitting bathing suit. She simply had a body to die for and to kill for. Looking at her sashay over to the deep mahogany leather, high-back executive chair I proudly occupied.

"I seemed to have forgotten what I was about to say."

"Well, you know what they say." China moved into position, sitting on my left leg then finished her statement. "When you don't know what to say, don't say anything." She leaned in, put her arms around me and kissed me. Her kisses had become more comfortable and effortlessly accurate. I felt our bodies warm to the touch of passion.

"So what do you want to do today?" She asked with the look of a sixteen year old full of adventure and quite sybaritic, hedonistic even.

"Whatever you want to do China. Remember I'm just a squirrel tryin' to get a nut." We both laughed.

"I haven't heard that one in a while, you must of went into your archives to get that one."

"Speaking of nut, could I interest you in a game of strip pool. I'll spot you two balls and guarantee you'll be naked before I will."

"You must really think I can't play, just for that I'm gone beat you like you stole something." She moved like a Victoria Secret model towards the sliding oak doors of the den.

"Where you going?"

"I'm going to put some more clothes on so I can even the playing field."

"Cause you know you're gonna lose." I shouted as she disappeared up the stairs.

My phone rang it's distinctive tone, displaying an unfamiliar 410 number.

"Hello."

"What's up Dee? We're gonna be out there this weekend coming up. I changed my ticket 'cause my friend couldn't get off from work."

"Yeah awight, where is my daughter? Let me holla at her."

"Hold on... NAISHAAA." Screaming in my ear.

"Heyy." I screamed back letting her know to stop screaming in my ear.

"What?"

"What you mean, what? Stop screaming in my fuckin' ear, that's what."

"Yeah whatever... Here Isha take this phone."

"Hello?"

"Hey baby, what's up with my favorite girl?"

"DADDYYY, Hiii. My mother said we gone catch a plane to see you daddy. I can't wait."

"I can't either baby. I love you Isha."

"I love you too daddy."

"Awight put your mother..."

She cut me off saying, "Hey daddy, can we go to Disneyland when I come?"

"I'll make sure you get to go to Disneyland okay. Now put your mother back on the phone for me."

"What's up?"

"I'm not paying for your boyfriend to be laying' up in no hotel fucking my baby-
mother."

"Boy shut up, plus he got money. He probably gonna pay for the hotel anyway or he can pay half and I'll pay half with the money you give me.

"Yeah awight, I just wanted you to know that that shit ain't happening, so tell him get his money right."

"Whatever, I'll see you next week."

"I'm out." I said and hung up as China walked into the den with stockings on under a pair of Khaki shorts, a white button down shirt, with a white V-neck tennis cardigan over it. She had over dressed, hoping that it would help her win.

"What the..."

"What?" China said with a sinister grin on her face.

"Why do you have all those clothes on?"

"Because you think you're slick. You didn't want to play strip pool until you saw that I only had on two pieces of clothing. So like I said, I'm evening the playing field."

"So you think all them clothes is going to help you? I got something for you. Let's play, go ahead and rack 'em up."

We played pool for about twenty minutes before we were naked and I had her all over the pool table, tonguing her down. We made love in every imaginable position. Then showered and we met Splizz and Myles at a restaurant inside the resort known for it's imported tiger prawns and they were huge. China and I chose the stuffed shrimp with coconut sauce. Myles ordered the curry platter of goat, lamb, and chicken. Splizzy ordered the house special recommended by the young, beautiful Jamaican girl. We drank Pina Coladas and Tropical Daiquiris until around 8:30pm. Then the Reggae band took the stage, China and I danced up a sweat. It seemed like the more I held her the more I needed to hold her. She was really starting to feel me too, as evidenced by the looks she gave me when other women gave me second glances as if to hint an interest.

Splizz certainly took advantage of my being with China and had no problem taking care of the girls who's attention we had attracted. He charmed at least three of them on the dance floor. Rude Boy introduced us to two of his Jamaican police friends. They were real helpful and offered to check on the house. They even told us about the Islands security genius named Renard, who came from three generations of locksmiths and alarm specialists.

The very next morning Rude Boy had the locksmith to come by. I had him install a serious state-of-the-art alarm system. Myles turned me on to the Tropi-Clean Maid Service. I hand picked from their online catalog, a young tender Jamaican beauty named Twyla, within twenty minutes she was there. Her figure was slim but muscular, her breast were erect and there was a girlishness about her movements. Her tropical sun darkened skin was naturally tight and smooth as if well preserved. Her hair was woven into micro-mini braids, burnt at the tips. There was something strange about the way China looked at this young beauty. I couldn't quite put my finger on it.

I tried to keep it professional as I could but I was definitely turned on by her sexy Jamaican accent and those sexy legs in the short skirt she wore as a uniform. I know that China felt the attraction between us especially when Twyla later came in the den where China and I were.

"Mister Dee, I'm finished with the bathroom d'want me to do sumtin' else now?"

I wanted so bad to say 'yes just turn around and bend over and let me hit it', but instead I held back waiting for her to make the first move. It's better that way plus I didn't want to risk it while China was there. But I did want to know more about her.

"Twyla, let me ask you a few questions." China left the room but came right back as if she didn't want to miss the interview.

"Sure."

"Do you have children?"

"Oh nooohh, I am too young to have a child right now."

"How old are you?"

"I'm twenty, soon to be twenty-one." Her beautiful smile told me she liked me but still I needed more to make my move, and it would have to be when China had left.

"So what do you do when you're not working?" China cut her eye at me as if I was getting too personal.

"I don't do much; I just take care of my mother and my brothers and sisters."

"How old are your brothers and sisters?" China joined in.

"There's, lets see, Donovan, Wendy and Mendy-the twins, Kymani, and Elani. Five in all."

China started to take over, "And you said you are taking care of your mother, so where is your father?"

"My father is dead. He was killed by the rebels when I was seven years old and my mum has terminal cancer. She is very weak from the radiation treatments. So I care for her along with my brothers and sisters." China left the room remembering that she was cooking something.

"So who takes care of you while you take care of everyone?" I inquired with a hint of interest.

"I take care of me, what about you, who takes care of you?" She shot back at me.

"Well right now you're taking care of me because this house would be a mess if you hadn't come to help me clean. Do you cook as well as you clean?"

"I cook the best jerk chicken in Jamaica. You ever tried jerk chicken Mister Dee? I can show your wife how to cook it."

"Who China, she's not my wife. She's my business partner and good friend and yes I love Jamaican food." That was sharp of her to find out if China was my wife.

"Well I'm gonna have to cook for you sometime Mister Dee."

"Yeah, I look forward to that Twyla I'll be waiting."

"I can cook for you when I come Thursday."

My phone's distinctive ring interrupted us. I excused myself and Twyla walked out, leaving me to take the call.

"Hello."

"You know what?" Candy's voice projected through the phone.

"No. What?"

"Why haven't you been by or called to check on me?"

"I told you what's going on. So you know my situation Candy. You know if I could get to your sexy chocolate ass, I'd be there."

"I miss you Dee."

"I miss you too Candy, but until I figure out how to get around this problem I gotta lay low."

"Dee what's going on? Does this have anything to do with the car?"

"No, the car is fine, but I got some problems."

"What kind of problems Dee?"

"Some people might be looking for me".

"What kind of people?"

"The FEDs."

"Oh my god, is it real bad?"

"It's bad enough, so I'm laying low that's why you might not see me for a while. So tell me how many months are you now?"

"You should know."

"Look Candy, my mind is not always remembering everything in a split second. So have you been to the doctors?"

"Yeah, the baby is fine, I'm gettin' big. Well, my stomach is getting big."

"Damn, this shit would happen to me."

"What?"

"Damn, this is the guy I gotta meet. I'ma have to call you back Candy, I gotta take this call."

"When you gone call me back?"

"As soon as I can Candy, but I gotta go so I'll talk to you soon."

"Awight, I love you Dee."

"Yeah, me too."

I clicked over to find out if my daughter was okay. "Hello."

"Dee I just called to let you know we're here, but it's late so we're just gone check in and get some sleep and I'll call you in the morning."

"Don't be doing nothing with that guy around my daughter either."

"What do I look like doing something around my daughter; you talk like a fool Dee."

"You heard what I said. You can wait until I come get Isha before y'all start jumping up and down."

"Goodbye Dee, I'm hanging up."

"I wish you would hand up on me Rissa."

"Well hang up then."

Before I could hang up my line beeped again. "Awight Rissa I'm gone."

When I clicked over I heard Splizzy's voice, "Come on, we're outside." He and Rude Boy had come to pick me up so they could take me to meet some of the key players in Jamaica.

We stopped by the resort, met the owners who gave me card Blanche, V.I.P. treatment, Cuban Cigars, Louis XIII, and a pass to return as a house guest. Rude Boy wasn't lying about his reputation. He knew everyone and they all treated him with respect. Myles also told me which banks who would wire money with no hassle.

I purchased a wireless modem for my laptop so I could take it with me wherever I go and not have to worry about finding a connection on the island.

That evening I returned, tired as hell after meeting Splizz, Rude Boy and Myles alone because China wanted to stay and rest. Only China was hardly resting, instead she and had a mouth full of pussy. I never in a million years would have thought China was gay, well, bisexual. But there she was her and the young Jamaican tender Twyla "bumping pussies" we call it.

Obviously they were so engrossed, that they never heard me enter. All I could think about as I stood at the door, motionless, getting hard as penitentiary steel, is how did this happen. I thought Twyla was a good wholesome young girl. As they moved into position to kiss each other, Twyla saw me standing there and nudged China who looked up at me and waived me over.

"You want to join us?" China said as Twyla pulled the covers over her cocoa complexioned body. China moved aside and patted the middle of the king sized bed, showing me where she wanted me. Twyla, probably a little embarrassed.

"I'm gonna go now. I have to be getting home."

That's when China grabbed her hand and put it on her breast; they began kissing then caressing each other. "I want you to stay." China said as the kissing ended.

I joined them and began kissing China while she fingered Twyla. China started licking and kissing me on my chest while I fondled Twyla soft, perky titties. Twyla began to respond by kissing me, her mouth tasted of pussy.

China started moaning while she licked up and down my shaft. Suddenly she was joined by Twyla. They took turns one giving me head while the other teased my balls with their moist tongue until I shot my load, and as soon as I was hard again China pulled out a condom from her purse, handed it to Twyla who started to gently roll it on with both hands, stroke after stroke. China finger-fucked her while she stroked my manhood. I was so ready to cum again and I hadn't even started fucking yet. I thought

Twyla was prepping me for China but Twyla mounted me herself and began to ride me while China watched. Then china started massaging Twyla's breast while she rode me. I started rubbing China's now wet and juicy pussy...

Twyla bounced up and down on the magic stick until she came. I didn't because she was going too fast, then Twyla rolled over on to her back exhausted from her hedonistic ride. China moved in and began sucking Twyla's beautiful golden brown titties, exposing her love hole to me. While China was positioned on her knees giving Twyla head, I couldn't resist sliding deep into her warm wet waiting pussy. The more I banged away, they both moaned, China, from my relentless pounding inside of her sugar walls, and Twyla from China's seemingly expert cunnilingus.

This was truly a dream come true, being the center of a pussy-bumping party. But what really blew my mind was when China left the room, temporarily leaving me alone with Twyla to enjoy a sixty-nine suck-a-thon only to return with two glasses of water, one with ice and one without. It didn't really hit me until china set the two glasses on the nightstand and set on the top edge of the bed. China then instructed both Twyla and I to scoot to the edge of the bed, open our legs and lay back. She began with Twyla by drinking some of the hot water then licking Twyla's young juicy pussy. I kissed and massaged Twyla's breast while china made her moan to climax from hot and cold pleasure from her kisses. Then it was my turn, she began licking my balls with her chilled tongue which sent chills up and down my spine. Then she licked up and down my shaft, teasing the head but not putting it all the way into her mouth until she started getting fingered by Twyla that's when she deep throated my swollen member, soft and slow until I shot my load or what was left of a load, because I was practically drained but that didn't stop me. I then had both girls put their feet on the floor and bend forward over the bed, exposing all ass and bushy pussy.

I started by placing my left hand on China's lower back just above the crack of her ass right at her waist. This was for balance while I guided my, swollen again, love muscle into her warm waiting hot box. I first moved both hands to her waist to hold her in place while I tried to insert every inch of my magic stick inside of her. Slowly at first then I sped up as she started moaning loudly. By this time Twyla had one leg on the bed and had moved in, put one of her hands under China's breast, pulled one outward to the side and began sucking. Then they began kissing until their teeth bumped as I started banging away Doggy-style. Then I pulled out of China and slid right into Twyla who was even juicier and easier to access with her leg still on the bed, spread eagle. I didn't last long at all inside this young Jamaican tender. Her pussy was so good I came after about ten or fifteen strokes, but kept pumping even after I got soft, until she came. Then we each collapsed from exhaustion.

The next morning I awoke, China was alone in the kitchen, the smell of fried potatoes and onions and fresh biscuits woke me up. Twyla had gone home. If China wasn't half naked in the kitchen I would not have believed last night was real, it was just too good to be true.

"Good morning baby." China turned and said as I seemingly startled her as she emerged from the refrigerator.

"Oh hey Dee. You scared me. I hope you're hungry because..."

"Let me save you some trouble. Anything you got, I wanna taste it." I moved in closer to her, hugging her form behind, smelling the Escada fragrance she wore so well.

Chapter 42

China and I had a beautiful day together. I took her to the resort and we had a ball. I felt closer to her because she had shared all of her with me and fulfilled my fantasy to be with two beautiful women at the same time. The next day it was time for her to go back to L.A. Splizzy arrived at 9:00 a.m., we had breakfast at the resort. While we were there, I got a dreaded call from Reecee. I took the call and walked out on to the patio.

"Hello?"

"Hey Dee, it's me Reecee. Did I catch you at a bad time?"

"Well, you did actually. I was having my breakfast."

"Well, this is important, look I'm at Mel's house he's not here though. What I wanna tell you is I think my sister knows."

"Why you think that?"

"Oh, it's just a feeling. She hasn't said anything, but it's the way she acts when we mention you. It could be the baby driving her crazy but I just feel something different. You know what I mean?"

"Don't you think she would approach you if she thought something like that?"

"Yeah, I guess you're right. Well I gotta go; I think that's Mel blowing the horn out there. Awight Dee, call me when you can, I miss. you."

"Yeah I miss you too. I'll call you soon, awight. Later." I returned to the table now thinking about what she just said. I got Splizz and china to the airport because

Myles had left two days ago but he was going back to the East Coast.

As I left the airport it seemed like my whole life flashed before me. The thought of being an R&B singer and movie star still remained in the background of my life goals. I just never stuck with it even though I knew that consistency would get me anything I wanted.

Who knows, my meeting Brishette could be destiny, especially now that she is a well known movie script writer she could write me right into a leading role of one of her movies, or better yet, I could even help her to write the role for me. It seemed like my thoughts of Brishette summoned her call or maybe we were just meant to be.

I answered on the second ring, "Hello."

"Hey baby." Her soothing, sexy voice emanated from the phone. "I missed you so much."

"You're not gonna believe this."

"Yes I will, try me."

"I was thinking about you and the baby at the very moment you called. That's a good sign."

"I'm back in L.A. and I went to your apartment hoping I would surprise you, but you weren't there and never showed up. So where are you?"

"I'm out of town; I'll explain it to you later."

"When are you coming home? And explain what Dejohn? Is something wrong?"

"Something like that."

"What is it? Are you in some kind of trouble?"

"I'll explain it to you when I see you."

"When Dejohn?" She panted like a nine- year old spoiled child.

"Soon, I promise. So how is your mother doing?" I quickly diverted her attention.

"She's fine; she's at home now and doing much better. Dejohn you still haven't told me when I'm going to see you. Oh yeah, thanks for taking care of my car."

"Can you take a trip? Because I got a surprise for you?"

"To come to you, sure I can, but when? Dejohn you know I just got back and I have a lot of catching up to do. My film premiere is in two days."

"Look, my daughter is going to be here on Friday or Saturday and I'd like you to come with her to where I am. I'll fill you in on the details later, but for now, get yourself settled in, make your appearance at the premiere and make arrangements to go away for another week, even if you have to bring your work with you."

"I thought you said you were gonna spend time with her alone."

"I did, but she's gonna have to share me with you, it's just that simple because both of you are my world."

Brishette's voice said it all; she was afraid, pregnant with my baby boy, now confirmed by the sonogram test, and now more uncertain about whether she'd be forced to raise him alone.

What kept running through my head like a sub way train was how I always wanted a family and to create and environment where I could bring both children from Brishette and Candy together with my other East Coast children would be a task.

"Okay, okay. I'll make arrangements, but where am I making arrangements to come to?"

"You just make arrangements to get the time off and I'll do the rest. Okay, just trust me, okay? I love you and I gotta go, I'll call you back."

Chapter 43

I couldn't get it out of my head that Reecee thinks Candy might know something if she did, she's one hell of an actress and would definitely deserve an Oscar for her performance, but also she'd have to be watched closely because that means she's sneaky and if she's sneaky, she's dangerous. But there was only one way for me to find out and that was to call her back and probe. Just like my grandfather said all the time, "Time reveals everything."

She answered the phone sounding as if she was out of breath, either she had ran to get the phone or she had someone else banging her back out and our baby's head in.

"Hello."

"What's up? What was you doing?"

"Cleaning the bathroom, why?"

"What do you mean, why? Because I'm calling to check on you, that's why?"

"All of a sudden you wanna check on me now."

"Hold up, what's wrong with you? First you said I didn't call and check on you, and now I call to check on you and you get smart. Make up your mind Candy."

"So where did you say you were at again?"

"We can't talk about that on the phone."

"I need some money Dee."

"Tell Larry I said to give you five-hundred. Is that enough?"

"Yeah, I guess. I just want to see you Dee."

"I know baby, I wanna see you too, but not right now. When this is over we gone take a trip somewhere okay."

"Awight." Something wasn't right; now I see what Reecee was saying, but she ain't got no proof of nothing ever happening.

That next day I went out sight seeing, finding my way around town. It gave me a chance to clear my head and think through my plan, and take it to the next level, even from Jamaica. And if China failed I'd have to have a contingency plan.

Twyla cooked for me and we almost had sex, except she was on her period. I had even thought of trying sexing her while she was on her period, she was fine as hell, or was it just that she was one of the women who made my fantasy a reality.

I knew I had to make some changes in my sexual appetite if I was to marry and keep Brishette. I often thought about getting some professional help like a therapist or something but decided against it each time because I always reasoned that just like my first love Myalisa used to say, "All men are dogs", but marriage would change me, it does that to a man.

Splizzy called the house phone with the late news, letting me know that Irissa and my daughter were finally in L.A., and had been trying to reach me but I hadn't answered my cell phone. "I just finished running on the beach, my cell phone is upstairs on the bed."

"Yo, you need to call them she said your daughter wants to see you. So what you want me to do, because you mentioned something about her meeting your wife. Plus I want to meet her too so I can see who got your nose wide open like 7-11." Splizzy chuckled.

"Yo, I already talked to my daughter and Rissa, she called me, but you know what? I'm glad you asked me that because I just came up with an idea."

"Uh oh, so what you got up your sleeve yo?"

"I need you to get two tickets..." Splizz cut me off.

"With what?"

"I'ma get China to give you the money for two first class tickets to Jamaica. I'll pick them up from the airport when they get here."

"So do wifee know about your daughter being here yet?"

"Nah, I just told her to get the week off from work, but I did tell her that my daughter was coming. That's right I sure did."

"So why don't you let her make the arrangements and I'll just give her the money.

"Yo, I can do that myself, this is supposed to be a surprise yo."

"Awight, so what day they gone leave?"

"Let me call you back. I'ma call Brishette and Rissa and set everything up, then I'll call you back. Where you at anyway?"

"I'm at the mansion spot."

"So is China there?"

"She was here; I'm in the girl Sizzle's room chillin'. You want me try to find her?"

"Nah, that's awight. I'll call her, or better yet, tell her call me yo. I'm out. Let me call them and set it up."

I called Brishette and confirmed the trip with details. Then I phoned my daughter's mother, spoke to my princess, then called Splizz and gave him the details. The next five hours I shopped at the mall, buying everything I could think of, from new outfits for my daughter which I had to call Rissa several times to get sizes and opinions, to new expensive Ralph Lauren and Laura Ashley bedding. Not to mention all the Victoria's Secret Lingerie for Brishette to model for me.

I had given Twyla the week off with pay after she cleaned the house so well you could eat off the floors, but she promised to come by and check on the house anyway. This young Jamaican beauty was growing on me, especially after the threesome I had with her and China. I had been warned about Jamaican women, and how crazy they were, so I didn't want to continue to mix business with pleasure at least not now when I'm about to get married.

Chapter 44

They arrived at the small airport fifteen minutes late, and I was right there to receive them with open arms. My daughter came running first; she was so excited to see me. I hugged her for a while as Brishette marveled at the way that we bonded.

"So how was your trip baby?"

"It was good. Your daughter is something else, everyone on the plane commented on how beautiful and well mannered she was. She is definitely star material."

"Daddy, Ms. Brissh bought me everything, she is so nice."

"I know princess, that's why she is going to be your stepmother."

"Stepmother, what is that?"

"That's a second mother because daddy is getting married to Ms. Brissh." I put my arms around Brishette and began kissing her in front of Isha. The response was favorable. She actually started smiling. My little princess was growing up so fast.

We made our way through the crowed airport to the parking structure where, just as we got into the car, Isha asked the million dollar question.

"Daddy, can I ask you a question?"

"Sure Isha what is your question?"

"Daddy, the baby in Ms. Brissh stomach, is it going to be my stepsister or brother? Because Ms. Brissh is my stepmother."

"No princess, the baby will be your sister or brother because even though your mother is not having the baby, your father is having the baby. Well not having the baby but the father of the baby."

"I understand daddy."

We made it to the house, unpacked and Brishette started having pains in her stomach, so we stayed in until she was feeling better. Meanwhile, Isha got in the pool.

"So do you think she likes me Dee?"

"Yeah, you heard what she said. She likes you or she would have been acting funny towards you. Don't forget you are not the only woman that she has been exposed to."

"What do you mean by that? Does that mean that you have a lot of women?"

"Listen to you, that sounds crazy. I'm getting ready to marry you and you're talking about other women. If I did have a lot of women, that is all in the past now. I love you Brishette, and only you."

"Do you mean that Dee, or are you just telling me what you think I want to hear?"

"Brishette, do you have any idea how much I love you? I am crazy about you. You are the first woman who could excite me to change and that should say it all. I think it's just the baby making you all emotional because you already know how much I love you."

The next day we all went to Montego Bay and spent the day being. catered to. When we returned, that' when the drama started. Splizzy called me and gave me the news that Rissa's boyfriend was a police and that he might be in L.A. to find me.

"Yo, I'm telling you, I know his face from anywhere. He was the one who put his foot all in Man Man's face that time they did that raid on the block. It could just be a coincidence but I don't think so."

"Did he recognize you?"

"He don't know me. I was just on the block that day coming out of the store."

"But you're sure it's him?"

"Yo, I'm positive. I'll never forget his face yo."

"You think Rissa's trying to set me up?"

"We gotta find out how she knows this dude, then we can figure out what's up and where to go from there."

"Yo, I wonder if it was a set up and they was gonna lock me up if I had showed up to pick up my daughter. Plus that makes me wonder whether they followed you to the spot?"

"I don't think so because when Sizzle took me to pick up your daughter we went to Rodeo Drive. Brishette met us there and then we went to Woodland Hills to her cousin's and stayed there until late. When we came back there were hardly any cars on the road. So like I said, I don't think so."

"Awight, we'll talk about this later, let me get back to the girls."

When I returned, I saw Brishette teaching Naisha to play pool. It was good that they were bonding because both of them would have to share me and there was no better way to do it than to be harmonious about it.

"Daddy, look I can play pool. You wanna play with me?"

"Yeah baby, but not right now. We can play some another time. Anyway you two need to get some practice if y'all want to play me."

Brishette was sharp, she picked up on my phony response, "Dee, is everything okay?"

"Yeah I'm cool. I'll tell you about it later." I walked out of the room and I must of thought her up because my phone began to vibrate on my side. And sure enough, I answered and it was Rissa.

"Dee where you at?"

"Why? Why you want to know where I'm at?"

"Cause I need some money, that's why and I wanted to give you Isha's sweater just in case it get cool inside or something."

"She don't need no sweater, she awight. And where your boyfriend at? Tell him give you some money."

"First of all he ain't here, and he ain't my boyfriend, he's just a friend okay. It ain't nothing serious."

"So where he at then?"

"He went to workout or something."

"Workout where, in the hotel?"

"I don't think he went downstairs, I think he went out to a gym somewhere."

"So how he know his way around?"

"He know people out here. Why you asking me all these damn questions? I don't keep no tabs on him. I told you we just friends."

"How long you been knowing this guy?"

"Why? Why you so concerned about this guy? You ain't been being concerned about nobody I'm seeing."

"Just answer the fuckin' question man."

"I told you stop callin' me fucking man too. I got you're fucking man, plus if I gotta go through the third degree every time I ask you for some money you can..."

I cut her off saying, "This ain't got nothing to do with no money. I ain't never tell you no when you ask me for something. so don't even fucking go there. I just asked you a simple question and I want a simple answer."

"That's you're fuckin' problem now, you think you my father, don't you daddy?"

"Just answer my question. How long you been knowing this guy?"

"I met him right before Isha's birthday, why?"

"Awight. look I'ma call you back at this number later on, and I'll put a few dollars together for you."

"When? "Cause I wanted to go shopping for me and Isha."

Brishette and Isha came into the room. Rissa heard Isha and asked to speak with her. "Is that Isha I hear? Let me speak to her."

"Here Isha your mother want you." I caught a quick look from Brishette as if she was thinking 'How long had this conversation been going on and maybe was I missing Rissa or wishing I was with Rissa instead of her'. All the crazy stuff women think when they are pregnant.

When I realized Isha was starting to answer too many questions I intervened, "Isha, let me talk to your mother." She said goodbye and handed me the phone.

"Awight Rissa, you'll have the money in a day or two, it might be today. I'll call you back and let you know. Awight?"

Just as I was hanging up, Isha and Brishette started looking for their bathing suits so they could go swimming.

"Dee, you wanna go swimming with us?"

"Yeah daddy, put your swim trunks on and come swimming with us daddy."

"Y'all go ahead; I got some very important business calls to make." I walked out of the room and went downstairs into the study and closed the door. I immediately called Splizz and filled him in.

"Yo Splizz, I just talked to Rissa ten minutes ago, and the guy ain't there. She said he went out to workout or something. Yo she said she need some money which is perfect. Just go over there, meet her and find out what she knows. Give her a few dollars after she tell you what she knows. Just give her about $500, awight."

"So she at the spot now?"

"Yeah."

"So who I'ma get to take me?"

"Hold on." I clicked over, dialed China and had us all on a three-way.

"Hello."

"China, it's me, Dee."

"I know who this is.

"Look, I got Splizz on the line with us."

"Where he at? Where you at Splizz?"

"I'm downstairs."

"Okay, what's up Dee?"

"China I need your help. I need you take Splizz to L.A. for me and wait for him while he take some money to my daughter's mother so she can get some things for my daughter."

"Why don't I just let him use the car?"

"Because he don't know his way around."

"Where is Sizzle? She can take him down there."

"I don't care who takes him down there China. I just need you to make sure he gets there for me please. And China give him $500 for me awight."

"I got 'chew Dee, I'll take care of it. Plus I need to talk to you too Dee, so call me back. Okay?"

"Call you back? Ay Splizz, hang up man, let me holla at China and call me when you know something."

"Awight, peace."

China and I spoke for almost thirty minutes during which time she got one of the girls to take Splizz to meet

Rissa. China could tell something was up because just when we were about to hang up, she let it out.

"Oh yeah, Dee I know when something ain't right. And you don't ever have to lie to me. I'd rather you say you don't want to talk about it, but please don't destroy my trust in you by lying to me."

I cut her off, "What are you talking about China?"

"Just the way you're acting, I can just tell that something is wrong Dee."

"Damn girl, what 'chew, a psychic or sumpin'?"

"You just don't hide shit well, that's all it is."

"Yeah, you right, but I can't talk about it now but I will call you back though."

"Awight, I'll be here most of the day Dee."

"Awight China I'm out." She was right, when it's going down inside, it comes out.

After I hung up I went for a walk on the beach, which was new for me. It offered a serenity I had never really known before. The waves rolling in consistently were like a message that no matter what, the show must go on, so that meant we needed to stay several steps head of the game. I had to find a way to get rid of a problem without causing a bigger problem.

Seeing a couple walking along the beach, holding hands and stopping to kiss immediately made me think of Brishette and I didn't want to lose her because she was my future. I thought of us having about five children and growing old with her. She was just that kind of girl. I made it back to the house and tried my best to get the sand from the bottom of my sandals, but once I found it to be a task I took them off at the sliding glass door.

I spent some time with Isha after her bath and allowed Brishette some "she time" in her dark, aroma-candle lit bubble bath. Once Isha had fallen asleep, I carefully and sensually ravished Brishette's yearning, juicy, pregnant pussy until my tongue became one with her little pearl universe and the force came flowing like Luke Skywalker in Star Wars. Her pussy became so wet like she was trying to fill a cup with cum. She laid on her side and I entered her from behind and short stroked her until I came.

The next morning, I was on the phone to Rude Boy setting up the surprise quiet wedding. Just the three, or shall I say four of us, Isha, our unborn son - I hope - Brishette and myself Rude boy had hooked me up with a priest who met us at Dunn's River Falls. It was so beautiful, the Botanic, exotic garden was so beautiful. There were exotic birds chirping in the background as we said our vows. We were all dressed in white; Isha wore a white sundress and sandals. I had a sharp white linen jacket with matching pants with a white, raw silk shirt with the first three buttons unbuttoned. Brishette was breathtaking with the beautiful white linen maternity dress that was fitting the hell out her ass, which seemed have gotten bigger.

The scenery was simply unbelievable, the fresh breeze from the beautiful greenish blue ocean. We exchanged rings, it almost made Isha cry. I could see the water welling up in her eyes, as young as she was, even she knew I was making the right move. Damn, this shit was like a dream because I never thought I would get married.

We had dinner in a quaint restaurant in the beautiful Run-a-way bay. We spent all day either on or near the beach. Beach bums for a day. I rode horses on the beach after Isha was made to get over her fear by putting her on a pony. We enjoyed the gorgeous sunset then made it back to the house. While getting Isha ready for bed, Rissa called twice asking about Isha, asking when she was coming back. The last time was different however, because she started talking about her friend.

"Dee, I think Splizzy might be right about him."

"What do you mean Rissa?" I asked as if I didn't know what she was talking about, but I knew exactly what she was talking about and what she said was music to my ears.

"He used me Dee, and I do not like that at all. You know I can't stand somebody to play me like a sucka, but that's okay, he'll get his one day."

"Rissa, where you at now?"

"I don't know, he said he was going out for a walk."

"He going for a walk alright. So did you get the money?"

"Yeah, thank you Dee. I guess I'ma go to the mall tomorrow."

"You just gave me an idea. Rissa, stay by the phone, I'ma call you right back.

I'ma call Splizz, awight."

"Okay."

I immediately hung up and called Splizz, who was right on point. As soon as I told him that I just spoke to Rissa, he told me that he had spoke to Rissa already and he tried calling me and got no answer all day when he tried to tell me what he found out.

"Dee, I been hangin out at the strip club some nights waiting for Sizzle to get off and I met these Spanish dudes that I buy weed from, well Sizzle turned me on. Anyway, one of them was jokingly saying if I ever have any problems they can be taken care of because one night was..."

"This ain't no long story is it?"

"Nah, I was just gone say that one night I had to straighten a dude out because he kept trying to grab Sizzle when she told him he couldn't touch. And when they saw I had been beefin' with the dude, he said for the right price it'll be handled."

"So what you saying?"

"I'm saying I just finished a real good book where the girl's boyfriend was on a gang's turf and while him and his girlfriend was shopping at the mall, it was close to closing and they got robbed by some Spanish dudes with red bandannas on. He tried to play hero and got himself killed, they didn't hurt the girl because she was down with the lick. That was her way of getting back at the dude for him beating on her."

"Damn, that sounds like a good assed book, especially the ending. So what happened to the girl when the police came?"

"Good question, well, in the book the people schooled her and she just tells them they got robbed. The cameras show what happened, and it matches her story so they let her go about her business. Believe me, you'll like it 'cause even the ending is good."

"So they never find out who did it?"

"Hell nah. Look, these Spanish boys is Bloods. They grew up doing this shit, so they were seasoned. You feel me?"

"So how much did they make for that?"

"I don't remember but it was probably around fifty thou. Plus that was nothing to the dude because that was the price of protecting his empire."

"Yeah, I know what you mean. I think I'ma have to cop that book if it's that good." I could trust Splizz with my life. He was like a brother to me and I knew he would die for me just like I would for him.

"You just need to authorize me to use the American Express card. You feel me?" Splizz was like the only one that I could just pick up on any code he threw out there.

"Yeah, I got 'chew. I'll have China or Steph to take care of that for me. So you spoke to Rissa already?"

"Nah, but I told her I'll talk to her tomorrow so she's gonna call me in the morning."

"Awight, if you need me, call me. Yo, I'm gone." I hung up and my mind started wondering. What if it goes wrong and somebody goes to jail and starts talking to save themselves? What if the dude being a police is just a coincidence and he's really into Rissa rather than being after me? That's when I got the strange call from Candy. She was sniffling as if she had been crying.

"Dee, I'm scared."

"Scared of what Candy? What are you scared of?"

"I'm scared that this ain't gone work out, and I'ma be stuck with raising this baby alone and that's the last thing I want to do, but if I have to I will Dee. I just don't want to."

"What are you talking about Candy? And you sound like you've been crying, you been crying?"

"Dee I gotta go. I need to use the bathroom. I'll call you back." Before I could say anything Candy hung up the phone on me. I called back repeatedly and got no answer.

Brishette came into the study after knocking, she was soaked and wet and the maternity bathing suit perfectly displayed her very round stomach. "I just came to check on you and make sure you're okay."

"I'm good baby. Thanks for checking on me though."

She could tell I was going through something, or up to no good, but it was all good. "Where is Isha?"

"She's in the tub. When she gets out we're gonna have some Chips-Ahoy chocolate chip cookies and milk, then I'm gonna put her to bed and take me a hot bubble bath. Then I want to curl up with you, my teddy bear." Her smile was, alone worth all the gold in Fort Knox. I couldn't let none of the drama I got myself into hit home.

"Brissh, I'll be in there in a few, I need to make a few more calls. Okay Brissh?"

Where most women are bitches, almost to the point of disbelief, she was so understanding during her pregnancy. "Okay Dee, let me leave you alone then."

"Hold up, come here." She walked over to the leather executive chair where I was seated at my desk, "Give me a kiss." She leaned in and kissed me. I grabbed the back of her head and whispered in her ear, "Later on I want us to make love in this chair. You on top so you can control how much goes in. I don't want to put a dent in the baby's head." We both laughed as she disappeared into the hallway.

I continued to try to reach Candy. No answers. I then dialed Reecee's number and found her half asleep, probably been fucking somebody with her hot ass.

"Hello." she sounded either worn out or half asleep, knowing her it was the earlier.

"What's up? What you doing? Were you sleep?"

"Umm, hey Dee, what's up baby? I thought you forgot all about me. I ain't heard from you in a while."

"You sound crazy girl. How the hell I'ma forget about you, good as you do the damn thing." I caught myself and lowered my voice just in case Brishette may have come back for something. "Have you spoken to your sister?"

"No. Why?" I could hear the concern in her voice.

"Because I spoke to her earlier and she started crying and told me she had to use the bathroom and that she would call me back. But she never did and when I called her she won't answer."

"Hold on, let me try her on the other line." She put me on hold and came back with nothing also, "She ain't answering the phone, she might be sleep or she might be going through something. You must not have believed me when I told you that I think she knows something. She's been acting funny every since.

"Every since what Reecee?" I knew it was something she wasn't telling me.

"Look Dee, we had an argument okay, and she blew it out of proportion and started accusing me of sleeping with you."

"So what did you say?" I was hoping she didn't say what I thought was about to say.

"I didn't say nothing. I told her if that's what she want to believe, 'cause she gone believe what she want to believe anyway. That's when she told me she wanted me out of her house."

"Why didn't you tell her it wasn't like that? Why did you let her believe something like that?"

"You don't know my sister Dee. She's gonna accuse me of sleeping with you whether I slept with you or not. She blames me for her not being able to keep a man when it's her; it ain't got nothing to do with me. She's the one that run them off cause she's evil and vindictive..."

I cut her off, "What do you mean, vindictive?"

"Like I said, she's evil. She goes way too far to get people back. It's like she sits around and plots on how to ruin people's lives. She's lucky ain't nobody killed her evil ass. That's my sister and I love her, but I swear her father, Mr. Earl must have been the devil for real."

I had heard enough, I knew it was too good to .be true. Her pussy was 'the bomb' and I just knew it was something that she was hiding. "Anyway, I hope she never find out the truth about us." I said to Reecee.

"Yeah, me either Dee cause she is possessed or something, cause she don't know when to stop. My sister is crazy. Especially over some dick and she got a nerve to be playing hard to get."

If I didn't tell Reecee I had to go she'd talk me to death. "Awight Reecee, I'm getting ready to go. I got to take care of some things but I'll get back to you awight?"

"Yeah, that's what you always say. You're just like the rest of them Dee. You get what you want from a girl then act like you don't know 'em."

"Don't start that shit Reecee. You staying in my apartment, if I acted like I didn't know you, you damn sure wouldn't be staying in my apartment. Reecee I gotta go." I hung up the phone and went upstairs.

Chapter 45

The next two days Isha, Brishette and I had a ball before I had put them on the plane back to L.A.. As I got a signal on my phone outside the airport bathroom, I answered the call. I didn't know whether to celebrate or start worrying about what I was hearing from Splizzy on the other end of the phone.

"Yo Dee, you not gone believe this shit man. Your baby mother Rissa just called me crying and shit talking about she's at the Fox Hills Mall in a store and that her and her boyfriend just got robbed by some Spanish dudes. She said they shot 'em yo, and she got away and ran inside for help. The police came while she was talking to me, but she told me she would call me back and hung up. So I'm just waiting for her to call me back."

"Hold up, what the fuck is you talking about Splizz? You said she just got shot!"

"Nah, not her, just her friend got shot."

"So where he at?"

"I don't know whether he's dead or not. I guess they took 'em to the hospital. Man that shit is crazy."

"Did they catch the dudes?"

"Dee, we only talked for a couple minutes before the police came, then she had to hang up. Yo, so I don't know. She'll call you back, she said she tried to get you first but that recording came on, 'Please hold while subscriber is located'. And it was taking too long so she called me, she said."

"Yeah awight. Well if you talk to her before she gets with me, tell her to call me. Plus Brishette and Isha should be there in a couple hours. I need you to go pick them up from the airport. Tell China give you the keys to the Bentley."

"Oh yeah, I seen that joint in the garage when Sizzle took me to the tennis court. We cut through the garage. Yo that joint is crazy. So what's that, the company car?"

"Yeah, I guess you could say that. Anyway, call me back when you pick them up. I guess Brishette could keep Isha until we find out what's up with Rissa. Then she can take them to the airport tomorrow."

"Awight yo, I'll call you back when I hear something."

"Awight yo."

The only thing I could think about on my way back to Ocho Rios was whether Rissa would crack under the pressure of L.A.P.D. or the feds if they ever got involved. But Rissa couldn't be stupid enough to tell the police that she set up a police officer to be killed. She's got to know that she would get the same life sentence as everybody else.

Even though she didn't know where I was, I was still concerned about her involving me in a murder-for-hire plot to kill a police, I had to try her cell phone. She answered on the second ring.

"Hello."

"What's going on? Are you alright?"

"Hell no I ain't awight. These fuckin' police got me down here asking me all these damn questions. Instead of them wasting all their time on me, they should be looking at the cameras trying to find out who robbed us. I know there was some cameras somewhere."

"So where you at anyway?"

"I'm downtown somewhere. Hold on... Excuse me, can you give me a minute. I'm on the phone checking on my daughter."

"What is he saying?"

"He wants me to get off the phone so I can talk to some agents or something. So where is Isha? Let me talk to her."

"She ain't back yet."

"Back from where? Hold up Sir, please don't rush me while I'm checking on my daughter."

I could hear him in the background saying she needed to get off the phone and now, "Tell him hold up."

"Dee, I'll call you right back as soon as I'm finished cause he talking about taking my phone if I don't get off now."

"You don't have to talk to them if you don't want to. As a matter of fact, tell them you ain't got nothing else to say to them. Nah, that'll make you look guilty of something. Just don't answer any questions outside of what happened. I'ma send a lawyer down there. So just tell them you don't have anything else to say until your lawyer gets there."

"Dee, I'll call you back. I don't think I need no lawyer. I didn't do nothing and I don't know nothing about what the hell you're into. I can't go to jail for something I didn't do. I gotta go."

The phone went dead. She hung up leaving me uncomfortable about this whole situation because it's no secret that pressure bust pipes. The first person that came to mind is Mel because he had turned me on to the lawyer who was handling the money trusts and teaching us the game.

I speed-dialed Mel, who answered on the first ring probably recognizing my cell number. "What's up youngster?"

"Mel I need your help man. My baby mother just got robbed..." He cut me off.

"What? Got robbed? Where?"

"In L.A. coming out of the mall."

"Aw shit, theses dudes are crazy. Is she awight?"

"Yeah, she's cool but her boyfriend ain't though, he got shot and he's a police."

"So how can I help?" He sounded sincere as if he really wanted to help me.

"Remember the cool lawyer dude whose house we went over for the meeting? Does he do criminal cases? Cause he seem like a good lawyer."

"I don't think so, but I could call him and ask him."

"Yeah that's what I need, and if he don't maybe he can recommend somebody. I need somebody to go to L.A.P.D. downtown now because my baby mother sound scared to death and I don't need any unnecessary drama. You feel me?"

"If you want to hold on I'll call him now or I can all you back. What's her name just in case?"

"Her name is Irisa Barkley and she said they got her at the station in downtown L.A."

"You ain't got an address?"

"No, let me try to call her back and see if she answers."

"Awight, call me back youngster and I should know something by then."

This whole thing was starting to come apart at the seams and as much as I tried to tie up the loose ends in one way, it unraveled in another. In particular, this situation with my daughter's mother being in custody or interrogated about the robbery-murder of her boyfriend, an undercover police I got to worry about whether Rissa's scared enough to tell them that she was in on it and that the whole thing was planned, the location, the time, the robbery and murder of the police officer because we believed he was using Rissa to get to me. Then with Candy possibly finding out that I was sleeping with her sister Reecee, especially where Reecee told me that her sister was evil and vindictive and would stop at nothing to get revenge by destroying people's lives.

Then to make matters worse, their young cousin who I really don't know all that well, just got locked up for cocaine and I don't know whether he's gonna include me in a conspiracy or not. Then finally there is the possible murder/drug conspiracy with Jay, my California connect. And I wonder if the Baltimore Police was investigating me and followed my trial to California, or did they already know and just waiting to get more evidence for a longer sentence.

Then I don't want to lose Brishette and that's exactly what might happen if she finds out that I have another woman pregnant in California. I needed some time to sort things out but instead I was quickly running out of time.

It didn't help that, as I pulled up to the house, Twyla, my housekeeper/new bi¬sexual lover was sitting on my steps with her face in her hands. Her eyes were puffy as if she had been crying her eyes out. "Twyla, what are you doing here?"

"I need to talk to you Mister Dee."

"What's the matter? You look like you've been crying." I reached out my hand, she took hold of my hand and pulled herself up from the steps and we went inside. "Have a seat and tell me what's going on."

She sat down next to me on the brown leather couch in the living room. "I'm sorry to bother you Mr. Dee, butI didn't have anyone else to talk to about this. I know I shouldn't be telling you my problems but you're the only one that might not take his side."

"Whose side? What are you talking about Twyla?"

"Mr. Dee there is a boy, his name is Gusta, he was my boyfriend since I was twelve years old, he is older by four years. Well, I told him I don't want to be with him anymore but he won't leave me alone."

"Why?"

"What? Why I don't want to be with him anymore or why he won't leave me alone?"

"Both." It's funny how listening to someone else's problems kind of makes you forget about your own just for a short while. Nevertheless it was a welcomed escape.

"Well, I don't want to be with him anymore because, because he makes me do things I don't like to do. And why he won't leave me alone, I don't know." She was leaning her head on my shoulder.

"So what kind of things does he make you do?"

"Just crazy things, ya know around his friends..."

"Crazy things like what Twyla? You can be open with me."

"I know, but I don't want to talk about it now okay. Please, let's just talk about something else." She laid her head in my lap. As much as I didn't want my dick to get hard and poke her in the face at a time like this, I couldn't control it's eagerness to get hard and obviously she couldn't help but put me out of my misery. Twyla unzipped my pants and began sucking my dick like she was trying out for the dick-sucking Olympics. And she was winning the gold until my phone rang on the coffee table. I reached out and could see it was Rissa's cell number. I had to literally stop Twyla by grabbing her hand that held the shaft. She was really into it, moaning just as much as I was.

"Hold up, I gotta get this call."

"Okay." Twyla got up and walked into the downstairs bathroom.

"Hello." I answered and heard what sounded like evil coming through the phone mixed with tears of fear.

"Dee, what the fuck are these polices talking about Dee, that you might be involved with drug conspiracy and murder of a federal agent?"

My world instantly became a nightmare based on my uncertain fate. What did they know?

"What are you talking about Rissa?"

"Dee they're telling me they can charge me with obstruction of justice and I could get five years if I don't tell them where you at..." I cut her off.

"Don't say nothing else to them. I got a lawyer coming down there, do you understand?"

She started crying even harder when she said they told her she would probably lose our daughter and child protective services would get her. It did not look good for me; a woman will give up her mother to save her only child.

"They said I can't leave L.A. Dee you really need to come and straighten this out Dee."

"I'm sending a lawyer to get you, awight?"

"Where is my daughter? Put her on the phone, I gotta go Dee. They are making me get off the phone. Dee you gotta turn yourself in so me and Isha can go hooommme." Her voice was very faint and full of fear. This was not a good sign. The phone went dead.

….TO BE CONTINUED….

The Saga continues in Part II...

FRAUD MASTERS

COMING TO A BOOK STORE NEAR YOU!!!

FRAUD CHRONICLES Part II

Preview

Chapter 1

I quickly dialed Splizzy. He answered on the first ring "Splizz, this thing is blowing up in our face, this crazy broad is telling me to turn myself in so her and Isha can go home."

"What? Are they saying she can't leave?"

"Yeah, I guess so." Then I remembered Mel was checking on a lawyer.

"Splizz, I'll call you back; I'm trying to get a lawyer down there real fast."

"Awight yo, call me back, I'm here."

Without saying another word, I clicked over and dialed Mel. He must have recognized my number because without saying hello he went straight into talking to me.

"Youngster what took you so long to call me back. He said he got you. He's on his way down there. So you can breathe a little easier now."

"When did you talk to him? Because I just got off the phone with her and she's scared to death. They're telling her she can't leave L.A. And they gone take my daughter and shit." He became instantly hot like he had a personal stake in this outcome and he sort of did. Because if something happens to me, his business goes back to normal "Man I hate them mutha fuckas."

"Look Mel, I need you to call your man and tell him that I need an update on the situation."

"I'll take care of it youngster."

"Awight, later."

Twyla came back into the room. "Is everything ok mister Dee? You seem upset, did I do something wrong?"

"No Twyla, everything is fine, I just got some problems, that's all." Just as I put the phone on the coffee table the sound of glass shattering and Twyla's scream scared the shit out of me, I turned towards the windows and noticed a brick and broken glass on the beige plush carpet. "What da fuck?" I was totally off guard. I didn't know anybody in Jamaica and nobody knew me or where I was so maybe it was a mistake. I walked over to the window pulled the curtain aside. Twyla's scream did not help the situation because the two Jamaicans obviously heard her and began screaming out Jamaican obscenities "You fuckin blood clot bitch, ya naw mi not gon let chu go, mi ki ya firs. You betta cum naw or mi gon cum get you."

"Mister Dee," Twyla joined me at the window "I'm sorry, that's the boy who I tell you about. He's crazy Mister Dee."

This kind of shit always happens to me. A piece of pussy always comes with a hidden price to pay. "Does he have a gun Twyla?" If so, I was definitely unprepared, "damn, I just got here and fucking drama following me here already." All I could think of was the golf clubs in the study room. I might not be a pro Golfer but I had busted a few heads in my day. And I hit many softballs over the fence, so I could swing that mutha fuckin golf-club. I grabbed one of the graphite golf-clubs from the dusty/leather golf bag and started for the door. That's when my cell phone rang. I stopped and grabbed my phone from the coffee table only to find it was Splizz. And I'm glad he called right then because if something happened to me at least somebody could know who it was and revenge my death.

"Yo, I'm glad you called..." before I could say what was going on with me Splizzy cut me off.

"Yo Dee, man what the fuck is going on man," I been tryin call you and I ain't get no answer so I called Rude Boy and sent him to check on you plus the police is here at the mansion.

"What? "What the fuck are you talking about man, my phone was right next to me, It ain't even ring. Plus you know how the signal is on this Island. That's when another brick or rock broke more glass. That was it, I couldn't take it anymore. I had to do something.

"Yo, what was that noise in the background?"

"Splizz, listen, some Jamaican dudes just threw some bricks through my windows."

"What?"

"Yo just listen, it's Twyla's ex-boyfriend."

"Who the fuck is Twyla?" Splizzy shouted into the phone.

"She's my housekeeper. Yo I'm going out there it's only two of them and I got a golf club.

"Yo, you don't know whether they got guns or what. Hold up let me call Myles he can call Rude Boy back and see how close he is. Don't go out there yet Dee let me see what's up with Rude Boy first." That's' the last word I heard before I threw the phone on the couch and it bounced on the floor and Twyla picked it up.

"Let me tell you mutha fuckas something cause yaw don't know who the fuck you fucking with..." before I could get out another word the skinny pitch black taller one came running at me with a bat. He swung and although I jumped back almost out of the way, while swinging the golf-club, the bat caught me on the left arm right by the funny bone. I felt it go numb, but I was already in motion, the golf-club smashed into the side of his head right at his ear. And all I saw was crimson red liquid starting to pour out. He screamed like a little bitch. That's when the other shorter lighter skinned dred started comin after me with a machete.

Twyla screamed "stop it Donovan, leave him alone. Okay, I will go with you."

The excruciating and debilitating pain in my left arm and the black suburban came at the same time. Just as the dred swung the machete at me I blocked it with the golf club but lost my grip from the impact and it fell to the ground, leaving me defenseless.

The next swing of the machete may have been fatal but it was interrupted by the loud gun shot that I also feared was for me. Until I heard the voice say "drop it or I kill you right here in the sand."

God was definitely on my side this day. Because after I realized I wasn't hit I turned towards the black truck and recognized Rude Boy. The Jamaican that Myles introduced me to who told me that if I ever have any problems to call him. "Dee you Awight man?"

"Respect, respect Rude Boy," the assailant said with the look of fear on his face.

"Yo why da fuck you cum here? huh?"

"Rude Boy, mi sorry mi jus com for da girl."

"Who her? "he turned pointing at Twyla "you want go wit him?"

"No," Twyla answered with the look of fear on her face.

"She don't wanna go. So you need to get your friend and take imm to the ospital, imm look like ee gone need stitches. And I don't want to see you around ear anymore because if I do, you gon ave prob-lums ya earre." Rude boy said

Yeah mon, mi didn't know Rude Boy, mi swear mi didn't know." Twyla's ex¬-boyfriend pleaded as he helped his friend to their whether-beaten Toyota. At that time I felt lightning strike inside my arm, it had to be broken. I let out a loud shreak and grabbed my arm.

"Dee, it look like you might need to go to the ospital." It was crazy how Jamaicans just refuse to pronounce the 'h' sound, the 'h' is always silent when they speak, that tripped me out. "Mr. Dee we need to go inside let me get you some ice for the swelling. And then go to the ospital."

"Rude Boy, do you know those dudes?"

"They are just a couple of punks from Kingston. Mi grew up in Kingston ya know. And everybody know me and my reputation. It look like I made it right on time."

"You sure did, what were you..." he cut me off

"Splizzee called me imm said something about imm couldn't reach you on your cell phone. I told imm oww the reception is on the Island."

We all went inside. Twyla fixed us a drink and made an ice pack for my arm to bring down the swelling. Rude Boy promised to hook me up with a gun so I could protect myself. But also explained that I better not tell nobody I got it because, unlike America, the Jamaican police will kill you just for having a gun. He went on to tell me that if I am ever stopped by police, I'd better shoot first because if they find a gun they will kill me. This Foreign Country shit is crazy.

He and Twyla talked me into going to the hospital. Where they took x-rays, gave me some Tylenol #3 with codeine, a sling and released me. During the drive back home I checked my messages. Splizz was cussing me out. Brishette, Candy, China, and Rissa had all called.

The lawyer had gotten Rissa released. Brishette had taken Isha to her house and Rissa was having a fit, she had called four times, so I returned Brishette's call first.

"Hey baby, what is going on? I've been trying to reach you. So you can tell me what to do about your Daughter."

"Where is she?"

"She's in the bed sleeping, she's ok. I just got a little worried when I couldn't get you."

"Well I'm glad you made it back safely and I miss you allraaaedy." I began to yawn from the codine in my system.

"You sound tired."

"I am. So what's your schedule like tomorrow?"

"Just writing most of the day. So I'll probably be at home. Have you talked to Isha's mother?"

"Naw, not yet, but she's called and left messages. I wasn't getting a signal for a while, the signal is bad in Jamaica. But I am going to call her as soon as I hang up with you so I can find out what time tomorrow you can meet her with Isha."

"Okay, let me know."

"I'll call you as soon as I talk to Rissa."

I started dialing Rissa on my cell and the phone began ringing at the house which means only one of three people could be calling, Twyla, China, or Splizzy. No one else had this house number.

"Hello, Rissa hold on." I picked up the house phone.

"Hello."

"Yo what's up wit chew? I told you we had a situation..."

"I cut him off "Hold up, I'm a have to call one of you back. Rissa?"

"You need to talk to me right mutha fuckin now..."

"Hold up, who da fluckk you talking to like that?, you done lost your damn mind girl."

"Where is my daughter, Dee? And you need to come talk to me, where you at anyway?"

"Splizz hold on one minute. Okay Rissa check this out, I got a problem on the other end. Isha is fine, she's sleep right now but I'ma bring her to you tomorrow morning. So are you still at the same hotel?"

"Yeah, and I don't have no money to pay them for any more days,..." I cut her off "Don't worry about money, I got chew. I'll send some money by Isha, but I gotta call you back Rissa, so you Awight until tomorrow?"

"No I ain't Awight."

"What did them people say to you anyway?"

"We'll talk when you come tomorrow, you are bringing Isha in the morning right'?"

"See you tomorrow Rissa, or I'll call you back tonight."

I hung up.

"Splizz,..." before I could say anything else Splizz told me to hold on and put China on the phone.

"Dee Why you just calling us back?... Oh, you called him." Obviously talking to Splizz.

"I just got back from the hospital."

"Hospital? For what? What's wrong? Are you Okay?

"Yeah, I'm good, my arm is fractured."

"Oh my God, what happened?" China said with sincere concern.

"I had a lil problem with some Jamaicans, they tried to jump me."

"So what happened? Where are you?"

"It's a long story, I'll tell you about it later. But right now, I need to know what happened."

"Well, I was getting ready to leave as I walked towards the door, I heard the chimes and the monitor lit up by the foyer. I saw the police at the gate along with a pointed nosed old white lady..."

"So what happened? What did you do?" I interrupted

"I did what you taught me to do; well I first answered them and let them in. Once inside, the lady started asking me who was I and how did I get in and who's cars were in the driveway? I just told her that we are leasing the property, well my fiancé is leasing..."

"Your fiance huh." I had to cut her off with that one. "So where did that come from?"

"Don't let it go to your head. So anyway, I went and got the paper work after the police asked me for my I.D. I showed them my driver's license and the lease agreement, then payment receipts, and the ad from the paper. The police told the lady that this is a civil matter just like you said. They asked could they take the paperwork I told them no. But I called Kareem and he said just make em a copy, so I ran a copy in the fax machine."

"Damn, China you sound like you been through this shit before."

"To be honest, I was scared to death. They could tell too but the paperwork was all they needed to see. Oh yeah, the lady said we'd be hearing from her lawyers. And they need you to contact them the police left his card."

"Yeah right, like I'm really gone call them back. I need you to start looking for another property, cause we ready to go legit anyway.."

"I'm already on it, got an appointment Thursday to see a property in Woodland Estates."

"You know what? I knew I made the right choice when I chose you as my partner."

"Yeah whatever, flattery get somewhere some of the time but not everywhere all the time. Dee I need to see you so we can discuss this next move. You need to be here if you can."

"We'll talk about that later. Let me speak to Splizzy, Awight, and I'll call you back. I luv you here?"

"Yeah, I luv you too Dee, hold on here go Splizz."

"Yo what up?"

"Yo how has China been acting since that situation?"

"What chew mean? How she been acting? I guess she been cool, I didn't see no change, she still handling her business as usual."

"Just keep your eye on her, make sure she Awight, that's my girl yo, I don't want nothing to happen to her you feel me?"

"Yeah, I got chu, you want me watch her back. Yo, you ain't even have to tell me that, that goes without saying cause that's why I'm here, for real for real."

"Oh yeah, what's up with the girl Sizzle? What she got you pussy-whipped or something? Tell me about her."

"What the fuck you talking about Dee? You done bumped your fuckin head man, It ain't never gone be like that if I can help it. But she's cool, sexy as a muthafucka, 5ft. 2, long hair, she's about a size 6, kind of petite, real petite. Yo, her skin is like bronze, no bullshit, guess that's how they make them in Brazil..."

"Yo... that's enough, that's just what I thought. She got chew wide open. Anytime you're about to go into her whole history, she must've put it on your ass."

"Yeah whatever, you the one be fallin all in love and shit. China got yo ass open too..." I cut him off

"Yo China is a millionaire in the making. Shiiit, you gotta love her. You need to be tryin to find out how you and sizzle can get some money together, that's what you need to be doin; because these days it's about a point-to-point relationship both parties gotta bring something to the table and meet in the middle. You feel me?" If it don't make money, it don't make sense. Hold on, that's my other line."

"Hello'"

"Dee, I need to come see you. Where you at?"

"You can't come see me Rissa, cause I ain't around. I'm out of town."

"So why I can't come where you at? And I thought you was bringing Isha tomorrow?"

"Rissa, I thought I just told you I'll call you back."

"Dee, I'm scared, I don't wanna be by myself; plus I'm horny as a mutha fucka right now."

"What the fuck you scared of, the Boogie-man? Hold on Rissa, damn I forgot I got somebody on the other line."

"Yo, Splizz, that's Rissa, on the other line talking about she's scared. Let me call you back, plus I don't want her to meet Brishette cause I don't know whether she tryin set me up or what. So I need one of the girls to drop Isha off to Rissa after you meet Brishette and get Isha, but we'll talk more when I call you back yo. Awight?"

"Okay, I'm back Rissa. So what are you scared of?"

"I'm in this hotel way out here in California, all by myself. And ain't nobody here to hold me, the poleeece..." she started her sniffin-crying act that I know oh so well. "Don't want me to leave cause they think I'm withholding information about a murder. Dee, they talking about taking Isha, if I go to jail..."

"Let me stop you right there, ain't nobody gone do shit to Isha or you cause you haven't done nothing wrong. And neither have I so you don't have nothing to worry about. That's their job to try to scare people into telling them what they need to build a case."

"Well, if you ain't do nothing why don't you turn yourself in so you can clear your name?"

"Rissa? You don't understand. You saw enemy of the state with Will Smith right? Well he didn't walk into their trap, he looked for a way to clear his name before they could get him. Because once they get somebody in their custody, innocent or not, it's impossible to defend yourself because they give you a lawyer that's down with them. People are in jail right now that they know are innocent but they need a body to close a case."

"Dee, I don't want to go to jail and let them take Isha..."

"What did I tell you? Ain't nobody going to jail and ain't nobody taking Isha so stop saying that. First of all, didn't I tell you I would take care of you? Didn't I get you out of the police station? Plus didn't the lawyer explain to you that you don't have anything to worry about? So stop worrying Rissa, I got chew. Use your head, you're my daughter's mother, I ain't gone let nothing happen to you girl. I still love you and I always will."

"You mean that Dee? or you just saying that so I'll stop worrying?"

"Both, I love you and I want you to stop worrying. You are safe in the hotel, so get you some sleep and tomorrow we gonna take care of the hotel and you and Isha can go shopping, alwight?"

"Yeah, okay. I love you Dee."

"I love you too Rissa, good night. Get your horny ass in the bed girl and get you some rest; you had long day. Get some sleep, awight?"

"Okay, so am I gonna see you in the morning?"

"We'll see. Good night."

She must think I'm stupid. I did not get this far being stupid. I called Splizzy and told him to get somebody to watch her so I'll know her every move. And I wasn't too worried about the phone being traced to my location because there's no GPS chip in it and the phone is hooked up through a routing service, so they will only see that the call went to a router but they can't see where it went after that. So I'm good on that.